Simply Fiona

Simply Fiona

JOHN DENISON

WHY KNOT
BOOKS ✁

Simply Fiona

ISBN (book)   978-1-927506-48-6
ISBN (e-book) 978-1-927506-49-3

CIP available

Front cover image by Michael Lee
Cover and book design: Gillian Stead

Published by Why Knot Books
5443 Eighth Line,
Erin, ON, NoB 1To
Canada
Editorial: 519-833-1242

For Fiona K.

Thank you!

Billy swears I can be a famous writer if I put

my brain to it — and Karen says get it down

while it's steaming. The hard part's going to

be slowing down, not sprinting to the finish

in four pages or something. Here goes...

THURSDAY
Time Unknown

I t's not every day you wake up to find a fecking marching band in your bedroom. Around and around they're marching this enormous black guy leading the way moving his baton up and down in time to the music, his kilt swaying, climbing up on my bed his bearskin hat — you know those tall, black, furry things the soldiers at Buckingham Palace wear — rubbing against the ceiling. He's followed by a row of snare drum players — rat a tat tat, rat a tat tat — followed by five cymbal players crashing their hands together, trying their best to drown out their pals the drummers, followed by two base drummers twirling their mallets beating the shite out of their drums like World War Three depends on 'em. Then when it seems things can't get any worse, they do, much worse. Bagpipes! Is that fecking *Mull of Kintyre?*

THURSDAY
Still Time Unknown

My best friend Darcy died six days ago. He went over the cliff up by the tower. There was a fierce storm that night, the wind howling, but even so Grandad Sky says clever fifteen-year-old boys don't fall over cliffs and I agree with that. No way Darcy fell, not without help. The truth of it is I should have been with him. Then we'd both be having funerals or better yet we'd both be at school laughing at something funny.

You would have liked Darcy. He was the Seth Rogen type; bit spastic, bit geek, but funny and caring and as smart as Stephen Hawking or at least that's how he seemed to me. There was never a dull moment with Darcy around. He could always see the irony in things, the absurdities, the hopelessness of trying to make sense of this world. Like now...

But there's one thing I know for certain. Darcy wouldn't want me moping about feeling sorry for myself, devastated because he's no longer around. He'd want me to live a life big enough for two of us. That's for sure.

Darcy's funeral is today and I think I've set my alarm but I can't be sure because there's a fecking Scottish marching band using my head as a parade ground. It's my own fault of course being hung-over and all.

Last night I was supposed to go with Grandad to The Betty, our local pub, for Darcy's wake but the thought of all that drunken testosterone kept me home. And to be honest I was hoping Gran might Zoom. She doesn't know anything about Darcy going over the cliff. I'm not sure I should tell her — I don't want to ruin her trip — but she'll know something's wrong as soon as she sees the tear tracks on my face.

My Aunt Nora — she's got more piercings than a hedgehog's mother — gave me a Mickey Mouse alarm clock for my fifteenth birthday. She bought it at The Charity Shop in Dublin claiming she had to fight off a bald, female wrestler to get it. It's round, with four tiny stick legs, and two bells with clangors on top. Mickey's standing in the middle, his arms moving around telling the time, except the poor mouse is missing his minute hand — Aunt Nora says he's an American war vet! You tell the time by staring at the hour hand and guessing the minutes.

Trouble is Mickey isn't where he's supposed to be, which is on the little table beside my bed. Darcy's funeral starts at 09:30 but whether it's 7 or noon I haven't a clue.

'Feister! I need to know the time. *Now!*'

Fiona's First Rule of Hangovers: Never shout.

Feister is Gran's boggart — she inherited him from her mum — and boggarts, if you're not knowing, are '*extremely ugly faeries!* — are you listening, Feister?' — that live in houses, are mostly invisible, and are supposed to be helping out with the chores except they have attitude if not kept in check. Gran's gone to Africa for three weeks — I'll be telling you about that later — so Feister thinks he's running the place, plus he and I don't get along. He thinks I'm a Changeling and I think he's Something-We-Can-Do-Without like dog shite on your wellies.

Mickey lands on the table with a thud. The trouble now is his hour hand is spinning around like a boat propeller.

I better tell you my name. Fiona O'Hara. That's it. No middle names, which is right unusual in Ireland I can tell you. Here mothers think if they give you four or five names they can appease their ancestors and chances are, with any luck, there'll be one suiting you.

My mum's name was Brigid Fallon Colleen Scarlet Dawn O'Hara and it was the Fallon she liked. It means fair one. She had long blonde hair like me so choosing Fallon made sense, plus it sounds dreamy like a celeb's name. *Casablanca Revisited,* starring Fallon O'Hara.

Darcy Casey Braden Regan Ryan O'Malley was my best friend and always will be. When he was being stupid arrogant — which was often enough — I'd call him *Mouthful* and he'd come back with, *Simply Fiona.*

We did everything together. Well, not *everything*, but that was Darcy's doing not mine.

Last night when Grandad Sky trundled off to The Betty, me and Bandit, Gran's cat, had Stonehaven to ourselves. Stonehaven is Gran's ancestral home. It sits by itself, on its own rise overlooking the sea, just north of the village. It's been in Gran's family forever and then some. Most of the houses in Gloire Bay are one-story shanties staying low to the ground, hiding from the wind, which can be right fierce coming off the Atlantic Ocean, but not Stonehaven. It's got two stories sticking up like a prizefighter flicking his nose saying, *c'mon you dumb ocean give me your best shot!*

Grandad Sky's from Texas so he's always bringing home bottles with names like Wild Turkey Bourbon, Kentucky White Lightning, Pappy Van Winkle Family Reserve and my favorite, Southern Comfort. He and Gran like a wee nip or two before supper, sitting on the porch watching the fishing/lobster boats chugging home. Grandad always buys multiple bottles so he never notices one gone missing or if he does, he doesn't let on. Southern Comfort tastes like fermented peaches, in case you're wondering, and there's an empty bottle lying by my bed so my mouth should taste fruity but it doesn't; it tastes like one of the marching band's bearskin hats has lodged in my throat.

'Feister, I need to know the time right now or else!'

Darcy and I have been best friends since the day we were born, which was the same day, Darcy and I sharing a birthday. His mum knew my mum growing up so when Gran brought me home from Africa, only days old, Darcy's mum volunteered to feed me because she'd just had Darcy. What they called *a wet nurse* in the old days. If you google that it'll tell you wet nurse was a job, sometimes looking after a baby when the mum died — there was lots of that! — and sometimes feeding babies when the rich mother couldn't be bothered.

Darcy says we're milk mates. That's when I say we're more like Nutella. I'm sweet and you're nuts!

I really need to know what time it is!

Fiona's Second Rule of Hangovers: Never get out of bed in a hurry!

Crumpled on the floor I realize I'm still wearing my black jeans and my mum's faded U2 t-shirt, yellow. I peek under Bono and find the black, lacey bra Aunt Ciara gave me for Christmas. I gave her platinum hoops from The Silver Cellar in Sligo. She thought they were *sick*.

We're supposed to wear our school uniforms to the funeral. Mrs. Barrow, principal at St. Barbara's, has decreed this. It's so us kids can go to school afterward. Mrs. B can be a battleax but mostly she's kind enough. She told me to take days off till I feel better which was good of her. If Darcy was around, I'd love days off but without him I'm probably better at school keeping my brain occupied with other things.

So, Aunt Ciara's black bra is a problem because it'll show through my thin white shirt everybody thinking I did it on purpose.

'Grandad?'

No answer.

'GRANDAD!'

OMG! The bagpipe players are back!

Fiona's Third Rule of Hangovers: Whatever you do, do not wake up the fecking bagpipers!

It's obvious I've got Stonehaven to myself. I cross the hallway and peek into Gran and Grandad's bedroom. The bed's made meaning Grandad either got up early — not likely — or never came home — likely. I step in so I can see the clock beside the bed except there is no clock.

'Feister! I am getting seriously miffed here! I need to know the time. **Now!**'

Once again I hear a snicker.

I storm to end of the hallway where there's an antique wooden desk with a Dell computer on top. I flip it open and look at the time.

09:46 SHITE! SHITE! SHITE!

I'm not dressed plus it's a fifteen-minute hike to the church/cemetery. Half that if my bike didn't have two flat tires. For sure I've missed the Mass but there's still the graveyard.

I am so fecked!

I approach my dresser with trepidation. I do my own laundry now so it's hit or miss whether I've done it lately. Once in a while Gran takes pity on me and fills the drawers which always gets her a kiss and a hug while she whispers in my ear, 'Fiona, you're going to make someone a wonderful husband.'

Top right drawer is... empty. Argh!

If I wear my school tie the black bra might not be too noticeable.

(Really my brain should be in a jar, pickled. It could be on a shelf beside Einstein's. Genius. Eejit.)

Now I can't find my uniform.

It's hard to lose a school uniform. It doesn't hide well and it doesn't look like anything else. Apparently, they debated long and hard whether St. B's students should be wearing uniforms. Darcy says I'm beyond sexy in my kilt and not many can say that he says, so I guess I'm in favor.

It suddenly occurs to me I'm not going to find my uniform by looking.

'All right Feister, that's it! I need my uniform, **now!**'

There! Did you hear it? That snort?

'C'mon Feister. I'm late for Darcy's funeral... *please...*'

I definitely don't have time for this.

'All right you little wanker, if it's war you want, you got it!'

I storm back into Gran's bedroom and go right to the SHP — Secret Hiding Place — where I anticipate yanking out Gran's *Book of Faery Spells* except it isn't there. Shite! Shite! Shite! I lent it to Darcy for his essay and now it'll be lying among the rocks getting pummeled by the Atlantic Ocean. Gran will kill me and I'll be helping her. How stupid can you be Fiona?

(Now there's a question with no answer!)

But! In the SHP is a pile of handwritten pages. Spells Gran's been collecting but hasn't put in the book yet. I return to my bedroom flipping pieces of paper as I go.

'Feister, are you listenin? If my uniform does not appear this instant, I am going to change you into a... (flip, flip, flip) ...**Horned Toad!'**

I have no idea what a Horned Toad looks like but it sounds bad.

'And the spell lasts...' I search the page... **'Five hundred ciorcails!'**

Whatever they are.

'Théann.'

Most of the spells are written in Latin but this one's in Irish.

'Tú.

My kilt falls on my head. It's a wool kilt made of County Donegal tartan — sea blue and heather green plaid. It's supposed to end a hand's width above your knees but mine stops a finger's width below my knickers. All the girls at school wear them hitched up, and the more the teachers bitch the higher they go so they've packed in worrying about it. Darcy says that's the trouble with rules. You can't break 'em if there aren't any.

'Isteach.'

My white shirt wafts down from the ceiling like a pillowcase in a washing powder ad. I put it on and look in the mirror at the flimsy white shirt with the screaming black bra.

'I.'

My navy blue knee socks whiz by my ears like bungees.

'Buairc.'

One navy blue blazer lands at my feet.

'Gran isn't here Feister and you shouldn't be either!'

There's only one more word. I run into the hallway staring at the clock on the computer.

09:54.

FECKED!

'I need my shoes. *Now!*'

I hear a muffled bang outside the dormer window followed by another. I'm just in time to see my black oxfords tumbling down the porch roof.

'Adharcach!'

They've sent Billy Ridout to fetch me. He's the best bike rider in the village so that's why. He's also Darcy's first cousin, their mums being sisters. Billy's in most of my classes but he's got his own mates he hangs with. The Kickers Darcy calls 'em cos football's all they talk about. (Note to my American cousin Alice: football = soccer. Your football shouldn't be called football, should it? Grandad Sky suggests Concussionball.)

'Hey Fion! They're waitin' for you. Hop on.'

Billy's rear wheel has a pipe sticking out both sides so I stand on the pipe my hands gripping Billy's shoulders and it's a good thing my kilt is short or I'd be doing the Isadora Duncan with my knickers. (Admit it Alice: knickers is a much better word than *panties,* which sounds like something small dogs do! And Isadora Duncan, if you're not knowing, is the mother of Modern Dance who died when the enormous silk scarf she was wearing — she's riding in a convertible —got entangled in the rear wheel!)

I shout in Billy's ear, 'Medvedev and Alcaraz are using my brain for practice.'

Darcy would have chuckled at this but Billy doesn't know Daniil Medvedev from Chris Martin.

Billy says over his shoulder, 'They've been callin your mobile.'

'Went over the cliff with Darcy.'

I'm amazed how strong Billy is. Here we are tearing up the hill almost as fast as Billy came down. Our Billy might not be the brightest light in the harbor but he's certainly one of the strongest and as I'm going to find out probably the nicest as well.

As we shoot through the iron gates of Gloire Bay Cemetery — a rusty angel looking down on us — I see the sea of folks gathered around the freshly dug grave. Kids in their uniforms — trying their best to behave — while the adults chat to each other. And I can hear Darcy laughing because in the middle of this ocean of humanity our pal, Fungal Fergus, is sitting high in his yellow John Deere digger (backhoe) waiting to fill the hole back in. He's got his headphones on listening to something that's got his head bobbing. (Fungal got his nickname from a massive dose of jock itch should have kept him out of the big match but didn't. Fungal scored the winning goal cementing his aka forever!) He waves to me and I wave back. Then my eyes land on Father Walter — *Wanker!* — McKenna who's scowling at me, put out he has to wait for an absentee schoolgirl and one who never comes to Mass to boot.

Billy stops his bike a respectful distance away and I clamber off. Every eye is on me but I'm okay with that. Darcy would want me to play my part.

The Grief-Stricken Girlfriend.

'Sweetjeesus! Would you look at that kilt? She might as well not bother. Just wear her knickers and save the lads all that salivating.'

'Next you'll be going on about the black bra but I do think you might be cuttin her some slack. First, she loses her parents — and not in a nice way — and now her boyfriend does a nosedive. You're just jealous of those legs that go on forever.'

That's me pretending to be Donna — *Big Mouth* — McLeish and Betty — *Wide Arse* — McDonogh who live side-by-side on Ascal Mhuire sharing a clothesline and all the village's gossip. Darcy said they were Gloire Bay's equivalent of Statler and Waldorf, the two old geezers on the Muppets always have something bad to say about everybody. They're standing in the front row staring at me so I stare back.

When I arrive at the grave the sea parts and Darcy's mum Debra — my wet nurse — comes barreling out her face streaked with tears. She gathers me into her arms and hugs me so tightly I can barely breathe. That makes her laugh.

'That's all we're needing me squeezin you to death. Does Gran know?'

'Not yet.'

'How's Grandad Sky?'

'Sad.'

'All of Gloire Bay is sad today.'

I look around for Grandad but can't find him.

'I'm sorry he's not here.'

'That's okay. There's some can't do these things. He'll be at The Betty toastin our Darcy.'

I can see Darcy's mum wants to ask me something but she changes her mind. Instead, she wraps her arm around my waist and leads me through the crowd to the front row. Father McKenna glares at me like, *how dare you be late,* but I just glare back. *Do your job, Wanker.*

Debra signals him to begin.

'We are gathered here...'

While Father McKenna is droning on I'm going to tell you about my parents. When I was little and feeling brave, instead of Gran reading *Cat in the Hat* or *Madeline,* I'd ask her to tell me the story of my mum and dad.

'They were such a handsome couple,' is how Gran always begins. 'Your father was from Texas, a big strapping fellow, gentle as a lamb but afraid of nothing. Grandad says no one tangled with Jesse Locking. If there was trouble Jesse would step into the middle of it and that would be the end of that.

'You'd think your mum would be petite like me but she wasn't. She favored your grandpa Ryan, the one you never met. He wasn't as tall as your dad but he was a fine-looking man with long limbs and a big smile. Your mum took after him. She was born right here in Gloire Bay on a beautiful summer night with a full moon. We named her Brigid Fallon Colleen Scarlet Dawn O'Hara, which is at least three more names than anyone is needing, but I wanted her to have a choice.'

"I don't have a choice,' I say to Gran the first time she tells me the story.

'Would you like to be called something different?'

I think about that. Fiona was a gift from my parents, the only gift I'll ever have.

'No. I like Fiona.'

'Me too.' Gran's big on hugs and she gives me one. 'Fallon was the name your mum liked and that's what everyone called her. Fallon O'Hara. She had two sisters –'

I interrupt here saying, 'Aunt Ciara and Aunt Nora.' Little kids like to answer questions they know the answer to. And I'm lucky I have two aunts I like so much. Aunt Ciara — in America you'd spell it Keira — is smart and proper; Aunt Nora is funky and silly. Different, but complimentary, like salt and pepper. We always have a good time when they're around.

Gran continues, 'I wanted to have a boy, someone your Grandad Ryan could take under his wing, but I was okay when it was your mum who popped out. I thought raising girls was much easier than raising boys but that was before Fallon came along. She might as well have been three boys for all the havoc she caused. Always getting into trouble and just for the fun of it too.'

Here Gran would tell some story about my mum and it was never the same story so I came to believe the stockpile was endless. 'But she was the smartest girl in the whole world when she wanted to be — like someone else we know...' Gran made sure I knew who the someone was. 'But oh, she was beautiful. Tall, lanky, long fair hair. She had legs stretched to the moon and when she smiled it was like the sun dimmed. I mean the local lads would walk into bins staring after her. They all wanted her but your mum had her sights set much higher.

'She came home one day raving about a young woman from Limerick who'd come to the school to talk to the kids. She was a nurse and she'd just spent three years in Africa working for Médecins Sans Frontières, which is French for Doctors Without Borders.' The first time Gran told the story she tried to explain all the conflicts around the world and how good men and women worked for organizations like Médecins Sans Frontières trying to help. 'Your mum was on fire that day. It was like all the energy inside her bursting to get out finally had a target. She never missed school after that and won the prize for smartest student. Then she was off to medical school in Dublin. She graduated at the top of her class and I was so proud of her.

'She did her residency in a big hospital in London.' Here Gran explains that all doctors have to work in a hospital for two or three years to get hands-on medical training. 'Then she joined Doctors Without Borders and her first assignment was in Haiti. She said she learned more there in six weeks than six years at university.' The first time Gran told me the story she stopped here and got the atlas. It's a gigantic book and my half was heavy in my lap. We found Haiti. 'Then they moved her to Cambodia... and then Afghanistan... That's where she met your father. I remember the email when Fallon mentioned your dad for the first time. *I've met this American doctor. His name's Jesse Locking. He's from Texas and he's LARGE. Bigger than O'Meara.* You know O'Meara, Fiona. At the petrol station. He's the one has to duck coming out the door.'

Me and Gran duck together.

'After that your dad was all she talked about. Nothing about the danger and the terrible wounds she was fixing. She knew that stuff scared me. Made me angry that the world is the way it is.

'Then fighting broke out again in Sudan between the North and South. It was a horrible war but they needed doctors to go and it was so dangerous no one would volunteer so, of course, your mum and dad stuck their hands up.' Gran sticks her hand up and so do I. 'They were sent to a village called Leer. There was a clinic there and they became the clinic's doctors.

'I went to visit them. I was so scared but I thought, if Fallon can do this so can I. I traveled the last hundred kilometers by Land Rover. They said it was a road but to me it looked more like potholes held together by ruts. When I arrived your mum was operating on a woman whose arm had been badly cut... (I'm sure by a soldier with a machete but Gran leaves this part out) ...so it was your dad who met me at the gates. He was gorgeous. Picture Grandad Sky as a young man. He gave me a hug and I suddenly felt safe like nothing can harm me. Your daughter's saving the world as usual, he said, so we're free to have a cold beer.'

The word beer jolts me back to Father McKenna. He's going on and on about Darcy like he knew him which he didn't. I turn my head so I can see Fungal sitting in his digger. He can't hear a word Father McKenna's saying so I'm wishing I was in the cab too listening to the music; probably The Pogues or Dropkick Murphys knowing Fungal. Now he's looking in a backpack and frowning. Ha ha, me thinks, probably staring at a-year-old ham sandwich all green and nasty. Now he's swinging up another backpack and taking out a Thermos flask and a sandwich wrapped in waxed paper. Teatime.

Even though he's ten years older Fungal was mates with Darcy cos they both played Marauders, Friday nights at the Parish Hall. Fungal's not quite right in the head, what they used to call *slow*. He speaks slowly — maybe that's why they use that word — thinking about every word, stringing them together carefully like a baby taking his first steps. Gran says Fungal was one of the brightest lads in Gloire Bay till Deirdre, his mum, painted his bedroom with old paint had lead in it and that night Fungal woke up screaming because the paint fumes were making his brain expand. They rushed him to the hospital where they cut a hole in his skull to let his brain come out. Fungal survived but his IQ didn't.

Gran says Deirdre will never forgive herself, even though it was an accident, everyone in the village swearing they wouldn't have known any different. The funny thing is Darcy said Fungal was murder when it came to Marauders. *Savant,* Darcy said, meaning Fungal had a gift for strategizing the others could only marvel at. Anyway, Fungal listening to music, chewing on a ham sandwich at Darcy's funeral would have pleased Darcy no end.

That's for sure.

Father McKenna: 'O God, who by the glorious resurrection of thy Son, Jesus Christ, didst destroy death, and bring life and immortality to light, grant that thy servant, Darcy, being raised with him, may know the strength of his presence, and rejoice in his eternal glory; who liveth and reigneth with thee in the unity of the Holy Spirit, one God, for ever and ever. Amen.'

I asked Darcy once if he believed in an afterlife? Reincarnation, he said, that's the way to go. And what would you be coming back as? I asked. Gran's cat, he says, knowing it will make me laugh. No, really?

A bird, he says, staring at the gulls circling above us.

Father McKenna loves the sound of his own voice and these days he rarely enjoys such a large audience so we're going back to the Sudan. Gran's been fired as narrator because she isn't going to tell her little granddaughter the truth. Well, that's not fair. She told me the truth — my parents died — but she left out the horrible details. Those I've discovered on my own searching the net for anything on Sudan. Now I know all the stats, all the players.

I know North Sudan is mostly Muslim with a strong Arabic flavor while the South is more Christian, more African. In twenty years of civil war, the North and South between them managed to murder over two million men, women and children. In 2011 South Sudan broke away from the North and became its own country. I even found articles about the clinic in Leer but those I can only read till I see words like machinegun and massacre.

So, I've turned what happens next into a Hollywood movie. Darcy says anything Hollywood touches becomes unreal. He blames the lighting and

I don't know enough to argue. All I know is it's the only way I can keep my heart from shattering.

I've cast Chris Hemsworth as my dad, Jesse. He's perfect for the part. Large, strong, big heart. Emma Stone is my mum, Fallon. This isn't quite right — she's too short to start with — but I love her froggy voice and all the expressions she has. Putting my two favorite actors together has to be magic, right?

As the titles run we see Gran (played by Helen Mirren speaking with an Irish accent) helping Angelina the midwife (Naomi Harris) deliver babies. Hard to bring babies into this mess, Gran says to Fallon at the end of a long day. That's when Fallon tells her mum she's pregnant. Gran asks, will you go somewhere safe to have the baby? Fallon doesn't answer which is answer enough. Gran understands. The people of Sudan live with danger every day. Jesse and Fallon won't desert them. Gran flies back to Ireland.

My movie — **The Parents I Never Knew** changed by the director (Ridley Scott) to **My Dead Parents** changed by the studio (Warner Bros.) to **Massacre!** — opens with my parents working together, wearing their gowns and masks, their faces glistening with sweat as they labor to save a woman with one arm. Fallon groans and Jesse glances at her. Fallon is nine months pregnant and this is the moment her baby (me) has chosen to enter the world. They're ecstatic about having a baby it's just there isn't time right now.

'It's okay,' Jesse says. 'I can handle this. Go and have that baby.'

Fallon lies down on the floor on a mat and Angelina the midwife brings some low screens for privacy. She says, 'It will not hurt as much if you squat.'

'Really?'

'Trust me.'

Fallon changes position. Now she looks like she's trying to poop out a bowling ball. She smiles over at Jesse and they both laugh but the laughter is short-lived because little Shaker (Dani Dare) comes running into the room shouting, 'SPLA coming! Convoy! Two trucks and SUV!'

The SPLA — Sudanese People's Liberation Army — have visited twice before. The first time they were looking for food and took everything they found. The second time they brought their wounded for the doctors to fix. Jesse tried to tell Makal Kuol, the young SPLA leader, that most of the people they treat are there because of the SPLA but Makal (Byron James) doesn't care. 'Fix my men so they can send you more patients,' he says, laughing like this is beyond funny.

Between contractions Fallon says, 'If they find Tayeb they'll kill him for sure.'

'We can't move him.'

Tayeb is a government soldier from the North, a Muslim of Arabic descent. The SPLA left him for dead but Tayeb managed to crawl onto the road and from there he ended up at the clinic where Dr. Jesse had no choice but to cut his leg off — the one with gangrene.

'Put him in the fridge.'

The fridge is a wooden box — coffin-shaped — in the ground deep enough to keep things cool. It lies beneath a trapdoor in the clinic floor. Jesse leaves the suturing to nurse Rita and helps Shaker lift Tayeb from his cot and place him in the fridge. There isn't room without first rearranging the medicine and what's left of the beer.

'Don't drink all the beer,' Jesse says and Tayeb grins. He knows enough English to understand Dr. Jesse is making a joke. He also understands everyone in the clinic is risking his or her life for him.

'Thank you,' he whispers as the trapdoor closes above him.

Jesse grabs the edge of the mat Fallon is squatting on and pulls till the mat covers the trapdoor. Then he looks between Fallon's legs hoping to see the top of a baby's head.

'The things you'll do to get time off.'

Fallon wants to laugh but — *OMG!* — it hurts.

'You can have the next one.'

'Not me. I just like being there for the good stuff.'

Jesse is heading back to the operating table when the clinic door bursts open. Makal Kuol strides in followed by five of his men. The last one is only a child. Ten at most. He looks ridiculous carrying a machinegun as big as he is but Jesse knows this little boy will die with that gun in his hands and when he does the gun will be handed to the next child warrior.

Jesse's surprised when more soldiers don't appear carrying the wounded. Where are the other soldiers and what are they doing? Makal takes a step forward. He's tall, lean and cruel, hardened by war into merciless steel.

'I hear you are hiding a government soldier. Is this true?'

Fallon cries out. Jesse glances at her head above the screen. He thinks she's trying to be a distraction but he can't be sure.

'Excuse me for a sec; my wife is having a baby.'

Jesse and Fallon aren't married but they've been living together for three years so the wedding certificate is just a formality, right? Otherwise, I'm a love child and that sounds okay too.

I'm not sure about this next part. Should we see my head emerging or just skip to the part where my dad holds me high in the air for all to see?

'Hey Fiona, welcome to the world.'

I know my parents have chosen names because they'd emailed Gran: *if it's a boy, Josh; if it's a girl, Fiona*. So, I'm pretty sure my dad would have said Fiona as he handed me back to Fallon. I picture him crouching down beside her, kissing her. 'Good job.'

'You have not answered my question.'

Jesse gets back to his feet. He needs to get Makal outside away from Fallon and the new baby. He starts toward the door but the nearest soldier raises his gun, shakes his head. Jesse isn't sure which way to turn. They've been betrayed, that much is obvious, and because they've hidden Tayeb, Jesse has, really, only one way to go.

'No soldier here as you can see. Mostly women and children who deserve better.'

A woman screams outside the clinic. Inside no one speaks until

Angelina the midwife — she's having a premonition and not a good one — says to Fallon, 'Give me the baby. I'll wash her in the sink outside.'

The camera focuses on Fallon's face. You can see her heart is breaking as she hands me over. Angelina walks outside cradling the baby. She takes one look back and starts to run.

I can't watch the rest. Instead, I follow Angelina running away, while on the soundtrack we hear Makal Kuol asking for a cold beer.

THURSDAY
10:30

Father McKenna finally finishes. He goes to Debra, who he's turned to quivering jelly, and tries to comfort her. Fungal starts his engine but Father Wanker glares at him so he shuts it down. Fungal's like me he wants this over.

Poor Darcy. Poor me. All our hopes and dreams dead in the dirt.

Everyone walks sadly through the iron gates. Even the angel on top has turned her back on everybody.

'Hey Fiona, would you be heading back to school? I could give you a ride.'

Billy has attached himself like handcuffs.

'Thanks Billy, I've got other plans.'

'I could still be giving you a lift.'

I can see Billy has instructions to keep an eye on me. Probably from his Aunt Debra or maybe Mrs. Barrow

'You'll get yourself suspended.'

'That would be ironic, wouldn't it?'

Mr. Davidson, our English teacher, has been teaching us about irony. He says it's one of the great human conditions.

'And what would be ironic about that?'

'You miss school so the punishment is you miss more school.'

So, me and Billy — Billy pushing his bike — turn away from the crowd trundling back to the village and follow instead the dirt laneway that leads to the top of the steep cliffs that overlook Gloire Bay. Sliabh Cloiche the cliffs are called in Irish — Stone Mountain — but Sean's Mountain is what we locals call it. It isn't technically a mountain — Grandad Sky says a hill has to be a thousand feet tall to be called a mountain — but Gran says calling it Sean's Hill wouldn't do the climb justice. It's all words to me till one night we watch Hugh Grant in an old movie called *The Englishman Who Went Up a Hill But Came Down a Mountain,* which is the story of these two English cartographers sent to measure a mountain near this little Welsh town only to find it isn't quite tall enough to be called a mountain it's only a hill. The town folks are so outraged they storm up the hill with their shovels and start building a mound high enough to make it a mountain again. Rotten Tomatoes only gives it 58% but Gran and Grandad and I liked it and when it's over I ask, 'So, who was this Sean that he has a mountain named after him?' Gran just shakes her head like haven't a clue, which pleases me. I like questions seeking answers.

Billy says, 'Dad says it's luck to have found Darcy's body.'

We're walking along the cliff edge now. The tide's in, the white waves crashing on the rocks far below sending up spray dancing with rainbows. I don't answer so Billy continues, 'He says most bodies aren't found. They wash out to sea and become food for the fishes.' I wince at this and Billy says, 'Sorry.'

Gran's taught me not to grieve for those who pass on. They're still out there somewhere, she says, in some way we don't understand. Don't you worry about them Fiona; they're fine.

'Darcy'd be okay with that,' I say after giving it some thought. 'He saw everything as interconnected; all of us part of a universal energy flow.'

'May the force be with you.'

'That's right, Billy. May the force be with you.'

I really don't want to talk so I send Billy back to the village. 'I'm okay Billy. I'm not jumping off these cliffs anytime soon.' Certainly not until I find out what happened to Darcy.

Billy doesn't want to but heads back and I keep going along the path that follows the cliff edge until finally it turns inward heading for the peat bog. Where the path turns a squat, circular tower made of stones stands guard, watching for intruders coming by sea. There's no opening in the bottom of the tower, instead there's supposed to be a wooden ladder leading to a doorway on the second floor the idea being, if you're attacked, you just pull your ladder in like a turtle hiding its head. Gran says the ladder disappeared after female tourists were complaining about the local lads looking up their skirts. Now there are wooden steps that are in much better shape than what's left of the stairs inside leading to the gun platform at the very top. I've listened so many times to Grandad Sky giving his American visitors a lesson in Irish history I could be a tour guide without even trying.

'The English built fifty of these Martello towers around Ireland's coastline to protect the island from Napoleon Bonaparte. They got the idea from a tower in Corsica built at Mortella Point. Two of their warships bombarded the place for two days but still the tower held. It was only when they sent land forces that they finally captured it and even that wasn't easy. The Brits were so impressed they started building them. Spelt the name wrong but what else is new, right? Some have been restored — Bono owns one! — but most are like this one, seen better days.'

This is our sunset picnic spot. Me, Gran, Grandad and, often as not, Darcy would hike up here to enjoy the view — one of the best in Ireland Gran says — and just before the sun waved goodbye for another day the horizon would erupt in a fiery lightshow of pinks and purples, oranges and reds, as if to say here's your reward for taking the time to enjoy the world around you. And then as we'd walk home the nightshift would appear: the white moon bouncing LED's across the dark sea while pinprick stars suspended in the night sky remind everyone that hey, there's a universe out here waiting to be explored.

I weep.

Crying's a strange thing like blowing your nose. After a while you're think-ing where does all this liquid come from? Darcy says you've got a sack of snot in your right buttock and a bag of salty water in the left, both just waiting for the right moment. Darcy had all kinds of theories most of them shite. Fiona, what would you think of an artificial intelligence run-ning the world? And me saying, it'll probably decide to eliminate human beings as we're the ones causing all the problems.

When the tears finally end I feel better, cleansed I suppose. Darcy's death has left a hole in my soul big enough to drive a bus through but somehow I'll go on, patching and mending, but remembering too and dreaming about what might have been. That's the thing about death you don't know till it knocks you on your arse. It's final. No second chances. No last goodbye. No last hug and kiss. No... *Stop it Fiona or you'll be blubbering again...*

Did I finish up with my mum and dad? They died that day in Sudan — the day I was born — but Makal Kuol and some of his soldiers died too so I figure my dad had some measure of revenge. All the deaths seem so pointless it's hard finding anything positive to hold onto. As for me...

Angelina, cradling Dr. Fallon's brand-new baby girl, reaches Adok a village ten kilometers from Leer. There she finds a young woman who's just had a baby of her own. The woman feeds Fiona and promises to look after her while Angelina returns to Leer but the next morning comes the horrible news of the massacre at the clinic and Angelina knows there's no point in going back. She talks the new mother — her name is Grace — into going with her and together they catch a ride to Juba. There, Angelina finds a woman who works for Médecins Sans Frontières. The woman promises to look after Dr. Fallon's baby but Angelina won't let go. 'I am not handing this baby over to anyone but Dr. Fallon's mother. She is the one who will love this child.'

And so, Angelina and Grace, with the two babies, wait for five days until Gran appears. A step behind comes a giant of a man carrying Gran's backpack and his duffel bag. Angelina hands Gran the baby and both women burst into tears. Then Gran turns to the giant of a man and says, 'Put the bags down Sky and meet your granddaughter. Her name's Fiona O'Hara.'

Gran and Sky met for the first time at the airport in London. On the flight to Juba they talked about everything — Fallon, her sisters Ciara and Nora; Jesse, his older brother, Luke; Gran's husband Ryan dead now six years; Sky's wife Beth taken by cancer ten years before; everything but the baby's last name.

The women hug as Sky cradles tiny Fiona. He's so big and Fiona so small. It occurs to Sky that they have no way to feed the baby but the women will sort this out as they always do. Women are good at sorting things out, thinks Sky, especially the things that matter.

'Angelina, this is Dr. Jesse's father, Sky Locking. He's from Texas.'

'Big,' Angelina says and Gran laughs.

Gran slips Angelina an envelope full of money. 'For you and Grace. We can never thank you enough.'

Angelina doesn't want to take the money — Dr. Fallon and Dr. Jesse were her friends — but Gran insists.

'Where will you go now?' Gran asks.

'Back to my village.'

'Is it safe there?'

'Nowhere is safe.'

'Would you like to come to Ireland?'

Angelina shakes her head but Sky Locking says, 'I would.'

To my left, far below, I can see my village, Gloire Bay, hugging the shoreline, hanging on for dear life as it has done for more than five thousand years. Where the cliffs vanish into the sea their tail forms a natural harbor, home to half-a-dozen fishing boats — Gran says there used to be 30 or more — along with sailboats and motor launches. Nothing grand but all you need to enjoy the big water on a sunny afternoon.

In the old days, before radio and radar, when a boat was late coming home the women would send one of the boys scampering up to the tower to look for it. That's when one of the best views in Ireland took on a meaning as deep as the Atlantic Ocean. Now I'm the one waiting for a ship that will never return.

I'm about to head home when I see a horse with two riders galloping fast, making short work of Sean's Mountain. I know the horse — his name is Tangent — and I know the lead rider is my buddy, Karen Hanlan, her distinctive carrot-red hair streaming out behind her. She's an American from Boston — 35 I think she is — speaking with the same accent as President Kennedy. *Ask not what your country can do for you but what you can do for your country.* She's a veterinarian though she doesn't practice here for a reason you'll soon be knowing and she's got pots of money so really, she doesn't need to work at all.

Karen arrived in Gloire Bay three years ago and promptly bought MacNamara's place, a heap of stones in need of resurrection. Now it's the prettiest property in Gloire Bay boasting a new barn and a scrubbed-clean piggery that has become the village's first yoga studio. The Downward Dog Karen calls it and me and Gran were the first to sign up for classes. Karen and I have been pals ever since. She's twenty years older but really, we're like two peas in a pod.

The man riding behind Karen, his arms wrapped around her waist, his face partly hidden by her hair, isn't anybody I recognize. He's wearing a dark suit and black, shiny shoes so maybe he was at the funeral. He looks daft wearing a suit on a horse but the grin on his face says he knows it. Tangent, Karen's Thoroughbred/Connemara cross, slows as he nears the tower.

Karen shouts, 'Hey Fiona, you there?' She's staring right at me but she doesn't see me. She might smell me if the wind wasn't blowing the other way.

Karen is blind and that's the first part of her story.

'Here!'

The man in the suit makes eye contact with me and slides off. He says something to Karen that I can't hear.

'This is Inspector Lawless. Isn't that a great name? He hasn't been on a horse since he was a little boy in short trousers.' Karen says trousers like she's lived in Gloire Bay forever — *trooosers* — then she turns Tangent around and disappears back down the path not worrying about Tangent knowing his way home.

I listen to footsteps on the stone stairs and then the Inspector's beside me. He's a tall, good-looking male — picture Colin Farrell in *Total Recall*. He sticks his hand out and I shake it.

'That's quite the view you've got here.'

I know I'm expected to say something but I've learned it drives adults crazy if you ignore them. He tries again.

'I'm the one looking into your friend Darcy's death.'

'What happened to Sergeant Leahy?'

In Ireland the police are called Garda or the plural Gardai, which is short for Gardai Síochána, which is Irish for Guardians of the Peace. Sergeant Leahy is mates with Gran so I see him often enough sneaking into Stonehaven for a cup of tea, catching up on the local gossip.

'It's usual in these cases to send a senior Inspector. Everyone seems to think the poor lad lost his way in the storm but that doesn't sit well with me.'

You've got that right!

'Why not?'

'Because I was a boy once.'

The Inspector doesn't say the rest, which is: a local lad would know to stay away from the cliff edge during a storm. I agree. No way did Darcy fall off this cliff. Someone helped him.

'My question is what was he doing up here in the first place?'

I can tell you that but not yet.

'How did you know where to find me?'

'Your grandfather said if you weren't at school or The Downhill Dog, chances are you'd be here.'

The Downhill Dog is what Grandad Sky calls Karen's yoga studio. He came with us once and ended up in bed for two days. Said there was another form of exercise he liked much better, which got him a punch in the arm from Gran!

'So, you started your investigation at the pub?'

The Inspector laughs at this. 'The hub of all knowledge.'

'And what was the consensus there?'

'The weather was fierce. Lad was probably walking backwards protecting his eyes. Or he might have been high on maryjane and lost his footing. Or...' The Inspector stops but I can guess. Or the young lad did a jumper, committed suicide.

'Faeries.'

'Fairies?'

'That's why Darcy was up here. We have to write a paper on Irish Literature/Irish History and Darcy was researching faeries. A E faeries.'

'A E?'

'Most people spell fairies with an I but Darcy said in Ireland they should be A E faeries because that's the way W.B. Yeats spelled it.'

I can see the Inspector isn't really following.

'Come away, O human child!
To the waters and the wild,
With a faery — spelled f a e r y — hand in hand.
For the world's more full of weeping than you can understand.'

Ah, I can see the data sorter in Inspector Lawless's brain has just pegged me as: too bright teenager, probably rebellious, for sure a pain in the arse.

'So why was Darcy coming up here?'

I walk to the other side of the tower and point. The Inspector joins me. In the distance you can see the land falling off leading to an island of vibrant green vegetation.

'He'd be going to the peat bog because that's where the faery fort is. And he'd be going at night because that's the only time you might see them.'

I can feel Inspector Lawless trying to hide his skepticism — like this is all I need, faeries and forts.

'You were his girlfriend, right?'

'We suckled on the same breasts.'

It's so much fun to startle adults. They double take; they flounder; they want to get into their Volvos and drive back to Sligo. Who cares about a fifteen-year-old boy falling off a cliff?

They strike back.

'So why weren't you with him?'

Now there's a good question and not one I want to answer.

'I was busy.'

'Busy how?'

There's suddenly steel in the Inspector's voice. The kid gloves are off. I imagine you don't become an Inspector without being able to smell a lie or an avoidance a football pitch away. Let's try misdirection.

'When they found Darcy's body did they find a mobile?'

'Mobile?'

'I got an iPhone for my birthday. Darcy borrowed it. That's what he was going to use to take the faeries' photos.'

'I don't know. I'll find out. Now, what were you busy with?'

The Inspector waits, not looking at me but staring out at the peat bog. I know he isn't going away till I answer.

'I went to my girlfriend's for a sleepover.'

We both know I'm lying but the Inspector lets it go. For now.

'I gather your grandmother is a witch.'

Whoa! And where would that be coming from?

'Of course, she is.'

And a healer and a feminist and a spiritualist and for sure the wisest person in Gloire Bay!

'Who told you that? It's hardly a secret.'

Probably Father McKenna the old reprobate.

'Do you think that had anything to do with this?'

'No. Do you?'

'She believes in faeries, right?"

"She talks to 'em. Helps 'em when they need a human. We've got a boggart livin in the house.'

'A boggart?'

'Do you know Dobby?'

This gets me a blank stare.

'Gollum?'

The Inspector shakes his head totally lost.

'Dobby's from *Harry Potter* and Gollum from *Lord of the Rings*. Feister looks like a mixture of those two.'

'Feister's the boggart?'

'Yes.'

'So, if we go to your house you can introduce me to Feister?'

Yes, except Feister is now a Horned Toad whereabouts unknown.

'You need a positive attitude. You have to believe.'

'Ah,' sighs the Inspector like there's the loophole you can drive the lorry (truck) through. 'So why wasn't Darcy just taking a picture of Feister?'

'Feister wouldn't let Darcy see him.'

'Ahhhhh.'

This conversation is suddenly making me angry. I have no time for ignorant people and their closed minds. It's why the world stinks. Unused brain cells. Rotting gray matter. I'm halfway down the stairs when the Inspector yells out.

'Okay, okay. I can see friendliness running away like Usain Bolt.'

'Bolting.'

The Inspector laughs and catches up to me outside the tower. He sticks his hand out.

'Hi. I'm Inspector Mike Lawless. Nice to meet you.'

His smile says he's sorry. His eyes ask: can we start over?

I think being a Garda's a shite job — dealing with everybody's crap and getting little thanks for doing it — so I say, 'Hi Mike, I'm Fiona.'

'Are you walking back? Can I join you?'

I nod, start walking. *Too bad you're not sixteen Inspector...*

'Tell me about your friend Darcy...'

I think about stopping in at The Betty to find Grandad Sky but my legs take me to Karen's instead. I find her in the living room playing her shiny black Yamaha grand piano, singing one of her own songs called, *Whisper in the Wind*. Here's the chorus:

'We had everything the world had to give,
Didn't need to think, just live,
Lover, dreamer, my best friend,
Gone like a *whisper in the wind*.'

Karen deserves a grand piano and a stage too but she says she's not that good if you hear the really good ones like Lady Gaga or Alicia Keys. She's being modest, believe me.

When she finishes, I say, 'I think Inspector Mike likes you.'

Karen looks like a tall Scarlet Johansson so males are attracted like boys to computer games.

'He seemed nice. What's he look like?'

'My, my, aren't we shallow. What about his character? His sense of humor? His E Quotient?'

'What's he look like?'

'Colin Farrell.'

'Yummy.'

'He wanted to know if you'd always been blind.'

Karen flinches. This isn't something we've talked about but I know all the rumors and I've read everything online I can find.

'What did you say?'

'I said you were in a bad car accident.'

Karen begins to cry and now I feel mean.

'I'm sorry. That was mean of me.'

I sit down on the bench beside her and now we're both crying leaning on each other.

'I'm already soggy.'

'I bet,' Karen says wiping her eyes with her fingers. 'There's tissues somewhere.'

I find the box and return.

'It's just not something I talk about,' Karen says.

'I know.'

Karen nods but doesn't say anything. I've been waiting forever for her to tell me about the accident but she never has.

'I want you to see again.'

Karen laughs at this, a bitter laugh without joy. Then the tears start again and I feel like a complete shite. I wrap my arms around her and we start bawling together. Finally, I say, 'I'm so sad I want everybody else to be sad.'

'Everybody *is* sad.'

Tears dried we go back to discussing the Inspector. I say, 'So we're walkin along the cliff edge, Mike asking me —'

'Mike?'

'Yeah, I was pushing his buttons.'

'You're good at that.'

'Thanks, I think. He's askin me questions about Darcy but then he switches to you, like have you got a husband or a boyfriend, so I told him you were a lesbian.'

Karen punches my arm. For a girl who can't see her aim's pretty good.

'You didn't.'

'Didn't. Anyhow we hadn't gone far when I hear a boat so I look over the edge and there's Adriana in her Boston Whaler. She's huggin the shore, one hand on the wheel and the other holding binocs. She's staring at the rocks.'

'That's weird.'

'She was looking for something and right where they found Darcy's body.'

'What'd the Inspector do?'

'Asked me who she was.'

'What did you say?'

'I said her name's Adriana de Santis. She's from Rome. She's young, attractive, speaks perfect Italian, English and French and is the new owner of the Gloire Bay Hotel, which she's renamed Inn With The Tide. Then I told him what you told me — I hope that's okay?"

'What did I tell you?'

'That Adriana's dad is a mega-rich hotel owner and he apparently bought the hotel because it was as far away from Rome as possible and told his daughter to stay there till she could prove she could run something without running it into the ground.'

I can see Karen isn't happy with me spreading rumors so I don't tell her what else I said which is in six months Adriana's managed to alienate just about every inhabitant of the village to the point where most refer to the inn as Out With The Tide. And how did she accomplish this?

She started by refurbishing the old hotel at great expense but instead of hiring locals to do the work — Adriana was heard to remark, 'the locals couldn't find their buttocks with two hands tied behind their backs' — she imported workers from Italy and a designer from New York. When the work was finally complete all had to admit the old hotel had been spiffed up to such a point it was hard to recognize the old place at all. Grandad says Duggan O'Malley said it was like seeing Joan Rivers after plastic surgery. 'The ol' girl's there somewhere but I'll be damned if I can find her.'

The Gloire Bay Hotel had been a Michelin 1 ★ establishment but the new Inn was ★ ★. It might have been 3 stars if Brenda Shaughnessy hadn't eaten the chocolate meant for the adjudicator's pillow. Brenda was let go and the doors opened but if Adriana was expecting a tsunami of well-heeled travelers to descend on Gloire Bay so far that hadn't happened. In fact, the few visitors who stumbled into the village — either lost or on their way somewhere else — took one glance at the Inn's rates and kept going.

Karen decides not to scold me instead she says, 'I like Adriana. She's interesting.' Adriana is one of Karen's private yoga students and because they've both landed in Gloire Bay from afar they confide in each other.

I want to protest but really the times I've eaten at the Inn Adriana has been nothing but nice. Grandad Sky's told me a story so I repeat it for Karen. 'Apparently one of her guests told her she could hardly call her bar an Irish pub when it was empty of anybody Irish and that if Adriana wanted to see a real Irish pub she had only to walk down the street to The Betty.'

'Bet she loved that,' Karen says.

'Slashed her beer prices till they were half of Stan's.' (Stan Bailey owns The Betty.)

'Good for her.'

'So, Stan empties his pub and they all show up at Adriana's. Drink up boys, Stan says, on me. Our Adriana's losing money on every pint.'

'Let me guess, Grandad Sky was there.'

'Of course, he was. So not only does Adriana lose pots of money but Seamus Pringle manages to burn a hole in one of the imported leather barstools while Brian Flood scrawls *Betty's is Better* above every urinal and Roxanne, the cook at Betty's, barfs on the carpet and refuses to clean it up because Adriana wouldn't know shite from Butler's Truffles.'

'I think that's mean.'

'They were teaching Adriana a lesson but don't ask them what it was.'

'She told me last week that if she doesn't get more guests, she'll have to sell the place and move back to Rome.'

'Bet her dad will love that.'

'She's afraid to ask for more money.'

Suddenly I'm feeling sorry for Adriana.

'But what was she doin down by the rocks?'

I'm doing the coin toss thing in my head. Is Grandad at The Betty or has he managed to stagger home? Betty's is sort of on the way so it makes sense to stop in and see and it's a good thing I do because I find Grandad at his usual table in the corner — the one with the best view of the harbor — surrounded by his friends, Jim Brennan, Shapoor McBride and Patrick Campbell. But I'm barely through the door when Stan Bailey gathers me into his strong arms. I nestle in letting him hug me till finally he let's go.

'I'm so sorry,' he says and I smile bravely back. 'Darcy was a good 'un. Had a brain in his head unlike most of the lads,' — Stan looks around — 'young or old.'

'Hey Fiona,' Grandad shouts above the din. 'Have you come to collect me?'

Neither of us wants to go home. Stonehaven is empty without Gran.

'Why weren't you at the funeral?'

'I'm still attending the wake.'

'He was sleeping is why,' Jim Brennan says, 'and no one had the heart to wake him.'

I try to look stern but inside I'm smiling. I love my big Grandad Sky from Texas. He is as out of place here as the cowboy hat he wears and yet somehow he belongs too.

'Bandit will need feedin.'

Bandit is Gran's cat and so fat he could live a month without *feedin*. Grandad pushes back his chair and gets to his feet. He doesn't do it smoothly more like rusted machinery needing oil.

'What would you say to some of Brownie's fish n' chips?'

Gran's packed the freezer with food but there's nothing thawing.

'I wouldn't say no.'

'See ya, Professor. Hang in there, Fiona.'

Everyone in Gloire Bay — everyone but me and Gran — call Sky Locking Professor because he taught history at various universities throughout the United States for over 40 years. As we exit the pub Grandad wraps his arm around my shoulders.

'Did that Inspector fellow find you?'

SUNDAY
11:00

It's Sunday, three days after Darcy's funeral. Still no word from Gran. Nothing from the Inspector. Grandad's in his study working ;on his latest book so I'm trying to be quiet. I'm so empty and so bored I decide to clean my room. If Gran was here she'd be taking my temperature. Darcy, how could you leave me destitute like this? Wanker. So, I'm doing laundry, tidying and sweeping, and crying and for a second I even miss Feister — did I really turn him into a toad? — which just shows how pathetic I've become. And then anger roars in and suddenly I'm my dad wrestling the machinegun from the child soldier and spraying Makal Kuol and all his rotten men. *Die wankers die!*

I fall on my bed and Bandit crawls in beside me wanting a cuddle.

'Life sucks Bandit.'

Did I tell you where Gran is? She's in South Sudan visiting with Angelina, the midwife who saved my life, and Grace the one who fed me. The government's erecting a new statue at the clinic in Leer celebrating the lives of the good people who died there. Gran's gone to be part of the unveiling.

'I should be there with her.'

Bandit doesn't say if he agrees or not, but it's definitely the truth. *I should have gone with Gran.*

After lunch Billy appears — uninvited but I'm glad to see him. Billy wants to go to the beach, which is a better idea than anything I'm thinking so we ride over to Karen's. We find her in the barn mucking out Tangent's stall. I introduce her to Billy.

'How do you know what you're doing?' Billy asks in his innocent, straightforward way.

'I feel the weight of the fork,' Karen says. 'If I'm still not sure I bounce the fork a little and if I feel lumps dancing around, I know I've got something.'

'Then how do you know where to put 'em?'

'I place everything in exactly the same place so my body's memory can remember what to do.' Karen swings her fork around and in one fluid motion deposits the dung in the wheelbarrow. 'But do you know what's even better?'

Billy shakes his head forgetting Karen can't see.

'He doesn't know what's better,' says me.

'Better is having a boy named Billy mucking out the stalls.'

It's obvious Billy doesn't know horses from horseradish and judging by the horrified look on his face he plans to keep it that way.

'We was hoping to borrow...' Billy looks at me.

'Sally.'

'We was hoping to borrow Sally for a mite ride.'

'That sounds way more fun than mucking out stalls.'

'Yeah,' agrees Billy.

We journey down the coast to Beg Head. I'm sitting in front Billy's arms wrapped around my waist and I'm liking the warmth of his body against mine. A flash of guilt courses through my veins but I don't see how a dead boyfriend is going to care.

'Your hair smells like straw,' Billy says in his no-nonsense way.

Sally's old — an Irish Cob workhorse her back as big as a chesterfield — but she seems pleased to be out by herself instead of having to keep up with that young upstart, Tangent. The tide's changing directions but still the beach at Beg Head is as wide as a football pitch and the sun's shining, which is a treat in Ireland, making the water a pretty cobalt blue color. There's a few other folk enjoying a day at the beach including Sergeant Leahy with his wife and two little daughters. He waves and I wave back.

Billy's wearing a backpack which he dumps out showing me the two cans of Guinness he's liberated from his large-mouthed father and a bag of crisps he says his mum sent 'and you be sayin hello to Fiona for me and tell her how badly we all feel about Darcy.'

Along with everything else — Frisbee, plastic bag, Irish Butter Toffee — Billy's brought a plastic squeeze bottle full of salt, which he proceeds to squirt into a hole on the beach. In seconds what looks like a piece of bamboo shoots out of the hole and Billy grabs it holding it up like a trophy.

'My dad loves these things.'

I've been razorfish fishing before. Inside the bamboo — the tube shell — is a long white clam. Whenever Mr. Davidson uses the word phallic it isn't penises I picture, it's razorfish erupting from the sand.

'He fries 'em in butter and garlic. The shell pops open.'

'Bit chewy.'

We search for more razorfish while Billy prattles on about last year's trip to Canada then — just like the Inspector — he wants to know about Karen. 'Dad says she's not really blind she just thinks she is.'

'Your dad says a lot.'

"Mum calls him Motor Mouth.'

Now there's the pot calling the kettle black cos if Billy's mother gets a hold of you she'll talk both ears off and tie 'em together too.

'Psychosomatic,' says me as if that should explain it. I can tell it's a new word for Billy but he gets the gist. There's nothing wrong with Karen's eyes; the fault's in her brain.

'Why would she do that?'

'She was in a really bad car accident. Her brother and her fiancé were killed. She was driving and it was her fault.'

'So, being blind is like her punishment?'

'I guess. On google it says she was charged with vehicular manslaughter but they suspended the sentence given the circumstances.'

'Dad says she inherited gobs of money.'

'Her brother was rich. He left everything to Karen.'

'Not married then?'

'No.' I know this and lots more from reading the American papers online but Billy takes my one word answer as meaning I'm not interested in adding to the gossip so he goes back to catching razorfish.

It's late afternoon now. We're still at the beach sitting on the sandy slope studying the waves rolling in. Wasting time really but the sunshine on my face feels good. Behind me Sally's found tufts of beach grass she's munching on. Billy's been helping Sgt. Leahy's little girls build a moat around their sandcastle but now he's back beside me, close enough I can feel the heat from his arm on mine. I go back to thinking about Karen not seeing.

'It's not quite the same but apparently hundreds of Cambodian women choose not to see because of all the horrors they endured.'

Ain't Wikipedia wonderful?

'I like seeing everything,' Billy says. 'I like seeing the girls building a sandcastle, then a wave comin in washin it away, and them not caring, just movin back, startin over.'

I decide I like spending time with Billy. There's more to him than I thought.

'Shouldn't you be watchin football or something?'

'I'd rather be with you.'

There it is again. Innocent. Honest. Direct. Darcy had to be the most complex person on the planet and keeping up with him was a challenge. This seems relaxed, simple.

'What do you think happened to Darcy?' Billy asks.

'Inspector Mike asked me that.'

'What did you say?'

'I said there's no way Darcy fell over that cliff without help.'

'That's what Dad says too. Somebody pushed him.'

Back at home I find Grandad Sky relaxing on the porch, petting Bandit.

'The Inspector called. He said to tell you they didn't find a mobile.'

I sit down beside Grandad and Bandit comes to me.

'Darcy borrowed my iPhone. It must have gone over the cliff with him.'

'We'll get you a new one.'

'Thanks Grandad.'

Grandad Sky begins to cry, big tears rolling down his cheeks. It scares me.

'This thing with Darcy has got me thinking about your mum and dad.'

He doesn't say the rest, which is just like Darcy they died so horribly, so needlessly.

Was Darcy screaming when he crashed onto the rocks?

I bury my head in Grandad's shoulder and we cry together.

I'm not much of a cook so I shift things around in the freezer till I find one of Gran's chicken potpies. This one's got phyllo pastry on top, bits of which get stuck in Grandad's cowboy moustache like oversized dandruff.

'Don't be kissin anyone like that,' says me.

'You're the only likely recipient.'

'It'd be like having another piece of pie.'

'Don't mind if I do.'

I get Grandad another helping and stick my plate on the floor for Bandit to lick. I'm about to say we should have gone with Gran but that'll just get us crying again.

'How's the book comin along?'

Grandad's writing a book about all the wars the United States has fought since World War II but instead of taking the American point-of-view he's going to show the other side and, if you need an example of that, did you know the Vietnamese don't talk about The Vietnam War they talk about The American War. He says the title's going to be *Bloodthirsty Nation* but I think he's pulling my leg. He says Americans like their wars because they're always far from the fighting. It's like playing a computer game till your nephew comes home with no legs or his brain scrambled like eggs.

Grandad finds *The Bourne Legacy* on the telly so we watch that. He likes the Bourne movies but prefers the ones with Matt Damon. I should be tired after that but I'm wide-awake instead. I start thinking again about my English/History essay trying to come up with a topic that interests me. Grandad's no help. He's opened a bottle of something called, Ten High Kentucky Bourbon Whiskey Sour Mash. He gives me a shot glass of the amber liquid — thank you Grandad! — and between sips suggests, The Great Potato Famine Mash-Up.

'No one had to die. The English let the poor Irish Catholics starve to death so they could amalgamate all the small holdings. It was genocide really.'

'I don't think that's what the Davidsons are looking for.'

There's two Mr. Davidsons at my school. They're twins, but the one teaching History is short and hairy, and the one teaching English is tall and bald. Dizygotic twins Darcy would say, meaning there were two eggs involved not one splitting in half. They're best mates so sometimes they tag team essays so they only have to read half, which is right smart when you think of it.

'Well, it knocked the stuffing out of Irish culture. A million died and another million emigrated.'

'I think I'm needin something more positive.'

'How bout Oscar Wilde?'

I know something about Oscar Wilde because one of Darcy's get rich schemes was makin T-shirts with Oscar Wilde quotes like: *I CAN RESIST EVERYTHING BUT TEMPTATION.*

'Barbara Lander's doin Oscar Wilde, I heard her talkin about it.'

'So, you do him better.'

Grandad can see I'm not in the mood to do things better.

'How bout craic? That's a word no one but the Irish use.'

Craic — you say it crack — means fun.

The frown on my face tells Grandad all he needs to know about that idea.

'How bout Curry Chips and Plastic Paddies?'

'Say goodnight, Grandad.'

'I love you, Fiona.'

I try to concentrate but my brain is like a dark hole. Every time I get a whisper of an idea it vanishes never to be heard from again. When Grandad goes outside to check on things, I liberate a mug of Ten High. Jenny Pearsall's lent me John Green's latest book, *Zorizontal*, and because I've tidied my room I know exactly where it is. I read the first page three times and still don't know what's going on.

Honestly Fiona, get your shite together!

That's when I remember Darcy borrowing Gran's *Book of Faery Spells.* I've got to get that back before Gran shows up. It might have gone over the cliff with Darcy but I'm thinking *no way* cos Darcy knew how important it was to me. He'd be doing everything in his power to keep it safe.

It suddenly occurs to me I haven't checked my messages for days. This is the dead boyfriend's fault. I'd have my iPhone if it wasn't for Darcy.

Sorry Darcy, you know I don't mean it!

Grandad writes his books on a MacBook and Gran and I share the Dell sitting on the desk at the end of the upstairs hallway. I log in and check my email. Shite mostly but there's one from Gran. *Ceremony was wonderful! I'll be back in Joba Tuesday. Let's Zoom Tuesday night 8pm your time. Love Gran.*

I agree to that then finish scanning the rest of my email. Delete,

delete, wanker, delete. Hold on, what's this? There's one from myself. Fiona O'Hara. I check the date. *OMG! Friday night. 01:17.*

There's no subject line or text, only a photo. A grainy photo showing various shades of browny-black. Are there shapes? Humans? The flash has gone off but it's obvious Darcy was too far away from his subject. No matter how I rotate the image — no matter how I manipulate it — all I've got is blurred darkness but I know exactly what it is. Darcy taking a photo of his killer/killers as he's falling.

Oh Darcy! That must have been beyond terrible!

My bones turn to jelly and my heart climbs into my mouth — *I mean it!* — and I'm falling with Darcy waiting for the impact that will break every bone in my body and there's absolutely nothin I can do about it...

Utterly unnerved I return to my bedroom and flop down in the window seat on the big cushy pillows Gran's made for me. It's a clear night and the stars are beautiful.

Are you out there Darcy? I hope so.

I know it's a dream because I'm a beautiful mermaid — silver-scaled, bare-chested, long platinum hair, playing tag with a school of silver fish while Darcy's empty body dances behind me moving to the rhythm of the ocean — but some irritating person — is that you Feister? — is tapping so hard and so insistently I've got no choice but to swim to the surface to silence the annoying sod. It takes me several seconds of disorientation to realize where the noise is coming from. A faery, no bigger than my hand, is frantically kicking the window glass beside my head. It's a boy faery wearing an animal skin over one shoulder like Fred Flintstone. He has long dark hair tied in a ponytail and slung over his bare shoulder is a bow and a quiver of arrows. He's barefooted so kicking the glass isn't making him happy. I crank open the window.

'Bout time. You sleep like a lumberjack.'

'That's rude.' I turn the crank and the window begins to close.

'Wait!'

'Say you're sorry.'

'I'm sorry.' I turn the crank the other way.

'Where's Gran?' the faery asks.

'Unavailable.'

'Oh.'

I wait as the boy faery thinks about things. It's easy to see his instructions are to bring Gran. But he can't go back empty-handed that's obvious by the perplexed/anxious look on his face.

'Are you any good with animals?' he asks.

'I don't think so but my friend Karen is. She's a vet.'

'Perfect! Let's go!'

I look down making sure I'm clothed — not a half-naked mermaid — and satisfied on that count — seems I fell asleep on the window seat with my clothes on — I make my way downstairs as quietly as I can. I needn't have bothered. Grandad Sky is snoring into the kitchen table the half-empty bottle of Ten High within reach. I don't want you thinking Grandad's a boozer because he's not; it's just this thing with Darcy has brought back his son Jesse's death and with Gran away Grandad's flirting with liquid oblivion till better times appear.

I put on my anorak (jacket) and hiking boots and step outside. The boy faery is waiting, hovering at face height like a hummingbird, giving off light like a firefly.

'What did you do to poor Feister?'

Feister? Forgot all about him is what I did. 'Where is he?'

The boy faery flies under the nearest holly bush illuminating a very large, very...

'Oh my,' says me. A Horned Toad is even uglier than I imagined. 'Sorry Feister. I'll fix you when I get back. Promise.'

The boy faery is obviously in a huge hurry. Agitated would be the word as we strike off for Karen's the boy faery buzzing around my head trying to speed me up.

'What's your name?'

'Benji. What's yours?'

'Fiona. Where have you come from?'

'Faeryland. Do you know how to run?'

'You're being rude again.' I start jogging. Bossy little faery but I like him. Too bad Inspector Mike's not here to witness this. He'd be a believer.

'Is Gran your grandmother?'

'Yes.'

'She's a great lady. She's helped us ever so many times. Is she away on a trip then?'

"Yes. She's gone to Africa to the place where my mum and dad were murdered.'

'That's terrible. Why didn't you go?'

I'm about to say 'school' but really that's just an excuse.

'I should have gone.' And that's the truth. I should have gone but my first reaction was to say no — why would I go back to the place where my parents had their lives brutally ended! — and then I was too stubborn to change my mind. Darcy gave me shite about it but that just made me more obstinate. Stupid really. And if I'd gone maybe Darcy would still be alive. He couldn't have borrowed Gran's book for starters.

'I should have gone,' I say again for emphasis.

'That's all right. We all make mistakes.'

'And what mistakes have you made lately?'

"Stickin around for one thing. As soon as Queen Caelia arrived with her entourage I should have taken off. That's what Tolly and Sapphire did.'

'Who's Queen Caelia?'

Benji looks at me like *don't you know anything?*

'Queen of the Irish Faeries.'

'Where's she come from?'

'Letterkenny. Stupid council built a housing development within a stone's throw of the faery fort and now all the dogs and cats are patrolling the area. A tabby ate Mrs. Ooster and that was it for Queen C. Horth says she screamed, 'That's it! We're out of here!' Then Horth says as they were leaving Queen C changed the tabby into a mouse and shouts, 'Let's see how you like it!' Then Queen C wanted to know where they were going and Major Domo says the fort at Gloire Bay is the closest and Queen C makes a face and says, 'The last time I was there the toilets backed up. I think they did it on purpose.'

I can see Benji thinking plugging the toilets might not be a bad idea.

'Then what happened?'

'Queen C arrives without warning. No flying pig, no Seelygram, nothing. I mean we had no idea she was coming and in the middle of a storm too. Fierce it was the wind howling, the rain comin in buckets, and we're all buttoned up in Sí Dún–'

'What night was this?' asks me, thinking of the terrible storm the night Darcy died.

I watch as Benji counts on his fingers.

'Nine sleeps ago.'

That sounds about right. 'What's Sí Dún?'

'That's what we call the faery fort.'

'What's it mean?'

'Faery fort.'

Of course it does. 'So you're buttoned up in Sí Dún...'

'Dancing and singing–'

'Like a ball? Or like a nightclub with a D.J.?'

Benji gives me the same look Darcy'd give when I was interrupting too much.

'Jalapeño Grande.'

'Jalapeño?'

No way, right? Faeries with jalapenos? Ha ha.

Now Benji's pissed cos I'm backing the conversation up just like the toilets.

'Sorry, I'm interrupting. Please continue, it's just that–'

'Irish faeries shouldn't know about Mexican jalapeños?'

'Yeah, I guess. It just seems (strange, odd, incongruous) unlikely.'

'Ulf traveled to Chihuahua and the faeries there — the Duendes — invited him to a Jalapeño Grande and Ulf says what's that? So they tell him whenever a hurricane's coming, instead of being afraid, they have a party instead, so Ulf came back raving about it so now whenever the weather gets extremely foul we have a Jalapeño Grande to raise our spirits.'

Sounds good, doesn't it?

'With mariachis and fiddlers,' continues Benji. 'The females wear tango gowns with long slits up to their waist and the males dark suits with white shirts. Surrounding the dance floor are palm trees with coconuts that light up makin the room blue or red or yellow. Big ferns hide the tables. Is that sufficient detail?'

'Yes, thank you. Now I can picture the whole thing.'

It sounds wonderful and now I'm hoping Darcy got to see it.

'Continue.'

'So, we're having a good ol' time oblivious to everything outside when the door bursts open and in marches Queen Caelia like she owns the place, which she does technically, but it's like we haven't seen her for ages and here she is blowin in like a cold north wind. Well, of course, nothing was good enough. The Boggies were beside themselves trying to please her. 'This is the fourth move in eight years,' she screams. 'I don't move for 500 years and now suddenly four moves in eight years!' You should hear her. She sounds like a cat having its tail stepped on. Then she wants to know what we're doin in these ridiculous costumes. Are we almost there?'

We are almost there. I jog up Karen's laneway. There are no lights on in the house but that's normal — Karen doesn't need lights — but what's odd is the torch (flashlight) shining through a window from outside. I veer to the left and the torch swings toward me shining in my eyes. I put my hand up but keep running toward the light. Standing beside the window are Rufus McLeish and Rory O'Flynn, seniors at my school. I once told Darcy that Rory wouldn't know shite from chocolate pudding and Darcy shot back Rufus is so dense light bends around him. Like bullies everywhere they're either up to something or putting somebody down.

I yank the torch out of Rory's hand and shine it in the window. Karen's in her bedroom wearing nothing but her bra and knickers her back to the window. As I watch she reaches behind and undoes her bra.

'You fuckin wankers!' I keep my voice low so Karen won't hear. 'I'm telling Mrs. Barrow about this. She'll have your testicles for tree ornaments!'

'No! C'mon Fiona. We didn't mean anything. Just having some craic.'

That's when I spy the mobile in Rory's hand. I lose it.

'And were you gonna be takin her photo too? Put it on the net? Come see Blind Karen? You fuckin scumbags!'

Before I can hiss something worse Benji swings his bow up and shoots both boys turning them into potbellied pigs. Down the laneway they scurry grunting all the way only changing back to boys when they reach the road that leads into the village.

'I don't suppose you could make that permanent?'

'I'd say it already was.'

Benji leads me back to the front of the house. I knock, then open the door.

'Karen! Get some clothes on! We need you!'

Less than ten minutes later Tangent is galloping up Sean's Mountain with Karen in front and me behind holding on for dear life. Karen turns her head and shouts, 'Why are you laughing!?'

'We're hell bent for leather, going God knows where, and you haven't asked any questions.'

'Good idea. Where are we going?'

'Don't know. We're following a faery.'

'Really?'

'Really. His name's Benji.'

'Is he flying?'

'About ten meters in front. Tangent seems to know to follow him.'

'How big?'

'Tinker Bell size. Lit up like a firefly.'

'That's so cool.'

'Two boys were looking in your window.'

'They're not the first.'

'You need a guard dog.'

'I like big goofy dogs but I hate vacuuming.'

'Blinds then,' shouts me instantly regretting my choice of words. Curtains. Drapes. Shutters.

Karen's good at changing subjects. 'Inspector Mike called. He asked me out.'

'He must have liked his horse ride.'

'I guess.'

I can tell by Tangent's breathing that he's tiring. Karen hears it too and says, 'We can't go much farther at this speed.'

'The tower's dead ahead. I can see more lights dancing around so I think that's where we're goin.'

Tangent slows to a walk his breathing heavy but that isn't the only sound. Another horse is neighing obviously in distress.

'What is it, Fiona?'

'A huge black horse. Lying down. Rolling back and forth. Something's terribly wrong.'

'Take me.'

Karen slides off beside me. I grab her elbow and lead her toward the black horse, which is thrashing on the ground, making a noise like a piece of glass is lodged in its throat. The horse's body is drenched in sweat, her eyes wild with fear. Benji and a hundred other faeries float above the horse providing light, quiet now that someone's here to help.

'It's a mare. She's trying to foal.'

Karen lets go of me and guided by the horse's noises, kneels down beside the mare's head.

'Easy girl, it's okay. Shhhhh. Shhhhh.' The mare rolls violently shaking her head knocking Karen backward.

'She's trying to change the foal's position. We need to get her up Fiona.'

I lift the mare's head till she has no choice but to stumble to her feet.

'Good. Now push her against the tower. Try to hold her there. Talk to her, stroke her.'

Karen runs her hand along the mare's side following her hand till she reaches the mare's rump.

'Easy girl, easy. We're trying to help... I should have brought my bag.'

But we didn't know, did we?

Karen removes her jumper (sweater) throwing it aside leaving a long-sleeved t-shirt, bright yellow. I've seen it before at yoga. In the middle is Da Vinci's naked man standing in a circle — arms and legs outstretched — except this time Da Vinci's drawn a woman. Karen pushes her right sleeve up and slips her hand into the mare's backside.

'Nothing in the vagina. Now I'm heading for the uterus where I feel...'

'Easy girl, easy...'

'It's a breech birth. It's not the head trying to come out it's the rear end... Her water hasn't broken yet.' Karen's eyes are closed, concentrating, and she's talking to me like I'm a first-year student at Vet school. I can see her arm moving inside the mare and it occurs to me that this is one time when being blind might be an advantage. Karen must be better at visualizing than most people.

'Good girl, good girl. You're being so brave.'

The mare is trying her best to cooperate but I can see the desperation in her eyes growing with every second. We're running out of time here and I want to tell Karen to hurry up but I know Karen's doing the best she can.

'Okay, I'm tearing open the placenta... now I can feel the amniotic sac... I can feel the foal's tail... and rump... It's in the upright position.'

I try to picture a little horse standing inside a big horse.

Suddenly the faeries above me gasp and shoot high into the night sky, scattering. The evening breeze, which has been warm and gentle through all of this, ramps up like a wind tunnel till my hair and Karen's are blowin sideways like the script calls for gale-force winds. None of this makes any sense till a strong light illuminates the mare like daylight. I turn my head to see where the light's coming from. Not ten paces away stands a tall man dressed all in black. A black cape flaps around his lean body as a beam of light as strong as an airplane's headlight lights him from behind.

'Fiona, what's happening?'

I recognize the man from Gran's fairytale books but I'm afraid to say the words.

'Fiona!'

'It's... The Dullahan.' *Doo-lihan* is how you say it.

'What's that?'

'The Headless Horseman.'

The Dullahan, his head tucked under his left arm, strides toward me. I know I should be petrified but I'm not. Thank Gran for that, I guess. *But stop staring at his head!* Gran's taught me that a lot of the things people don't believe in, like ghosts and faeries and angels, actually exist but it's like they live in a different dimension and to access that dimension you have to believe. If you're skeptical, cynical, suspicious, superior, have the empathy of a Donald Trump, then you're right, beings like The Headless Horseman don't exist. But if...

OMG! The head just winked at me! The Dullahan halts by the mare's head and strokes it with his right hand. *The mare is his, of course it is!*

'What's her name?' I ask.

The Dullahan's head chuckles. 'I have to be careful about what names I say out loud. I'm sure you understand.'

Legend says if The Dullahan speaks your name you won't live to see the sunrise.

'But I could spell it for you. B E S S. And who would you be?'

'Fiona O'Hara.'

'And your friend?'

'Karen Hanlan.'

'Damn!'

We both stare at Karen.

'I had one leg in the vagina but it's pulled it back in. But hey, it's alive. I'm going to try again... Okay, I've got one of the hind legs...'

I can see Karen straining, pulling hard. Soon one hoof appears and then the other.

'I need help! Quickly! I'm not strong enough.'

I start to move but The Dullahan stops me.

'Hold this, would you?' The Dullahan hands me his head and rushes to the back of the mare. The head's heavy and the neck feels wet and yucky on my palm. I'm so freaked out I'm beyond freaked out in some frozen place where you hold a human head like it's no big deal, I can do this. I bring the head up and it grins at me like isn't this good craic? Then it says, 'Perhaps, if you turned me around I could watch as well.'

We're just in time to see The Dullahan place his hands above Karen's and give a mighty heave. The foal slides out in a gush of fluid and Karen catches it, lowering it gently to the ground.

'It's a colt,' Karen says meaning male.

The Dullahan stands still for the longest time staring down at Karen inspecting the foal. The wind dies down. The light that seems to be always behind him dims. Benji and his friends return to their spot above our heads. Bess pushes me out of the way, turning so she can see her new baby.

The Dullahan takes his head from me, tucks it under his arm and says, 'As a reward I would like to grant you a wish. Is there someone you'd rather not see again?'

The Dullahan chuckles at this so I assume he's making a joke.

'I would like my friend Karen to see again.'

'Ah, that is a wish easily granted, isn't it Karen?'

Karen is still crouched down beside the colt but now she looks at me.

'I can see Fiona. I was so fixed on delivering the foal I forgot I couldn't see. Doctor Maynard said that might happen.'

The Dullahan winks at me again and says, 'I haven't had this much fun since Aughrim. Now, we're not going to count that wish. Try again.'

This time it's Karen who speaks. 'Show us what happened to Darcy.'

Suddenly it's raining so hard I can barely see Karen getting to her feet and the wind is so strong I couldn't walk into it if I tried. A bolt of lightning changes night to day while the thunder's crash sends Tangent rearing up pawing at the sky! And, for one brief second, I see human bodies, no more than shadows, huddled around another shadow lying unmoving on the ground. As the light from the lightning dissipates two shadows pick up the unmoving body by its wrists and ankles and pulling back their arms swing forward throwing the body like a sack of potatoes over the cliff.

I rush toward the cliff edge the wind pushing me so hard I think I'm going to go over too, so I drop to my knees stopping myself. I see Darcy falling, his arms moving toward his face, no sound but the wind and the waves, and then I see a flash of light. Poor Darcy taking his photo. Then he disappears into the darkness. Lightning flashes again but this time the sound of thunder is faint and far away as the wind dies around me.

When I finally turn back The Dullahan, the mare, the foal, Benji and his mates, the shadow people, all are gone. Only Karen and Tangent remain.

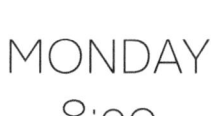

MONDAY
8:00

I keep reliving Sunday night — The Dullahan, the foal being born, Karen getting her sight back — and seeing Darcy being tossed over the cliff. (It'll haunt me forever!) At least two people were doing that and I keep thinking there were more watching, standing near the tower hiding from the wind. Karen says she only saw the two doing the tossing.

Karen telling me what she saw is new. I could tell she was excited about getting her sight back, but trying to temper that because practically the first thing she saw was Darcy going over the cliff. Karen didn't know Darcy, other than the few times he tagged along with me, but she knows he was my best mate so I sense she's trying to be subdued about seeing again. It's only when she realizes how excited I am for her that she relaxes. Gran's been right about everything so far so I'm trying really hard not to worry about Darcy. He's probably already back as a big goofy Golden Retriever, but wait till he sees he's in Shanghai with dogs hanging in the butcher shop!

(*Ugh. Trying to make a joke of things and it's not working.*)

What I am is feeling sorry for myself and more determined than ever to nail the smarmy bastards who'd throw a fifteen-year-old boy off a cliff.

I go to school my head still spinning. I don't hear a word anybody says till History class when Mr. Davidson — the short hairy one — takes off on one of his rants this time about Christopher Columbus getting credit for *discovering the New World*. 'I mean there were folks living there and there was nothing new about it!' Mr. D can get worked up about this stuff. 'So Columbus doesn't *discover* anything and he's not even the first to *visit* because the Vikings were there way ahead of him. And adding insult to injury what's CC do but compound the whole wretched thing by calling the locals *Indians* — the eejit thinks he's landed in India! — thereby cementing his name forever as one of the Grand Masters of White Person Arrogance.'

As I said Mr. D can get worked up about this stuff but he makes you sit up and listen which is more than a lot of teachers can say.

After school I make my way to The Downward Dog. Karen has an after-school yoga class for students, Monday and Thursday, so there's a bunch of us girls walking together chatting away. The odd boy comes because there's girls in leotards but they don't last which is just as well. Most of the girlie/flirty stuff I don't like vanishes when there's no boys to be practicin on.

'I'm sorry about Darcy,' Helen says. 'He was smarter than the others and funny.'

'What do you think happened?" Alicia asks and the other girls fall silent.

'I think he had help goin over the cliff,' says me.

'That's what my dad says. But why?'

That's the question, isn't it?

'He must 'ave seen something,' Heidi says making us all think. 'Something at the tower.'

'Or the bog.'

'Fiona, why weren't you with him?' Helen has finally found the courage to ask the question I imagine everybody's asking.

Because I had a date with somebody you don't know. Somebody older. Somebody who could give me what I thought I wanted. And why was I cheating on Darcy? Because my best mate Darcy was GAY! but you don't need to know that either.

Unlike Darcy I can't think of anything smart/funny to say so I clam up cementing — as Mr. D would say — my reputation of being stuck-up, aloof, removed, remote, self-important, snooty — take your pick and the funny thing is, whichever word you pick, I'll agree with it. Gran says Fallon was like that too. 'She wasn't a girlie girl,' Gran says and I get that. Not that I don't use cosmetics and such it's just that my nails aren't my whole life and never will be.

Karen's waiting at the door for us, smiling. She says to Alicia, 'I love your hair.'

Alicia can't believe it. 'You can see!'

'I can.'

'When did this happen?'

'Last night.'

'But how?'

This should be good but Karen laughs instead like it just happened, but she can see the girls aren't going to let this go without some explanation, so she tells them the truth — leaving out the part about Darcy — and of course they don't believe a word of it. The Dullahan? Faeries? *Please! Next, you'll be wanting us to believe in the Immaculate Conception.* 'You should be a writer,' Alicia says laughing and that's the end of Karen seeing for now.

I stay after class.

'Must be strange seeing everything for the first time.'

'Nothing's quite how I pictured it.'

'Better or worse?'

'Better. I love my house. I love my view. I like knowing what everybody looks like.'

'Including yourself?' Karen never wore makeup before but now she's wearing enough for an Estée Lauder ad.

'I was like a little girl getting into her mummy's makeup bag.'

'You're gorgeous without anything.'

Karen gives me a hug and says, 'Cuppa?'

We're sitting at her kitchen table drinking mango white tea discussing Alicia's blue, green and purple highlights when I change the subject and say, 'Tell me again what you saw last night.'

Karen doesn't say anything just keeps staring at her tea. Finally, she says, 'I'm someone who's grounded. My feet are firmly on the floor. I have just enough imagination to picture changing my bedroom walls from gray to yellow.' She looks at me over her cup and I nod. 'So when someone starts talking about faeries or goblins or God in His Heaven I stop listening. It's just more Santa Claus to me. And that's what makes me so angry about religious fanatics. How can they be so blind I ask myself? Why can't they see how manmade their religion is?'

'For some it's all they have.'

We've had this discussion before. About good religions and bad religions, about racism and gender inequality, about an evolutionary stepladder we need everyone to be climbing.

'Sorry,' Karen says, 'my mind's all over the place. What I'm trying to say is last night my eyes opened and I saw things that in my old life couldn't have existed.'

'Your old life. I like that.'

'You've always known about these things, haven't you?'

'Gran showed me.'

'You're lucky.'

'I am lucky. (Except for my parents and Darcy!) Now, tell me what you saw.'

Karen shuts her eyes, which makes me smile.

'I had the foal's hoofs in my hands but I wasn't strong enough so I called out and then I felt this male body behind me and powerful arms wrapping around me and then the foal's coming out and I realize I have to catch it but I need to see and next thing I know I'm not blind anymore. I catch the foal and lower it to the ground. Then I look up and there's The Headless Horseman, without his head, and everything inside me screams: NO! NO! NO! This can't be! — but there he is as real as you and me. Then

I see you holding his head — the look on your face! — and I want to laugh hysterically because all this has to be a dream but I know it isn't. Then I see the huge black mare licking her foal and above her a flock of faeries lit up like fireflies.' Karen opens her eyes. 'I can't believe I'm saying this.'

'What about Darcy?'

"The Dullahan showed us."

'You used our wish.'

'That was okay, right?'

'Absolutely. It was what I would have wished for.'

'After my sight.'

I nod.

'But are we taking what he showed us as gospel? I mean was The Dullahan there when Darcy went over the cliff?'

This makes no sense to me. Is Karen saying The Dullahan made it up? Or is she having trouble accepting the fact The Dullahan can conjure up past events at the drop of a hat? I decide to ask a question.

'When it was all over and everybody but us had vanished were your clothes wet?'

'Drenched.'

I can see Karen still wrestling with this because it goes against everything she thought she knew. But I can also see her brain cells are churning. *My sight's brand new so why shouldn't I look at everything in a brand-new way?* Now she's grinning because her size four world just expanded to XX-LARGE.

'Try again.'

Karen shuts her eyes remembering. 'It's raining so hard it's almost solid water and the wind's so powerful the rain's more horizontal than vertical. At the cliff edge I see two shadows, human, holding a body between them. I see them swing the body back then forward letting it go. I see you run to the cliff edge. You're not a shadow like the others. Then there's a flash of lightning and everything disappears. Everything but you.'

'Did you see more than two shadows?'

'No. Did you?'

'I think so. At least two more holding back by the tower, not moving.'

I tell Karen about opening my email and finding the photo from Darcy.

'When I ran to the cliff edge I saw a flash so that would be Darcy trying to take his killers' picture.'

'Four seems like a lot. And what would they be doing up there?'

'Something bad or they wouldn't be killin Darcy.'

Now it's me closing my eyes rerunning the images in my mind.

'When they were holding his arms and legs did it seem to you that Darcy was struggling?'

'No, not struggling. More like he was unconscious.'

I nod at this because that's what I remember too.

'But he must have been awake when he took the photo.'

That makes it worse. It means Darcy knew what was waiting for him at the end of his fall.

'But Fiona, The Dullahan, the mare, the foal, the faeries, they just vanished. I mean do they really exist or was it like some kind of hallucination?'

'Shut your eyes.'

When Karen opens them, I'll have vanished too.

TUESDAY
10:30

I go to school Tuesday but only make it through English class. Mr. D asks how our essays are coming along and I answer 'brewin' which makes him smile. But what it really does is remind me I've got to find Gran's *Book of Faery Spells* or she'll have my bones for school paste. (She won't but I will!)

I walk into Gloire Bay stopping at the Owl's Nest Café. It was Dunleavy's Tearoom till Martha Dunleavy, the owner, could see the writing on the wall. The Catholic Church is in the toilet and tearooms aren't far behind. (The times they are a changing!) I'm there because Debra, Darcy's mum, works at the Owl's Nest but I don't see her.

'She's taking the week off," Martha says staring at me like she's trying to read my mind. 'And how are you holding up Fiona?'

I think about that. 'I was sad but now I'm angry.'

'I can see that. My dad died in a motorway accident. Hit by a drunk driver. Puts me in a rage every time I think about it.'

Folks do that. Tell you a story from their life so you know we're all in this together. A young man wearing an Ohio Buckeye sweatshirt comes in looking for an Americano so I say goodbye and head for Darcy's place. I find Debra sitting out back crying. I go into the kitchen and make two cups of tea.

'This is so hard,' she says. 'Me heart's a grenade that's exploded and now I'm supposed to put the pieces back together.'

Then she finds the courage to ask what she wanted to ask at the funeral.

'Now Fiona, you wouldn't be pregnant by any chance?'

Darcy's mum doesn't know Darcy was gay though I think she might suspect. She never objected to me spending time in his bedroom so that could take it either way. Either she knew I was safe, nothing would be happening, or better still something is happening... I decide it's not my place to say anything. Darcy said he was waiting to come out till he was off to university so he could get through St. Barbara's without being called *faggot* or *fudge packer*. I was his camouflage, his subterfuge.

'Not pregnant, sorry.' We have a moment of silence and then I say, 'Darcy borrowed Gran's *Book of Faery Spells*. For his English essay. It's big.' I move my hands around showing Debra how big it is.

'Haven't seen it but I haven't been spendin time in Darcy's room.'

Debra gets to her feet and leads the way. The tidiness of Darcy's room surprises me. You can see the walls for one thing. They're a light gray color with white trim. The only decorations are two framed posters. One shows a bunch of animals staring at a teacher at a desk. The words underneath come from Einstein: *Everybody is a genius. But, if you judge a fish by its ability to climb a tree, it will spend its whole life believing it is stupid.* (Every school should have that one hanging by the front door!) The other poster shows a brain surrounded by the words: *If the right side of the brain controls the left side of the body then only lefthanders are in their right minds!* (Needless to say, Darcy was left-handed. He told me once the Latin word for left was *sinister* and then he made this really evil face making me laugh.)

Under the Einstein poster is a single bed covered in an Arsenal bedspread — more camouflage — and a bedside table with reading lamp and a framed selfie of Darcy and me at the tower, a gorgeous sunset painting the sky behind us. Beside the bed there's a rag rug with Darcy's slippers neatly placed. Under the room's only window sits a wooden bookcase full of books all right side up and organized. Opposite the window is Darcy's desk. On it sits a lonely gooseneck lamp. No stacks of higgledy-piggledy papers, no discarded gum wrappers, no pens that don't work, no forgotten post-it notes, no...

'When did Darcy get this neat?' I ask shaking my head.

Debra laughs. 'A few weeks ago. He came home from your place saying your room was like an archeological dig. There was no tellin what you might find.'

Now I laugh. 'You're kidding?'

"No, I'm not. He said seeing your room was like seeing the future.'

Now we're both laughing. That was the best thing about Darcy; he was hilarious. Even when he said something that wasn't funny it came out funny. Stand-up comic for sure.

'Is it okay if I look around?'

'Help yourself. Apparently, I have laundry to do. Audrey's already wearing her school blouse four days runnin.'

Debra leaves and I start looking. (To be honest I'm not expecting to find Gran's book here but I've got to start somewhere.)

Gran's book's not in the bookcase that's obvious so I open Darcy's wardrobe. It's neat too so it doesn't take much poking around to know Gran's big book isn't hiding there. Next I check under the bed and under the mattress. Then the desk drawers. Everywhere I see memories — a photo of us on the beach — a notebook full of doodles, most of them rude but ha ha too. A gold plastic trophy for winning the Under Fourteen Kenpo (Chinese street fighting) Tournament in Sligo. (Darcy making sure no one could push him around!)

Short of a secret cubbyhole Gran's book's not here.

I find Debra hanging up clothes.

'Any luck?'

'No. What about Darcy's backpack?' As soon as I ask the question something about backpacks itches in my brain like something you can't quite remember. Then I picture Darcy going over the cliff. I would have noticed his backpack if he'd been wearing it.

'That's a good question. I don't recall seeing it. Maybe it's at school?'

'No, he had it at my place Friday afternoon because that's where he put Gran's book.' And my iPhone but I don't say that. We go back into the house and search for the backpack without success.

'Has anyone else been in Darcy's room?'

Debra knows what I'm really asking. Could someone have taken something?

'There's been lots in and out of the house but...' I can see Debra debating with herself whether to tell me or not.

'Uncle Danny?'

Debra nods. Danny is her younger brother and always in trouble either with women or gambling. The women are usually married and as for the gambling everyone says, if you want a sure bet find out which team Danny's betting on and bet the other way.

'I saw him coming from Darcy's room lookin more than guilty but then that's how he always looks so I didn't think much about it. You think he took Gran's book? It sounds too big to be hidin under his shirt or something. Course he might have dropped it out the window, retrieved it later.'

I think about that. Possible but something about it doesn't feel right.

'I've got to find that book before Gran gets home.'

'Have you talked to your Gran?'

'Not yet. She's calling tonight.'

"Will you be tellin her?'

'She'll know the minute she sees me.'

While I'm walking to The Betty to find Uncle Danny I'm going to tell you more about Gloire Bay so you can picture where we are. Gloire Bay — Gloire is Irish for Glory — is a little village high up on the coast of Ireland. To the west is the Atlantic Ocean and to the east the border with Northern Ireland. Our county, Donegal, is like a dog's ear sticking up.

By rights Donegal should be part of Northern Ireland but there were too many Catholics in Donegal so when they formed Northern Ireland they put together the six counties with the highest percentage of Protestants so the government would be Protestant, not Catholic, and loyal to King George sitting on his throne in England. In 1922 all the

Catholic counties joined up becoming the Irish Free State changed in 1949 to the Republic of Ireland.

The Troubles you hear about in Northern Ireland were the Catholics there — the Irish Republican Army (IRA) — fighting for equal rights and work opportunities and trying to join with the rest of Ireland so the whole island would be one country again.

It was the women in Northern Ireland who finally put a stop to all the bloodshed saying we've had enough of you eejits killing each other. No religion is worth dying for so put your differences aside and get on with things. Betty Williams and Mairead Corrigan were awarded the Nobel Peace Prize for that. There. That's today's history lesson for my American cousin, Alice*, who for sure doesn't know Belfast from Belarus.

(*Cousin Alice is my dad's brother Luke's daughter. She's sixteen going on six or twenty-six depending on her mood. She came to visit last summer bringing all of America with her. Fortunately, she ditched me after Day Three deciding Liam O'Connor was much more fun. He was willing to put up with her for reasons I won't mention here. Darcy said she was ADHD with nothing there when she was paying attention and even Grandad found her ignorance and lack of curiosity about the rest of the world appalling. But Grandad says it's not all Alice's fault. For instance, in America J.K. Rowling's first book is called *Harry Potter and The Sorcerer's Stone* not *Harry Potter and the Philosopher's Stone* the way it's supposed to be. Grandad says everything in America gets Americanized to the point that the rest of the world ceases to exist.)

I remember asking once how many folks live in Gloire Bay and Gran replying 1100, give or take, but that sounds inflated to me Darcy agreeing saying if you count the dead fishermen you might get close.

Downtown Gloire Bay consists of about twenty buildings spread out along Front Street most of them stone wearing plaster and most freshly painted so tourists are getting those quaint/romantic vibes makes them feel Ireland is pretty nice if it'd only stop pissin rain. If you're coming from Gran's the first building on Front is the Post Office. Miss Carmichael is the postmistress and Grandad Sky says sure as shootin no one else would have her as a mistress, which gets him a punch in the arm from Gran for being mean. Across the road, the back of the building a wall of windows facing the sea, is The Betty Ford Clinic Neighborhood Pub shortened to The Betty after Stan Bailey, the owner, received a solicitor's letter from The Betty Ford Clinic in California — it's where the Hollywood celebs go to rehab — saying he couldn't use the name or they'd be sending in the Marines. The letter's framed on the wall and all the regulars give it a pat as they stagger home.

Beside the Post Office is The Owl's Nest, the café/bakery where Darcy's mum Debra works. Beside The Betty is Maudie's Off Licence (Liquor Store) without a Maudie in sight. Story is Boss O'Brien, the owner, had a girlfriend named Maudie who didn't approve of Boss's drinking so after they broke up he named his new store Maudie's to irritate her. There's a lot of that in Ireland. Boss O'Brien is pals with Grandad Sky — they both love history — so he goes out of his way to import American whiskies and bourbons so Grandad doesn't get homesick.

This is taking too long so I'll just be saying there's a small supermarket, two B&Bs, a petrol station/convenience store with ATM, an insurance office, a hardware/hobby shop and at the far end Brownie's Fish & Chips which gets a 4.8 rating on TripAdvisor — *Best I ever had!* — and rightly so. What's missing is a shopping center to hang out in, a cinema to watch Jennifer Lawrence, a supermarket with more than three aisles, a charity shop with rich lady castoffs, and how about a pool hall where all the bad boys hang out? For those you have to travel to Sligo 120 kilometers away which, if Gran's driving, takes three hours or more but two-thirds that if Grandad Sky's showing off in his '66 Chevy pickup truck imported from Texas and nicknamed Dale, after Dale Earnhardt the famous race car driver, one of Grandad's favorites.

I walk to The Betty. Grandad Sky's not there which surprises me — probably working on his book — but I do find Uncle Danny sitting at a table with his mates, Clyde Dunleavy and Clyde Vivienne, better known as the Clydesdales. They work together at Stevenson's Auto Repair.

'Danny, could I talk to you for a moment?'

'Sure Fiona, have a seat.'

'In private.'

Uncle Danny raises his eyebrows like hey boys, here's another female craving me attention. The Clydes chuckle as Uncle Danny gets to his feet and leads the way outside. We walk around the building going down the alley that leads to a low stone wall overlooking the harbor.

'What can I do for you?'

'Did you take a book from Darcy's room?'

I can see he doesn't want to answer but he takes too long making up his mind so we both know he did.

'Would you be tellin Debra?'

'No.'

He nods at this. 'I sold it to Father McKenna.'

Shite!

'And what about Darcy's MacBook?'

The one that should have been sitting on his desk.

Uncle Danny laughs at this. 'Audrey beat me to it.'

Have you seen the movie *Spotlight?* It's about the Catholic priests in Boston abusing little boys. Well, it's the same all over the world so those folks who believed heart and soul in the Church are finally waking up. In Ireland the Catholic Church was everything, the priests more powerful than the politicians, but not anymore. Now the Church is fading which I think is a good thing because it forces folks to think for themselves instead of having some puppet in a pulpit telling them what to do.

Grandad says there are three everyday sayings that need to be revised:

Common sense isn't common.

You're guilty until proven innocent.

Man created God in his image.

I find Father McKenna at the manse. He knows I'm no friend of the church and worse knows influential Gran holds him in the same esteem reserved for dung beetles, so the look he gives me when he opens the door is less than friendly. He's a big man filling the doorway. I figure that's as far as I get but he surprises me by standing aside ushering me in.

'I'm sure you're not here to confess,' Father McKenna says trying to make a joke of it. He leads me into his study, which has more books than the Gloire Bay Library.

'You bought a book from Danny Flaherty. I want to buy it back.'

'Why?'

'It belongs to my Gran.'

'Really? I doubt that.'

Something's not right. 'Why would you doubt that?'

Father McKenna doesn't answer instead he goes to a pile of books on his desk and finds the one he wants. He hands it to me. *Hitch Hiker's Guide to the Galaxy.* I look inside. It's signed by the author, Douglas Adams, and underneath is written, *To Darcy, love Mum xox*

'You're disappointed.'

'I'm lookin for my Gran's *Book of Faery Spells*. It's big.' I use my hands again.

Father McKenna waves his arm around. 'As you can see I have nothing like that here but bibles and atlases.'

I stare at the *Hitch Hiker's Guide*. Darcy loved those books and was always quoting them. 'This is the book Danny sold you?'

'Yes.'

'Is it worth a lot?'

Father McKenna doesn't answer meaning none of your business. I can google it so it doesn't matter.

'Could I buy it?'

"Perhaps if I hadn't already sold it.'

'That's quick.'

'It's what I do Fiona when I'm not saving souls. Buy and sell books.'

I think I knew that. Church attendance is so low priests are forced to do other things to make ends meet and someone told me the Pope doesn't help his minions despite being one of the richest men in the world. I think about asking Father McKenna if he fences jewelry too? I stop there. No one's accused Father McKenna of anything so I'm being hard on him, letting my prejudices tar him with a brush he probably doesn't deserve.

'If someone comes in with Gran's spell book...'

'I'll call you first. I promise.'

'Thank you.'

It was easier not liking Father McKenna. Now I'm forced to change black & white into fifty shades of gray. And, if I was being honest, I'd admit that most priests are good men trying their best to care for their flocks...

I wander aimlessly till Billy finds me by the harbor staring out to sea. He doesn't say anything just waits for me to come back to the planet.

'I've lost Gran's *Book of Faery Spells*. I think it's in Darcy's backpack but I can't find that either.'

We talk about where the backpack might be and decide to start at the tower. Billy doesn't mention the possibility that it's gone over the cliff with Darcy, I think because he'd rather spend time with me looking. We're halfway up Sean's Mountain when Billy says, 'I hear Karen can see again.'

'That's right, she can.'

'Alicia says Karen met The Dullahan and it scared her so much her eyes started workin.'

'Now Billy, would you be believin in The Dullahan?'

"Mum believes in faeries and such but Dad says it's all shite.'

'And whose side are you takin?'

I can see Billy has to think about this. It's a hundred percent certain me and Gran believe in faeries, so him believing will get him points with me, but deep down he agrees with his father, *faeries are shite*.

'It's an honest answer we're lookin for not what you think I want to hear.'

Billy stops. I look back. I've insulted Billy. Worse. I've kicked him where it hurts. Billy turns around heading back down the hill. I run to him, stop him.

'I'm sorry Billy. I shouldn't have said that. You've never been anything but straight with me.'

I do this all the time. I think for other people. I assume I know what they're thinking and then hold it against 'em. For sure it makes me an Upstanding Member of White Person Arrogance.

I give Billy a hug, my lips finding his ear. 'I'm sorry.'

Billy's quick to forgive, that's obvious, because he's soon smiling again and talking. 'I don't know what I think. I want there to be faeries but I've never seen one.'

'If we find Gran's book, I'll show you a boggart.'

When we get to the tower we find an empty, four-seater ATV — wearing Inn With The Tide logos — waiting outside and inside a clutch of female Chinese tourists on the gun platform taking selfies. They've even got the telescoping pole holds your Samsung farther back so with any luck you can tell you're in Ireland. How they got up the crumbling stairs in high heel shoes is beyond me. The only male in the group is staring out to sea except now he's staring at me. He's young, late twenties maybe, and very good-looking. I stare back till finally his mates join him and he's forced to turn away.

I'm still trying to figure out this male/female thing. Yin/yang. This pulling together and pushing apart. I mean I get that males want to impregnate the planet — and doing a good job of it, they are — but what's my motivation? Sex, love, validation? I haven't a clue.

Billy and I search the grounds around the tower but find nothing but bits of garbage mostly plastic water bottles. They say it was dust from a giant meteor took out the dinosaurs and I'm betting it's plastic finishes us off.

Billy's looking at me for instructions so I say, 'It was raining hard that night so you'd think Darcy'd be puttin his pack somewhere dry.' That thought sends us back inside the tower to the second floor where there are rooms for the soldiers who were stationed here. One of the doors is locked.

'I wonder why this room is locked?' I ask but Billy just shrugs.

'Didn't used to be.'

'What would it take to open that?'

The other doors, all of them open, are made of thick hardwood, the locks black metal boxes with keyholes.

Billy says, 'Battering ram maybe,' pushing on the door with his shoulder. 'We could try pickin it.'

We look around and find a twist tie left over from someone's lunch. Billy plays around with the lock while I wonder if there's a spell in Gran's book — maybe on the other side of the door — that would be doin the job? Darcy loved Catch 22's.

The Chinese tourists descend and the handsome male comes over looking interested. 'You want to go inside?' he asks smiling.

'Yes please,' says me smiling back.

'In my experience the key is usually close by.'

Billy and I start looking and sure enough I find a long skinny key hiding under a rock not far from the door. It's one of those old-fashioned keys you see in pirate movies, has the long shaft and the hole at the far end for hanging on a nail or the jailer's belt. I hold the key up to show the Chinese tourist but he already has the door open. He can see Billy and me are more than impressed so he laughs.

'Would you be a locksmith then?'

'Thief,' he says still laughing.

I push the door fully open and we all look inside. It's a small room probably for the Officer-in-charge thinks me remembering Grandad Sky's talks. One officer, twenty men. The room is empty except for a double bed with a mattress, pillow, sheets and quilt. Beside the bed is a wooden crate covered in white candles, puddles of wax, and two empty wine glasses. Inside the crate, lying on their side, are wine bottles, some full, some empty. Above the bed's a square opening with a wooden shutter closed and bolted. To the right of the bed is a fireplace full of ashes, a pile of peat bricks close by.

I go inside makin sure Darcy's backpack isn't hiding under the bed or behind the crate. No such luck. I close the door and relock it.

'A love nest,' says me putting the key back under its rock and we all exit the tower.

The thief's name is Liang. He's gone to university in Toronto so his English is near perfect and he is a locksmith, in fact his father owns the largest lock factory in Wuhan, the largest city in central China with a population over ten million twice that of all of Ireland. When he hears me telling Billy we're going to the peat bog he asks if he can tag along?

'Sure,' says me. Liang's female companions aren't interested so they hop into the ATV and head back to Gloire Bay. 'Are you stayin at the Inn then?'

'Yes.'

'What do you think of it?'

'I would prefer something more authentic.'

'You're not goin to the McDonald's in Borneo I guess.'

This is a daft thing to say but he gets it right away.

'Americans are good at exporting their culture.'

"And annihilating everybody else's.'

'Perhaps the world needs to be one place to survive.'

'With an AI runnin it.'

'Now you're talking.'

Darcy says that's Google's endgame — an Artificial Intelligence capable of running the world. That's why they collect all the world's knowledge, all the books, all the maps, all the photos of places, all the languages. Darcy says it's a race to see if Google's AI can take over before we destroy everything.

It's a twenty-minute walk to the bog. On the way I tell Liang about Darcy going over the cliff and the backpack Billy and I are looking for and why. Finally, we're standing at the edge of the bog, a huge egg-shaped area covered in purple moor grass with pockets of standing water dotting the surface like mini-lakes. 'Grandad says this is a blanket bog as opposed to a raised bog. He says the early Irish farmers cut down all the trees trying to make fields and then all the soil ran downhill makin meters deep deposits of organic material saturated with water.'

'They find bodies in the bog,' Billy adds joining in. 'Well-preserved like mummies. One they found in County Offaly was 2,000 years old. A young guy stood almost two meters tall. (That's 6' 6" if you're living in America, one of only three countries left in the world still using British Imperial Measurements like inches and feet. The other two countries are Liberia and Myanmar.)

'I thought our ancestors were short,' says me.

'Not this guy and they figure he was a king because his nails were manicured and he was wearing pleated leather armbands with bronze mounts.'

Now Billy's sounding like Wikipedia so I give him a look.

'It's my essay topic. The king's height is my tidbit.'

That's another thing I've got to worry about. Every essay has to have a *tidbit*, some fact of special interest.

'So, what happened to him?"

'They figure he was sacrificed to the gods because the harvest was poor.'

'They sacrificed a king?'

'Apparently they blamed the king for poor harvests.'

'That's a switch.'

'Had a stab wound to his chest and deep cuts under his nipples.'

This gets my eyebrows up.

'And why would they be doing that?'

'No one's sure but they think he was sacrificed to ensure good harvests of cereals and milk.'

I don't see how cutting a male's nipples is going to help with milk production but it makes as much sense as Isis terrorists thinking they're going to be rewarded in paradise with forty virgins.

'Gran says they find wooden boxes of butter in the bog.'

Now it's Liang looking at me for an explanation.

'The theory is butter was worth a lot of money so you hid it in the bog to preserve it.'

'But you didn't always come back for it.'

I nod at Liang like *that's it.*

All the way to the bog we've been following wide tire tracks carved deeply into the soil meaning it was probably raining when the machine was out here.

'These look recent,' I say and the other two agree.

'Don't the Irish use peat for heating?' Liang asks. 'Like we saw in the tower?'

'We call it turf.' I tell Liang about the United Nations' Global Peatlands Initiative to save the planet's largest carbon sink and how Ireland is doing its bit for climate change by buying up bogs and trying to get people off heating with turf. Trouble is it's an ancient tradition in Ireland so some folks are loath to change.

We follow the tracks till we're almost halfway around. Sure enough we find where someone's been turf cutting. The grass is torn away and a raw wall of peat lies exposed black and damp. There's no turf lying about so whoever it is has taken it away already.

'Maybe the bog owner doesn't allow turf cutting,' says me thinking out loud. 'Maybe whoever's doing it is workin at night so no one notices.' And maybe they were working Friday night and Darcy saw them. It was raining hard that night but it didn't start till later. Could be.

The tire tracks continue on but I turn left. 'The faery fort's on the other side.'

'Faery fort?' Liang is liking this.

'There's a mound. It's where the faeries live.' I can see Liang is as skeptical as Inspector Mike.

'Don't you have faeries in China?'

'Mogwai, little demons, but I've never seen one except in cartoons.'

By the time we reach the faery fort we've come to the conclusion that every culture has its fairylike creatures which makes you wonder, doesn't it? Like believing in ghosts. Just cos you can't see 'em doesn't mean they're not there and as I said before why would we have words for things if they didn't exist?

We stop on an island of grass, the faery mound in front of us. Gran says it's a bigger mound than most. I'd describe it as one of those giant anthills you see in Australia, the ones they flatten out to make tennis courts. We can't go right up to it because it's surrounded by water like a castle with a moat. I know this is where Darcy was headed because we'd talked about it. We search the grass for a wide area but come up empty-handed. No backpack. Probably just as well or Gran's book would be mush.

Darcy, what did you do with Gran's book?

Darcy may be listening but he's sure not answering. When we reach the bottom of Sean's Mountain Billy heads home and Liang heads for the Inn. Me, I head for Karen's because I can see Inspector Mike's silver Volvo glinting in the driveway. When I arrive I find Mike and Karen having tea in the kitchen. Karen's telling him about getting her sight back and I can see his policeman's brain has him not believing a word of it.

'The Dullahan?'

Now Inspector Mike's looking at me like I'm spreading a disease.

'This is all your fault Fiona.'

I laugh. Reason crashes into The Impossible.

'It's only a matter of time till you'll be joinin us,' I say sharing a smile with Karen over my cup of tea.

'Well, however it happened, I'm glad you can see again.'

Karen nods and I begin feeling those yin/yang vibrations again. Time to ask my questions and get out of here.

'Grandad said you didn't find a mobile.'

'No, nothing in Darcy's pockets but some loose change and soggy gum.'

That makes sense. There's no point asking about Darcy's backpack because it'll just get the Inspector sidetracked. 'What about Adriana?' I ask.

Now the Inspector's got a different look on his face.

'She says she wasn't out in her boat Friday afternoon.'

I can't believe this. 'We saw her!' I say, louder than I intend.

'We saw somebody.'

'It was Adriana, I'm sure of it.'

'There are witnesses who say she was in the pub that afternoon.'

'Like who? The people who work for her?' I'm gettin worked up now. It's one thing not to believe in faeries but it's another not to believe your own eyes.

'Like Stan Bailey.'

'What?'

'It seems Adriana was tired of folks saying her pub wasn't Irish so she invited Stan Bailey in to consult on the matter.'

Too funny except I'm still sure it was Adriana I saw in the boat. Had to be.

'So, she was there all afternoon?'

The Inspector nods at this.

'So, who did we see?'

'Don't know.'

'Did you ask Adriana if someone borrowed her boat?'

'She says there are three other Boston Whalers in the harbor.'

'So, you're askin the other owners?'

Inspector Mike doesn't answer just stares at me. None of this is making sense. We saw someone suspicious in Adriana's boat using binoculars to search the rocks where Darcy died and Inspector Mike's treating it like it's Colonel Mustard in the Library with a Candlestick.

But I'm not the only one getting worked up because Inspector Mike says, 'Maybe it's time you told me where you were Friday night?'

'I was out on a date.'

'But not with Darcy.'

'You should be a police inspector.'

Have you heard the phrase *bristling with anger?*

'Who with?'

'Peter Sullivan.'

'Where do I find him?'

'Sligo.'

'How old?'

'Twenty, twenty-one. Somewhere in there.'

The Inspector's eyebrows go up at this.

'Did Darcy know about this date?'

'Of course.' Not.

'And he wasn't upset?'

No way I'm telling the Inspector Darcy was gay. He'll be asking everybody if it's true.

'Nope. Darcy was me mate not my boyfriend.'

'That's not what everybody says.'

'Everybody knows shite.'

'Did your grandfather know about this date?'

'No.'

'Where did he think you were?'

This is bad. I told Grandad I was having a sleepover at Kylie's.

'I told him I was havin a sleepover at Kylie's.'

'Who's Kylie?'

'Girl in my class.'

'So where did you spend the night?'

'Things didn't go well with Peter so I slept in Karen's barn.'

Now there's X-ray vision streaming out of the Inspector's eyes boring into my skull. I figure there's so many lies here he doesn't know where to start.

'What happened with Peter?'

I don't have to tell him but it might distract him.

'He wanted sex but I wasn't interested.'

I can see Inspector Mike thinking if you're dumb enough to go out with a twenty-year-old what were you expecting?

'Was he... forceful.'

Yeah, he was but that was mostly my fault because I'd led him on.

'No. I told him to drive me back to Gloire Bay and he did.'

Not.

'Then you slept in Karen's barn? I don't suppose there are any witnesses to that?'

'Just Tangent and Sally.'

'Why not knock on Karen's door?'

'It was late. I didn't want to wake her.'

The Inspector's eyes keep moving between me and Karen. Karen's not saying a word, which is one of the things I like about Karen. She's not a talker. Inspector Mike turns back to me.

'I still don't get why Darcy wasn't upset with this or did you lie to him too? Did he think you were going to Kylie's for a sleepover?'

I didn't tell Darcy about Peter because I knew he'd be asking me a million questions and when he found out how old Peter was he'd be giving me supreme shite. So, I told Darcy I was having a girls' night out with Kylie, that we were going to the cinema in Sligo, hitching a ride with Marianne and Laura. The lies are piling up so high they're threatening to come crashing down like a five-car smashup. I decide it's time to take the offensive.

'So, Inspector Mike, did you ask Adriana out?'

'What?'

'Is that why you're letting her off so easily?'

The Inspector's face storms through baby girl pink into beet red into cardiac arrest crimson. He is very, *very* angry. Darcy says it's a talent of mine, making folks furious. I remind myself to ask Gran if my mum Fallon had this talent for pissing folks off.

Karen's eyes are as big as dinner plates. (Writers are allowed to exaggerate but you get the idea.)

'You didn't answer my question. Did you ask Adriana out?'

Inspector Mike gets to his feet. He's vibrating.

'Do you know what I think Fiona? I think Darcy was so despondent you were going out with someone else he threw himself off that cliff.'

He tries to say goodbye to Karen but he's too upset to do a good job.

'Did you see him turn lobster? For sure he asked Adriana out.'

'And why is that any of your business?'

'She may be Darcy's killer.'

'You heard the Inspector; she was in her bar when you saw the boat.'

'It was definitely her boat. Hers is spankin new, the other three in the harbor are practically sinkin.'

"Even so she couldn't have been driving it.'

Now I feel like a five-year-old getting scolded. Sure, the person driving the boat was wearing a hoodie and he/she was a long way off but still it felt like Adriana. I try a different tack.

'He asked you out first.'

'It's not a crime to ask two people out.'

'It stinks and you know it.'

I can see Karen is *disappointed* in me. I'm being *immature*. I try again.

'He's divorced.'

'And how do you know that?'

'Facebook.'

I can see Karen doesn't want to ask but can't help herself. 'Children?'

'One son, Jamie. Ten years old. Lives with his mum.'

Karen nods at this not letting on what she's thinking.

'So, are you still goin out with him?'

'None of your business.'

I nod but then Karen ignores her own advice.

'Why were you going out with this Peter guy?'

None of your business hangs in the air between us but I need a new best friend/confidant and Karen is definitely the leading candidate.

'Can you keep a secret?'

Karen crosses her heart.

'Darcy was gay.'

'I wondered about that.'

Gran calls just as Grandad and I are finishing supper. I hear the ringtone buzzing upstairs and take off. 'C'mon Grandad, it's Gran.'

Gran's smiling face fills the screen and my heart does a backflip.

'What time is it there?' Gran asks.

'We just finished supper. Grandad's mustache is full of tuna casserole.'

Grandad appears behind me his big hands resting on my shoulders. He bends down so the camera captures the grin on his face. Gran grins back.

'It's eight thirty here. I'm back in Juba in an internet café could be in Dublin or New York City for that matter.'

'How was the ceremony?'

'Wonderful. The President was there and the sculptor who made the memorial. I took a ton of photos and I bought a DVD of the ceremony from a fifteen-year-old entrepreneur named Alek. She's got frizzy blue hair and wanted to come home with me.'

Normally I'd be hooting at this egging Gran on but not tonight.

'Something's wrong, isn't it?'

Gran's staring at me like she's got a third eye and she's just turned it on.

'Is it Bandit?'

On cue Bandit jumps into my lap.

'It can wait till you're home,' Grandad says.

'No, tell me. Better to know. Is it Darcy?'

I can't sleep. Everything's gone to rat shite and even Fungal Fergus would be figuring out the common element is me, Simply Fiona. If I hadn't had that date with Peter *Wanker* Sullivan I would have been with Darcy and then he'd still be alive or worse case we'd both be dead which would mean I wouldn't be drowning in this pool of despair I'm sinking into.

Inspector Mike dislikes/loathes/hates me and who can blame him? Me acting like I know more about investigating than he does and now he's concluded Darcy did a jumper thinking about me getting fondled by some asshat from Sligo. He'll probably stop digging and all cos I had to be the cheeky smartass.

Karen still likes me, I think, but I don't make it easy for her being outrageous and all and lying, with her listening knowing I'm lying, and Gran's beyond sad which brings it back to me making poor decisions. If I'd just gone with Gran...

My downward spiraling halts here because there's mad tapping at the window and I know who it is.

'Benji! Are you needin me again?'

'No, everything's as fine as it can be considering. That was exciting wasn't it, The Dullahan and all?'

'My friend Karen got her sight back.'

'I saw that. Is she happy?'

'She is. Not seeing was a kind of punishment so seeing means she's forgiven herself.'

'That's good. Is Gran home soon?'

'Sunday.' The look on Benji's face tells me the word *Sunday* might as well be *Someday* for all it means. 'Five sleeps.' Benji likes that better. 'How are you makin out with Queen Caelia?'

'It's such a mess. Nothing pleases her. Nothing's good enough. Why is she, Queen Caelia, Queen of the Irish Faeries, stuck in the boonies like a second-rate Contessa? On top of everything else there's rumors The Unseelie Court is on its way wanting to take over Ireland.'

'What's The Unseelie Court?'

'Dark side faeries. King Kade, their ruler, is considered the nastiest faery in faerydom and that's saying something.'

'Why are they coming?'

'Because The Seelie have finally chased them out of Scotland.'

'The Seelie are the good guys?'

'No. They're terrible too just not quite as terrible as The Unseelie.'

That sounds like choosing between hanging or the guillotine.

'So now The Unseelie want Ireland?'

'Queen C says she's going to summon Sir Max to save us but Major Domo says...' Benji stops here lookin around for what? Spiders with listening devices? '...Major Domo says Sir Max's an old drunk who isn't saving anybody even if he does get here in time.'

'Who's Sir Max?'

'He's the fiercest warrior ever lived. Defeated Lubber Fiend and Robin Redcap among others and on the same day too. Saved Queen Aine at Dunany Point. He wanted to marry her but she said it was his destiny to travel the world righting wrongs, dispensing justice, helping the good guys win battles.'

Now there's a female who knows how to let a lad down easy.

'But now he's old and a drunk?' Benji nods looking sad about it. I blurt out, 'But I didn't think faeries got old?'

'We get old and then we rejuvenate.'

That sounds good, like reincarnation. Darcy'd like that.

'When will The Unseelie arrive?'

'No one's sure but Queen C says she can feel them.'

'What about askin The Dullahan for help?'

Benji's eyes go wide like I've said a really bad word or something.

'He doesn't interfere in things like this.'

'But you helped him.'

'No! We thought we were helping the poor horse. We didn't know who it belonged to.'

'But you still would have helped?'

'Of course, we would just have been scared shiteless earlier is all.'

We laugh at this.

'Do you remember the night Queen Caelia arrived you said it was a fierce night with lightning and thunder and rain falling in buckets?'

'That's right. Mally said it was like Mother Nature and Father Time were having a domestic dispute. A good one.'

'Did anything else strange happen that night?'

'Else?'

There's nothin for it but to tell Benji about Darcy and Gran's spell book and how Darcy was going to change himself into a faery.

'That's a great story except for the ending of course. Is it okay if I tell my friend Mally?'

'Who's Mally?'

'Girlfriend.'

That's so cute. 'Sure,' says me.

'There was so much going on that night with the Jalapeño Grande and Queen C arriving unannounced I don't think anyone would have noticed a stranger.'

I can see Benji thinking.

'Do you think you'll find Gran's spell book?'

'I'd better.'

'I'd be interested in seeing it.'

WEDNESDAY
9:00

Once again, I go to school with the best of intentions — *liar!* — but I'm no sooner in the door when everybody's staring at me like I'm wearing my knickers on my forehead. I take five paces — now they're whispering! — spin around and march back outside again. Talk about that wankers!

My feet put me on the path leading to the Inn. I have to find Gran's book and the only lead I've got is Adriana not being in her boat.

I'm on Front Street beyond downtown walking beside a stone wall covered in lime-green moss. Ahead of me is the Inn and beyond that the blue Atlantic. It's sunny, which is lifting my spirits, and already there are sailboats out gliding along guided by folks smart enough not to be working. I'm fifty meters from the Inn when Adriana flies by in her BMW. It's a silver Z4 convertible roadster that Darcy says he'd die for which seems ironic now that I think about it. Adriana waves to me but doesn't slow down which is probably just as well. I'm still in a mood to hurt someone, sunshine or no sunshine.

Now there's no reason to go to the Inn but my legs have a mind of their own and keep going. As I head down the Inn's expensive brand new/antique cobblestone driveway I see a red and black Mini Cooper waiting with all its doors open and boot (trunk) too. Standing under the Inn's porte-cochère — yes, I had to look it up! — are Liang's three female friends chattering away totally ignoring Liang struggling to fit four large suitcases into a space made for two. Liang sees me striding toward him and breaks into a big grin. I decide to be outrageous.

'How would you like to be stealing my virginity?' says me and Liang's eyes explode with laughter.

'I would like it very much but there would appear to be several impediments.'

You gotta love an English-as-a-second-language guy who can conjure up the word *impediments*.

'Who are the impediments anyway?'

Liang glances over at the three females giggling at something said.

'One sister, one friend of sister, one girlfriend.'

'We need to eliminate the girlfriend.'

Liang laughs out loud enjoying himself.

'How bout helping me break into a room?'

Now he's not laughing. 'Here?'

I nod.

'Show me.'

Liang follows me into the Inn. His girlfriend — I'm assuming the one looks like a runway model is the g.f. — asks something in Chinese but Liang just waves his hand like I'll be right back. We march by reception, which is empty, and down the hallway I know leads to Adriana's suite of rooms.

'Did you find your grandmother's book?'

'No, that's why I'm here.'

We turn a corner still not seeing anyone and now we're staring at a door with a sign that reads: Manager's Office. I knock on the door and when no one answers I try the knob. Locked.

I nod at Liang. In less time than it takes to read this sentence the world's best locksmith/burglar has the door open.

'Stand guard.'

I go in and close the door behind me. There might be a security camera in the office and I don't want Liang getting in trouble for helping me.

In seconds I search the office and come up empty. Gran's spell book is too big to hide easily. I go through the next door and now I'm in Adriana's apartment with a wall of glass and a view of the ocean good enough for a magazine. I check the living room and kitchen. I even peer into the oven and microwave. No book, no Darcy backpack. Nothing left now but the bedroom. Some sixth sense is telling me to be quiet so I open the door silently and peek in. There's a body lying in the bed!

Holy shite, right!?

Now what? It's a young man's body I can tell by the bare back and he looks to be out cold but I may be imagining that. He's facing the open bathroom door so I slide over to the other side of the bed and peek underneath. Not even dust bunnies. There's a wardrobe with mirrored doors left open. Inside, the wardrobe is crammed with Adriana's clothes and shoes. Lying on the floor is a duffel bag full of male clothes.

I take one last look then retrace my steps to the hallway. Liang is there waiting for me. I shake my head. We're halfway back to reception when Gail Murphy appears pushing a hoover (vacuum cleaner). Gail is Fungal's girlfriend. She's not winning Schools' Challenge anytime soon but she's a real sweetheart, *salt of the earth* Grandad Sky would be saying. Do anything for you and be thanking you too.

'Have you got a card?' I say loud enough to make Gail look our way.

Liang reaches into his pocket, pulls out his wallet and hands me a business card, which I pretend to read. We're still walking trying to look nonchalant till we're on top of Gail.

'Dia dhuit,' says me meaning 'god be with you' and you don't have to be religious to be using it.

Gail shuts off the hoover and gives me a hug. 'I'm so sorry about Darcy. He was one of my favorites.'

'Mine too,' says me trying to make a sad funny. 'Have you seen Adriana? I knocked on her door but no one answered.'

'She just left, I think. I'll tell her you're looking for her.'

'No, that's okay. I'll come back later. Gail, this is Liang. He's from China. We met up by the tower,' I say staring into Liang's eyes flirting but meaning it too. 'He's going to be my pen pal.'

'Oh, that's grand,' says Gail. 'I've got a pen pal you know.' I do know;

everyone in Gloire Bay knows. 'Stella her name is. Lives in Brisbane, Australia. It's so much fun hearin 'bout the rest of the world. Broadens your horizon so to speak. Nice to meet you Liang. I'd better get hooverin or Adriana will have me backside.'

After Liang left — not before taking a hug and a kiss from me both of us ignoring the shocked girlfriend looking on and Liang whispering, 'I'd like to be your pen pal' — I returned to school and managed to do Maths and Science. Mrs. Barrow said she was glad to see me back and we shared a hug too. Now school's over and me and Billy are riding his bike down to the harbor and I'm tellin Billy about Liang helping me break into Adriana's office.

'That was ballsy of you,' Billy says.

'Yeah, we need to change that,' says me still pissed off at everyone and everything including the universe. THE UNFAIRNESS OF IT ALL let's say if you're lookin for a label.

'Change what?'

'Ballsy. We need the female equivalent.'

'Brave.'

'Clitsy.'

I don't think Billy's blushing but he's riding in front so I can't see.

'Are you a virgin?' I ask. I am in such a mood.

Billy doesn't answer instead he comes back with, 'Are you?'

Darcy and I stuck together like Velcro so everybody assumed we were doin the wee beastie. Or at least I assume that's what everybody was assuming. Debra hoped I was pregnant so we know what she was thinking. I lean my head over Billy's shoulder bending it around till I can kiss Billy full on the lips. Billy, startled and totally blinded, cranks the handlebars nearly sending us over the curbstone into the Atlantic. I pull my head back laughing because I've come up with one of my theories; *corollaries* Darcy called 'em. Here it is: *Girls are fifteen going on twenty-five; boys are fifteen going on five.* Probably something to do with menstruation but that's enough about that.

'So, you think the bloke in Adriana's bed is the one driving Adriana's boat?'

'Got to be.'

'But who is he?'

'Boyfriend I reckon.'

We're walking among the boats now making our way to Adriana's Boston Whaler. I know this is a waste of time but I've got to be doing something.

'Maybe Darcy was wearing his backpack when he went over? Lost it in the water?'

'No. I would have seen it when The Dullahan showed me that night.'

Billy's not buying The Headless Horseman till he sees him with his own eyes. We reach Adriana's boat and stare down at it. It's as simple as a boat can be; two seats, an outboard motor, and a central console holding the steering wheel and controls.

'The door's not locked,' Billy says staring at the little door on the side of the console. We look around. No one seems to be paying attention so I clamber onboard and open the door. There's nothing inside but lifejackets. No backpack, no spell book. I scramble out and we head back the way we came.

'What are you doin tonight?' I ask not figuring on the effect this will have on Billy who's just been asked about his virginity. Billy can't speak and I start laughing. Peter Wanker Sullivan would have been in my knickers faster than a rollerblader on goose shite and here's Billy struck dumb.

I say, 'I want to go to the bog after dark. See if we can see who's leaving the tire marks.'

'I'll have to sneak out the window.'

'Me too, unless Grandad passes out again.'

'He's taking it hard then?'

'Reminds him of his son dying.'

When I get home Grandad's making supper. He does this when he's craving Cajun blackened fish or Texas chili. The blackened fish recipe calls for a frying pan so hot it's glowing red — I'm not kidding! — so I'm happy when it's chili he's making and not burning the house down.

'Chicken or beef?' asks me giving Grandad's arm a squeeze.

'Chicken.'

My favorite. I'll include the recipe here and a warning cos Grandad says the chili won't taste right if you're not wearing a cowboy hat when you make it. (Apparently the hat is an essential ingredient of true Texas chili the idea being, I think, that the hat keeps Gran from mucking with the recipe.)

'There's a package for you on the table.'

It's my new mobile! An iPhone 15 and what a beauty!

'Oh Grandad, thank you so much.' As well as the words Grandad gets a hug and a big kiss. Within seconds I've taken Grandad's photo, Bandit's, and I even go outside and take one of Feister the Horned Toad. Sorry Feister, I keep forgetting to change you back. (On purpose but we're not telling Feister that!)

A minute later Grandad and Bandit are on their way to Gran's mobile in South Sudan.

'How's your essay coming along?'

'It's not.'

'Isn't it due soon?'

'Monday.'

Grandad lets Monday hang in the air like I'm an inmate on death row and Monday's the day.

'What are me choices again?'

'My choices.'

'That's what I said.'

Grandad gives up because he knows I'm using me instead of my to be irritating because that's what teenagers are for, right? Cosmic payback for all the grief parents caused their parents.

'Potato Famine, Diaspora or Craic.'

'What's diaspora?'

'The scattering of a population, like the Jews being kicked out of Judea, or Africans taken from their homes to be slaves, or the Irish scattering to the wind because of the famine.'

'So the potato famine in a bigger context?'

'Gives you more chance to fill pages without really saying anything.'

'That's cynical.'

'I've been reading student essays for forty years. I know all the tricks.'

I'm doodling at the kitchen table when Grandad says he's going to The Betty to check on the latest. We don't have local newspapers in Ireland (ha ha!) you go to the pub/hub instead.

'I may go to Karen's,' mumbles me waiting to see how that goes over.

'Essay,' shoots back Grandad.

'I'm overwhelmed by me choices.'

'Now you're using another unique Irish word, blarney.'

I tear a page out of my drawing pad and write three words on it circling each one. CRAIC, DIASPORA, POTATO. Then I get three of Bandit's cat treats and put one on each word.

'Bandit will be castin the decidin vote.'

Grandad laughs at this. Then he says, 'There are G's on those words you know.'

I give him my blank stare.

'Cast-ING, decid-ING.'

'That would be bor-ING.'

Grandad shakes his head.

'So is it the one Bandit eats first?'

'No, it's the one he's not eat-ING.'

Grandad snorts and heads out the door putting on his cowboy hat.

'Are you not waitin to see then?'

Of course, Bandit eats all three treats so I take that as a sign I can ignore the essay and go to Karen's.

It's dark by the time I get there and all the lights are off just like the old days. When I reach the door I hear music so I let myself in. Karen's playing Lady Gaga's *The Edge of Glory* and belting it out too. I stand in the living room doorway joining in. Three lit candles are clustered together on the piano so I can see Karen grinning at me.

It's almost eleven when Karen shuts down the sing-along and asks how I'm doing?

'Sad, mad, empty, guilty. Take your pick.'

Karen nods. 'That's how it was after my accident, this overwhelming feeling of helplessness. Like I've caused all this incredible pain and loss and there's absolutely nothing I can do to redeem myself.'

After a while I say, 'I keep wondering if I'd been there with Darcy if that would have changed things?'

'Hard to know.' I expect her to say more but Karen's brain is thinking about something else because she asks, 'How did you meet that Peter guy?'

'He was at the Arcade Fire concert. Stood beside Darcy and me. Made sure I knew he went to Trinity. When Darcy went to the loo he asked for my number.'

I can hear *Big Mouth* and *Wide Arse* from here: '*Slut!*' I can see Karen's thinking it too.

'This virginity thing's botherin me and he seemed a likely candidate. Wouldn't be fumblin around like a rookie.'

I can't believe I just said that!

'I was fifteen,' Karen says. 'My parents sent me to this summer camp in Canada. Camp Tanamakoon. I was a CIT, a counselor-in-training. It was all girls except there was a boys' camp at the other end of the lake. We'd have campfires together.'

'What was his name?'

'Aiden'

'Your age?'

Karen nods.

'Was it wonderful?'

'I was in love for the first time so that made it wonderful.'

'Was Aiden in love too?'

'He's the one who died in the accident. With my brother.'

There's a conversation stopper.

'What would you say to a midnight ride?' asks me using my new iPhone to text Billy.

It's just after midnight when we reach the tower, Karen on Tangent, me and Billy pulling up the rear on Sally. We slide off the horses giving them a rest. I run up the steps and poke my head through the doorway to see if there's any light coming from under the locked door. There isn't so we keep going, the horses walking beside us, following the path that leads down to the bog. It's a pretty night, the stars twinkling above us, a sliver of moon suspended in the darkness like a slice of melon, the whole scene reminding me of another night. I say to Billy, 'Were you there when Tom Highmore lit off the lanterns?'

Tom Highmore, lead singer for Ransom — Darcy called 'em Rancid — owns a castle on the coast past the beach at Beg Head. For his seventieth birthday he bought seven hundred Chinese sky lanterns and invited everybody to come light one and watch them fly away. It was an east wind that night confirming Darcy's theory Tom Highmore was born with shamrocks up his arse the breeze blowing the lanterns over the sea on their way to Newfoundland. Had a cake as big as a Rolls Royce too. It was something.

'Mum and I went. She said it reminded her of *Midsummer's Night Dream.*'

A traveling Shakespeare company came to Gloire Bay a few years ago. They put the *Dream* on under the stars down by the harbor all of Gloire Bay sitting on the seawall. They'd strung lanterns from boat to boat. It was magic I must say and that's when I decided if I couldn't be a doctor like my parents, I'd be Hermia and travel the world.

Karen brings me back to earth asking, 'What are we looking for exactly?'

Billy's brought a tiny LED torch which he turns on shining it at our feet showing Karen the tire tracks deep and wide.

'We think someone's cutting turf illegally.'

'We don't know that,' Billy says.

Karen says, 'This is for heating, right?'

'Right. Some folks like the old ways of doing things.'

I give Karen the peat/turf lecture and by the time I get to four-hundred-year-old butter we've reached the bog. The path splits here. We can go right to the faery fort or left following the tracks.

We leave the horses munching on tufts of grass and follow the tire tracks for some distance till we come upon the place where the machine's left a straight wall in the black peat. There's no turf lying around drying, which there should be, so none of it makes much sense unless whoever did this took the turf away wet drying it somewhere else. We follow the wall to the end and the tracks keep going so we do too.

Now we're walking downward and I can feel the temperature dropping with us and suddenly there are patches of fog floating over the bog obscuring the moon. My heart starts pounding, my imagination taking over like Harry and Hermione heading into the Forbidden Forest and not feeling good about it. Like there's evil lurking ahead and we're walking right into its open mouth. That's when Billy grabs my arm and hisses, 'Look!'

We all stop and stare where Billy's pointing.

'I don't see anything.'

But then I do. A red glow, small like a cigarette. Moving. I can see a shadow holding it and then the shadow disappears behind something black then an overhead light comes on and I can see everything except it's too far away.

'It's Fungal's digger!' I whisper. 'Who's that inside?'

The person inside isn't tall and skinny like Fungal. The light goes off and the cigarette reappears going the other direction.

Billy says, 'I think that was Crash or Burn.'

Karen laughs. 'Who?'

I answer. 'Crash and Burn O'Reilly. Brothers. Conor and Brian really but everyone calls 'em Crash and Burn. Their dad's the biggest wheeler-dealer in the county. Always into something, most of it clem.'

'Clem?'

'Illegal. Like if you were up to something and needed help Ol' Man O'Reilly would be the bloke to talk to.'

We're moving again, heading toward the digger, walking slowly trying to be quiet and invisible.

'Maybe this is where they're dryin the turf?'

That would make sense — out of sight of the tower — but why not dig the turf down here too? Then my brain starts thinking about Darcy. Did he see Fungal's digger? Did he go to investigate and get caught? Would you kill a fifteen-year-old boy because he caught you cutting turf? No way, right? But then I remember it was pouring that night. No way they'd be cutting turf in a monsoon. Because there's three of us we're brave and we keep going until finally we're close enough to see for sure it's Fungal's digger, the oversized Man U sticker on the door sealing the deal.

'You two stay here.' Karen and Billy nod like you bet your arse we're staying here.

I stay low circling around until I'm behind the digger. I creep forward stopping when I reach one of the big back tires. There's faint light ahead but I still can't tell what I'm looking at. I crawl under the machine and wiggle to the front. Straight ahead there's a hole in the ground about the size of Darcy's grave and I can see the top of a ladder sticking up. The hole's leaking light but nothin substantial. More like the light a torch gives off just before the batteries die. I crawl forward leaving the safety of the digger till I'm at the edge of the hole. I peer down. The grave's empty but there's a tunnel leading from it heading underneath the bog. I can't see anybody but I hear voices. I reach into my pocket and pull out my iPhone. I'll take one photo then get the hell out of here.

Click. Flash.

SHITE! I forgot about the flash and now the voices have stopped talking. I scramble backwards, get to my feet and start hoofing it, staying low like a soldier in a war movie dodging bullets.

'C'mon!' I hiss sprinting by Karen and Billy who are clambering to their feet trying to catch up. I look back. I can see shadows scrambling up the ladder, staring into the darkness. Then for sure I see the digger's overhead light blink on. Then I hear the engine starting.

THURSDAY
9:00

I go to school Thursday. In the morning I have Maths and Irish. They're trying hard in Ireland to keep the old language alive and my county Donegal has the highest percentage of Irish speakers so teaching the old language here makes sense as there's people you can be practicing on.

Billy and I eat lunch together away from the school sitting on the seawall gazing at the harbor and the Atlantic beyond. I'm eating a pupusa — a thick corn tortilla stuffed with spicy pork — thanks to Gran freezing some for Grandad Sky who learned to love them on an archeological dig in El Salvador. I'm dipping it into Thai peanut sauce thinking how far we Irish have come from a diet of potatoes.

"Can I try that?' Billy asks in his straightforward way and I hand him my other pupusa holding out my Tupperware container so he can dip it into the peanut sauce.

'Ummm,' he says. "What's that inside?'

'Chicharrón.'

That gets me the *I'm-no-further-ahead* look so I take pity on Billy and say, 'spicy pork belly,' which gets me the *I-wish-you-hadn't-told-me* look. Billy the boy of a thousand looks.

'What have you got?'

'Tongue.'

Now it's my turn to make a face. Billy dips his pupusa into the peanut sauce as I say, 'You know this peanut butter allergy is a new thing and growing bigger all the time.'

'How come?'

'Gran blames the peanut oil in nipple cream but Grandad blames Monsanto.'

I can see Billy thinking about this. The European Union has banned GMO but they're getting sued by Bayer, Europe's biggest Agrichemical giant. Finally, Billy says, 'The world should be getting better but it's not.'

Now there's the truth in a nutshell.

We're walking back to school when Billy asks, 'Are we going back to the bog?'

I can't tell from his voice if he wants to or not.

'After yoga class when it's still light. We'll have a picnic at the tower.'

Now we're both thinking about last night. Billy says, 'We were lucky Fungal's digger wouldn't start.'

Lucky indeed!

'Fungal says it's mental, has a mind of its own.'

'Do you think Fungal was there last night?'

I don't want Fungal to be there cos he and Darcy were mates from playing Marauders together.

'I hope not,' says me. 'We could ask him.'

'He must know somebody's using his digger.'

'He rents it out sometimes if he trusts you.'

'I wouldn't be trusting Crash and Burn with shite.'

(This is the first time I've heard Billy swear so it makes me smile. I must be rubbing off on him.)

Crash and Burn, who are Fungal's age and about as clever though they can't be blaming paint fumes, got their nicknames as kids ramming their two motorcycles together while flying over Quinn's school bus. Apparently, it was stupid but spectacular.

Billy says, 'I still can't figure out what they're doing diggin a hole in the bog like that?'

I can't either but the fact they're doing it at night means something's not right and Darcy visiting the bog and dying, can that be a coincidence?

We're halfway back to school when Billy asks, 'Why didn't you tell Sergeant Leahy what you saw?'

Last night — it's like two in the morning, all the world sleeping 'cept Stumper, Mrs. Burn's three-legged cat — Billy and I are walking home from Karen's striding up Front when Sergeant Leahy pulls up beside us in his Guardia Land Rover.

'Bit late, isn't it?' he says trying to make sense of Billy and me together again. First the beach and now this. What about grieving for poor ol' Darcy?

'We were at Karen's singing. Lost track of the time.'

I don't think Constable Leahy believes me but he nods.

'I hear she can see.'

"She can.'

'And is she likin everything?'

'She is.'

'I guess now the lads will stop gawkin in her window.'

'You knew about that?'

'I warned them off but...'

Sergeant Leahy isn't scary like Inspector Mike. If the Inspector's a nasty German Shepard, Sergeant Leahy's a goofy Labrador.

'Where is Inspector Mike?' asks me. 'Haven't seen him around.'

'They gave him the double homicide in Sligo. I doubt we'll be seeing him till that's resolved.'

'Double homicide?'

'Husband murdered his wife and girlfriend.'

'You think he might have liked one of 'em?'

'It was the wife had the girlfriend.'

Sergeant Leahy waves as he drives away.

Billy steps in front of me and stops, startling me. Oh yeah, Billy asked a question which I have yet to answer.

'I don't know why I didn't tell him about the bog. Maybe I want you and I to solve this thing.'

Billy doesn't move. Finally, he says, 'Can I kiss you?'

'You just want more peanut sauce,' says me leaning forward.

I skip English — I'm not needing Mr. D asking about my essay — so I go to the library instead and google Adriana's father. There's no shortage of information, he's mega-rich after all, but most of it's in Italian so I turn on google translate. His name's Enzo Salvatore de Santis and he's 57 years old. He owns a chain of hotels including the Hotel Giorgione in Rome. He started as a bellhop at sixteen and by twenty-seven he'd created his first luxury hotel, the Hotel Luna Convento in Amalfi, by buying an abandoned convent overlooking the Tyrrhenian Sea. It was a wreck of a place but he talked his wife's father into paying for the renovations and the rest, as they say, is history... Married three times, has five kids, three with the first wife and two with the second. The third wife is young enough for kids but none so far, so maybe Enzo has had himself snipped or something. He's still partners with the first wife's father so that's saying something. I google the names of his children and that's when I hit pay dirt. The second wife had twins: Adriana and *Alessandro!*

Karen's upbeat at yoga. Alicia asks her if she'll be going back to being a vet and Karen laughs. 'I don't know. I've gotten used to being a woman of leisure.'

'She's gonna be the next Lady Gaga,' says me grinning. Karen lifts her eyebrows and the other girls leave.

'Did you know Adriana has a twin brother?'

'No. She's never mentioned him.'

'I bet that's who was drivin the boat.'

'He's here?'

I tell Karen about seeing the male lying in Adriana's bed.

'You snuck into her apartment?'

'I was looking for Gran's book.'

I can see Karen wrestling with this so I try to change the subject.

'Me and Billy are havin a picnic at the tower, then we're goin back to the bog. In daylight. You're welcome to join us.'

'Sorry, can't. You be careful now.'

I don't say anything, just stare at her. Finally, she pushes me out the door. As I trundle off I hear, 'None of your business.'

It makes me mad actually. Inspector Mike hasn't got time for Darcy because of a double homicide but he's got time to take out Karen *and* Adriana. Maybe it'll be a double date.

Half an hour later, Billy and me are striding along the path, beside the cliff edge, that leads to the tower but now Billy's stopped tying his shoe. I look back at my little village nestled like a baby in its mother's arms.

'Billy, do you think you'll always be livin in Gloire Bay?'

'I think I may end up here,' Billy replies, 'but I'd like to see the world first.'

That's how I feel too. Live a whole bunch then settle down where it seems right.

'Darcy had this verse he liked from T. S. Eliot:

> *We shall not cease from exploration,*
> *And the end of all our exploring,*
> *Will be to arrive where we started,*
> *And know the place for the first time.'*

Billy looks impressed like it's not everyday someone's spouting poetry. 'Say it once more.'

I say it again watching Billy's lips move as he says it with me, committing it to memory, just like I did with Darcy. Then he grins at me like I've just handed him a prize no one can take away.

We reach the tower and clamber up to the gun platform. The view's spectacular or would be if a carload of over-stuffed Germans, wearing expensive hiking gear and loud voices, weren't about to have their own picnic.

'Excuse me, is that your Mercedes at the bottom of the hill?'

'Ja.'

'You've got a flat tire.'

Before you can say, *Hitler saved his mother's Jewish doctor* — (It's true!) — we have the gun platform to ourselves.

'What?'

Billy's staring at me like, *I can't believe you just did that!*

'Think how happy they'll be when they find out they don't have a flat tire.'

Darcy'd have a comeback — something like, *other than that Mrs. Lincoln how did you enjoy the play?* — but Billy's just shaking his head.

I ignore him and say, 'How come it's always the female who makes the picnic?'

'I offered.' Billy was sweet, he did offer except we both know his mother would have made everything.

'You would have brought blood pudding and sweetbreads.'

Billy laughs. 'I'm hoping for more pupusas,' he says watching me pull things from my backpack.

'Nope. Corned beef on rye and we're splittin a Kilkenny.' I hand Billy the tall brown can and he moves it back and forth listening to the plastic widget inside.

'Tell me again what Fungal said.'

After school, while I'm contorting myself at yoga, Billy found Fungal behind the manse installing a new septic tank. Fungal tells Billy, Father McKenna is full of shite so he's not surprised.

'Fungal said he has a standing agreement with Ol' Man O'Reilly that Crash and Burn can use the digger at night. Has to be back by daylight. Fungal says he gets a thousand Euros a month, diesel and repairs extra. Even had another key made so they don't need to bother him.'

Fungal lives at his mum's place on Parnell. There's a metal garage out back where he keeps the digger.

'That sounds good. Makin money while you sleep.'

'Fungal says he and Gail are savin to buy Betty's.'

'Is Stan sellin?'

'No, but Fungal says someday he'll be sellin.'

I'm impressed. Seems Fungal has more smarts than he lets on. Course his mum is sharp. After Fungal lost his IQ she's the one arranged the loan for the digger. She's probably feeding him ideas.

'And how long has this been goin on for?'

'Fungal said he's been paid twice.'

Two months! You think Gran and me would have noticed the digger coming and going but maybe they're taking the long route up Columbine rather than going by the tower. That would make sense if you were trying to be inconspicuous. (I love long words like *inconspicuous* that are anything but.)

Something about Fungal is bothering me. Something from the funeral.

'Did you ask him what Crash and Burn are using the machine for?'

'He assumes they're cutting turf. Says the digger comes back covered in black muck.'

'How often do they use it?'

'Two or three times a week depending on the weather.'

There's the catch. The weather. It rains a lot in Ireland, which is why the place is so fecking green and why a container full of wellies (rubber boots) is always a sure bet.

'Do you remember the night Darcy died?'

Billy nods.

'When did the rain start?'

I'm asking Billy but I'm trying to remember myself. Peter picked me up on the outskirts of Gloire Bay around seven. Then we drove to a pub in Donegal Town called The Forge. I used my fake ID and the bartender knew it was fake but didn't care. As long as I had it he couldn't get in trouble if the Gardaí appeared. We were a couple of hours in the pub. There was a middle-aged couple playing mostly old stuff like Neil Diamond and The Eagles but they were talented so it was good craic. They take a break. I have to pee so I head off and I remember glancing at the clock behind the bar and it saying 22:30 (10:30 pm) or thereabouts.

The couple comes back playing something slow and Peter pulls me onto the dance floor his hands on my butt and suddenly I'm wanting to get this virginity thing out of the way so we go outside and it's not raining. I remember looking at the stars as Peter took my hand and led me to his car. He tries to get me in the backseat but I say not here so we drive out of town to a layby with a view of the water. Like the view matters when he's already got his hand up my shirt.

Billy interrupts my thoughts saying, 'I was at Ethan's that night. We were in his room playing Overwatch so we weren't paying attention to outside. But when I tried to head home it was raining so hard Ethan's mum said I should stay the night so I called home and mum said okay.'

It was the rain pounding on the car roof that stopped everything. It was like all the drummers in a marching band were beating on the roof at the same time. Then there was a flash of lightning and I see Peter's face and he looks like the devil. That's when I realize he doesn't give a damn about me — which was what I thought I wanted! — but suddenly it's not what I want because it's making me feel small and dirty. I have to leave that tiny space so I push open the car door and scramble out. Peter gets out on his side and he's screaming at me to get back inside. But I can't. My mind's changed. I don't want to be someone having sex in the back of a car with someone I feel nothing for. But it's not Peter's fault. I've led him on like a whore getting paid for it.

'I'm sorry!' I scream over the drumming rain and the thunder. 'I can't do it!'

I start walking back to town Peter following in the car his headlights showing the way. There's so much rain it's like a shower with a broken head. I go back into the pub looking like ten drowned rats glued together. I expect Peter to follow me in but he drives off instead. I try to be mad at him but it's myself I'm angry with. I think I'm a smart person so why do I keep making these stupid mistakes?

I need to get to Gloire Bay I say to the bartender but he just shakes his head. Won't be anybody driving in this he says. How 'bout a room? So that's what happens. I rent a room upstairs in the pub and that's where I spent the night, listening to the rain my virginity intact.

'You know when they say it's rainin cats and dogs?'

Billy nods.

'Gran says in the old days the cats and dogs would sleep in the thatched roof and if the rain got too hard they'd jump down.'

I can see the word *dubious* fly across Billy's face and I laugh. 'Yeah, I don't believe it either.' I put what's left of the picnic in the backpack and we clamber down the crumbling stairs heading for the bog.

There's a green tarp covering the open grave — held down by stones at the corners and sticking up where the ladder is — so we take that as a good sign. And no sign of Fungal's digger, which we take as an even better sign. The idea of coming in daylight is to not meet anybody. What I hadn't noticed before — it was dark! — was the mound of dirt piled behind the grave spread out and smoothed looking somewhat like a wannabe faery fort.

Billy pulls one corner of the tarp aside exposing the ladder. We climb down and peer into the tunnel. The tunnel's got wooden beams supporting a ceiling made of rough boards. Off to the side is a box full of car batteries with wires running up the wall to a lightbulb on the ceiling. I'm for finding the switch but Billy's brought a torch so I follow him down the tunnel into the darkness. The walls are black and slippery, the smell of peat overwhelming. I'm not big on confined spaces but this seems okay. Then we find digging instruments — picks, shovels and rakes — leaning on the wall behind two wheelbarrows. There's no way the digger's getting in here so shovels make sense.

The tunnel's been sloping down so now there's water at our feet glistening in Billy's light but we step forward onto a wooden walkway leading somewhere. 'What the...' Billy's shining his flashlight ahead not understanding what he's seeing. I push in beside him.

We're staring at a miniature city made of silver and gold. It seems to stretch on forever till Billy moves his light and I realize there's a wall of mirrors behind making it all seem much bigger than it is. But still the little city's impressive and putting a smile on my face because everything's wonky. Nothing's level. Roofs, floors, walls, windows, doors, all are at crazy angles like some clumsy janitor has tripped on his mop sending everything this way and that. We move closer.

'Don't move,' says Billy disappearing with the torch.

I wait in the dark knowing he's gone to hook up the batteries. All at once the city lights up! It was striking before but now it's glorious!

I bend down peering through the tiny windows.

'They're dancing!'

Billy leans in beside me staring at the tiny faery figures moving and twirling to music only they can hear.

'Jalapeño Grande,' says me thunderstruck by the skilled workmanship and the sheer audacity of it all.

Twenty minutes later we climb out of the grave putting the tarp back the way we found it. It's still light out but the sun's low in the sky and when I turn my head to follow after Billy a glint of reflected light catches my eye. It's coming from the bones of an old tractor abandoned on the edge of the bog.

'Hang on, Billy.'

I head for the pile of rust, Billy coming behind me.

'Shite.'

I assumed it was a piece of broken headlamp glinting in the sun but now I can see it for what it is, a rectangular black case with a round lens.

'It's a trail camera,' Billy says.

I pull the case from its hiding place and open the door on the back. Four new batteries stare back at me along with a memory card pushed into its holder. Instructions on the back of the door talk about setting the sensitivity of the motion detector. Billy and I stare at each other.

'For sure we're on the card.'

Any way you look at it we're screwed. If we steal the camera, they'll know someone's been here. If we leave it, they'll see our faces. If we take the card, they'll know someone's been here.

'Take the card,' Billy says at last. 'We'll erase it, put it back tomorrow. With any luck they won't notice.'

I hand the card to Billy and put the camera back. Billy's right. With any luck no one will show up tonight. With even more luck we'll see *their* faces on the card!

We're headed back to the tower when Billy asks, 'What was that back there?"

'I think that was supposed to be the inside of a faery fort.'

'Was it old?'

'I think it's brand new tryin to look old.'

'But why are they building it there? The faery fort is over there,' he says pointing.

'And surrounded by water.'

Billy nods at this. 'Maybe they didn't want to disturb the real thing.'

Inside I'm chuckling at this. Nobody believes in faeries but nobody's tampering with the faery fort either. You never know, right?

'One thing's for sure,' says me. 'Crash and Burn are only doin the diggin. Somebody talented is building the city.'

We reach the tower and climb up to the gun platform to enjoy the sunset, which is spectacular as usual. Billy stands right beside me and I can feel his warmth mixing with mine saying, *we're alive in a beautiful place, enjoy it.*

We're about to head out when we see headlights coming toward the tower. We duck down. 'Did you see who it was?' Billy shakes his head but starts rhyming off everybody who owns an ATV.

We're afraid to stick our heads up in case they see us.

'Maybe they're going to the bog?'

That theory doesn't last long because we hear the machine stop right below us and then the motor dies. Billy pops up looking over the edge.

'It's Ol' Man O'Reilly and Father McKenna.'

I grab Billy's hand and race him down the stairs. Quick as a flash I've got the key to the love nest and the door open. We go inside and I relock the door stupidly leaving the key in the lock. We sit on the bed and wait.

Soon we hear two men coming across the stone floor.

'The key's gone,' Father McKenna says. I'd know his deep voice anywhere.

Nothin happens for a moment and then I hear someone approaching the door getting down on his knees, making a noise about it.

'It's in the lock,' Ol' Man O'Reilly says. Then he starts pounding on the door.

'Who's in there?'

'Go find your own cubbyhole!' shouts me trying to disguise my voice, the words coming out sounding like Natalie Portman on steroids.

Now they're outside the door whispering.

Then a piece of paper slides under the door and I think they've written us a note. *Get out of there or else!* Too funny only that isn't it. Suddenly the key is falling from the lock and lands on the piece of paper. I'm on my feet now lunging for it when the piece of paper with the key disappears under the door.

'Goodnight Fiona. Try not to drink all the wine.'

I don't like to state the obvious but I do just to get things rolling again.

'We're fucked.'

Billy looks at me like, *no shite, Sherlock!*

I watch as Billy climbs on the bed so he can slide back the bolt holding the wooden shutter closed. That accomplished he pushes open the shutter and leans out. While he considers his chances of jumping without breaking his neck, I grab a bottle of wine and consider my chances of opening it without breaking its neck.

A Swiss Army knife lands on the bed beside me.

'What are you a feckin boy scout?'

I pry the corkscrew thingee from the knife and turn it into the cork.

'Some of the bottles are screw top,' Billy says, grinning.

I've got so many comebacks I don't bother but pull the cork instead. I take a long swig and hand the bottle to Billy. Back and forth the bottle goes till we start leaning/sniggering like two pirates just landed in Tortuga after six months at sea.

Billy sticks his head out the opening again then comes back in saying, 'If we take all our clothes off and tie them together, we might make a rope long enough.'

'I like your first idea better.'

That's when a little square package lands on the bed beside me.

'You are a feckin boy scout!'

Now that it's finally happened, I find I don't really want to talk about it other than to say I'm glad it was Billy...

My new iPhone says it's 22:37, 06:37 in Shanghai where it was made. Billy's lying beside me giving off heat like a furnace and I can honestly say I have no idea where my body stops and his begins.

'So, I guess it's obvious Father McKenna and Ol' Man O'Reilly are a gay couple and using this as their love nest.'

I try to make something ugly/sordid out of this but my brain and my heart won't go there. And besides the sheets don't smell like dirty old men they smell like an Irish Spring ad.

'Darcy was gay,' Billy says.

'You knew?'

'I guessed.'

'Cos he didn't care about football?'

Billy can't put it in words so he doesn't try.

'More wine?'

Billy shakes his head. We finished the first bottle, we don't seem to need another.

'I'd like to stay here forever but I guess we better start thinking about getting out of here. Grandad Sky will worry.'

'Me mum, too.'

'Our clothes are off, do you want to try your rope idea?'

'We'd be walkin home starkers.'

'You're right,' says me picturing it, laughing.

'Only person I can think to call is Karen.'

Billy nods at this. 'Send her a text.'

<Help! Me and Billy are locked in a room in the tower!>

A minute later I get: <You're joking!>

<Not! We need help before Grandad Sky calls the Gardai!>

<I've got the Garda here beside me! We're on our way!>

The condom looks like Moby Dick was wearing it so we toss it out the window — damn tourists! (Have you noticed tourists and terrorists sound the same after a bottle of wine?)

We get our clothes back on but we can't get the grins off our faces. That's when we hear a horse galloping up to the tower and Karen knocking on the door.

'How do we get this open?'

'There may be a key hidin under a rock.'

Next thing you know the door swings open and there stands Inspector Mike scowling with Karen leaning around him grinning. Inspector Mike takes in the bed, the wine bottles, the fireplace, the two unstoppable grins and says, 'Well, isn't this cozy.'

He pushes in marching around like a detective while Karen and I are staring at each other our eyes telling stories and Billy's standing still like he's the guy you can count on to keep his head when everybody else is losing theirs. Finally, Inspector Mike says, 'Smells like sex to me.'

No shite, Sherlock!

FRIDAY
OO:30

I'm home now lying in my bed thinking about everything that just happened. I can still smell Billy on my skin so that's good. I was going to have a shower but I'm glad I didn't. I didn't tell Billy I was carrying a little foil package too. Better him thinking he's the hero.

Inspector Mike was pissed again, this time cos we wouldn't say who locked us in the room, me and Billy pretending we didn't know. Billy almost spilled the beans but he took his cue from me and kept his mouth shut. I don't know why I didn't tell the Inspector other than he annoys me. Probably means we're alike, that's what Darcy would be saying. Bit arrogant, bit stubborn, bit full of ourselves. He went off with Karen muttering something about underage drinking/underage sex, but you could tell it was one of those idle threats adults use when they're flabbergasted.

Then I find myself feeling sorry for Father McKenna till I remember he may have something to do with Darcy going over the cliff. But still he and Ol' Man O'Reilly look like two men who've found forbidden love and it would never be me throwing rocks at that.

That's where my thoughts stop because there's a little faery named Benji knocking on my window. What's different is Benji is wearing armor like he's auditioning to be a Knight of the Round Table. Before I can ask him about that he says, 'You look happy.'

'I am happy Benji. How bout you?'

'It's been a day.'

'Tell me all about it,' I say pushing my backside into the pillows, getting comfortable.

'You remember I told you about The Unseelie Court?'

'Bad guys from Scotland.'

'Exactly. They've landed at Marble Hill.'

'Did they fly over?'

'The Unseelie don't have wings.'

'So ships then,' says me trying to picture it.

'You should hear Queen C going on about it.' Benji throws his hands in the air talking in the Queen's voice. 'If I'd known The Unseelie were coming I never would have come here!' Benji's voice returns to his own. 'We're all going, hey, feel free to leave anytime. (Queen's voice) I could have gone to New York and stayed with my aunt, Princess Littia.'

'That's funny.'

'Yeah, isn't it? Then she says where the hell is Sir Max? He should have been here ages ago.'

'Sir Max is the fierce warrior who's now a drunk?'

'That's right. He's the one beat King Killoe at Killiecrankie.'

'So, where is he?'

'No one knows so Queen C sends out six of the fastest flyers to scour the neighborhood and find Sir Max.'

'I bet you were one of them.'

'I was. But before we leave Major Domo calls us together...'

'Who's he again?' I meant to ask about Major Domo before but forgot.

'Major Domo, he's like Queen C's second-in-command. Been with her forever like before Saint Patrick.'

'Wow.'

'Yeah, anyway he huddles us together where nobody can overhear him and says Sir Max is an old reprobate, couldn't fight his way out of a burlap bag, so look for him in a bar or a ditch.'

'That doesn't sound good.'

'My mate Godfrey says, if Sir Max is useless why are we looking for him?'

'Good question.'

'Yeah, I thought so too. You're lookin for him, the Major says, because the Queen has ordered you to find him.'

I mean what do you say to that? An order's an order, right? Like when Gran tells me to clean my room I do it though we both know it's strictly temporary.

'Then what happened?'

'We divided up into the six directions.'

'Six?'

'North, East, West, South, Up and Down.'

Hard to argue with that. 'Which one did you get?'

'South. But I was smart, I brought Mally with me.'

'Was that allowed?'

'Not really, but I figured if I was wasting time I might as well do it with someone I adore.'

Adore. Nice. I *adore* Billy. Maybe I do.

'Then what?'

'All day we're galloping around–'

'Galloping?'

'Yeah, the Major let us use the pterippi–'

I put my hand up. *What?*

'Winged horses.'

Okay. I nod. Winged horses, that's cool. I picture Pegasus with Benji on top.

'Mally and I can fly but not that far or that fast so we mount two of the pterippi and take off. We're galloping south asking everybody we meet if they've seen Sir Max? Mally has a photo so we keep showing that in case they don't know who we're talking about.'

'Who's everybody?'

'Boggarts, brownies, goblins, water nymphs...'

'And these guys are everywhere?'

Benji nods like it's a dumb question.

'Okay, okay. So had anybody seen Sir Max?'

'Nobody's seen him until finally we meet this old geezette who says she may have seen Sir Max in The Fox & Thistle in Letterkenny. But he was by himself, no Alonzo.'

'Who's Alonzo?'

'Sir Max's Faithful Companion. Been with him since Day One. Polishes Sir Max's armor, makes sure the horses get fed, collects the gold when Sir Max defends somebody. That kind of thing.'

I don't know about you but I'm picturing Sancho Panza looking after Don Quixote.

'This is a great story.'

'It gets worse.'

'Worse?'

'We find Sir Max in the Fox & Thistle and it's a good thing I've invited Mally along because Sir Max is puking his guts out in the Ladies Toilets.'

'What's he doing in the Ladies?'

'He thought it said Laddies.'

Too funny!

'So, you brought Sir Max to the Queen?'

'We did but not that one.'

'What?!'

'That one died.'

'I didn't think faeries could die.'

'Only under *unusual circumstances*.'

'What happened?'

'Sir Max was sleeping under his horse and his horse fell down.'

'How did that happen?'

'Alonzo tripped him.'

'Sir Max?'

'No, the horse.'

'You're makin this up.'

'I'm not. The horse collapsed and crushed Sir Max.'

'Was the horse okay?'

'Yes.'

I can see Benji doesn't give a tinker's ass about the horse but I do.

'What's the horse's name?'

'You're not always this irritating.'

'Just tell me the horse's name and I'll shut up.'

'Promise?'

I nod.

'U.C.'

'You see, what?'

'U.C. Short for Unusual Circumstances.'

LOL. Poor Sir Max. Finally, I nod but don't say anything — per our agreement — but I'm waving my hand like, *go on I'm loving this!*

'So, we have dinner-'

'What did you have?'

Benji points his finger at me and the next thing I know my mouth won't open.

'Mmmmm!'

Benji continues, 'So we have dinner — badger & chips — at the pub, with Alonzo, trying to decide what we're going to do next because we know if we return to Queen C without Sir Max she's going to have the biggest hissy fit since The Great Cat Massacre.'

'Mmmmm!'

Benji ignores me.

'It's pitch black when we finally decide to go outside in hopes the fresh air will help us think better and that's when a miracle happens.'

'Mmmmm!' I want to know about the Great Cat Massacre, then the miracle, but Benji's having none of it.

'We're standing in the middle of the street when we see this ball of fiery light rocketing toward us. As it gets closer, we see it's a faery totally out of control. Instead of flying, the faery is doing somersaults! It crashes into the road in front of us but doesn't stop; it comes bouncing toward us and before we can get out of the way it bowls us over like we're bowling pins.'

'MMMMMMMM!'

Benji waves his finger and my mouth unsticks.

'Who was it?'

'Sir Max.'

'No! Sir Max is dead!'

'Reborn, replaced, recycled. Take your pick.'

'But who is it?'

'The new Max.'

'Young?'

'Yes.'

'Wearing armor?'

'Yes.'

'Big sword?'

'Yes.'

'Knows how to fight?'

'Yes, except–'

'–except for flying. But you could teach him that.'

'Yes. Mally did. Didn't take long. A few minor adjustments. Like riding a bike with one wheel.'

'A unicycle.'

'That's it.'

I can see Benji is hesitating, like a kid having to own up to the fact he's stolen gum from the convenience store.

'There's something you're not telling me.'

'Yes.'

'Tell me.'

'The new Max is a she.'

OMG! This is so good!

'How did that happen?'

'A mispronunciation I gather.'

I'm loving this!

'Like she said too-**may**-toe instead of too-**mat**-toe?'

'Exactly.'

'Can't you reverse it? Have her say it again?'

Benji shakes his head. 'The new Max rather likes being female.'

'You go girl!'

Benji rolls his eyes.

'Then what happened?

'We headed back to Sí Dún.'

'Queen C is ecstatic you've found Sir Max?'

'Not exactly. She pulls me aside and says, you eejit, Sir Max is a he not a she! So I have to explain that Sir Max has undergone a sex change. What's the world coming to snorts Queen C looking for a target for her anger and me the only one within reach. But can she fight, she asks, and I say better than before. She's got the spirit of Joan of Arc combined with the skill of Ronda Rousey.'

'How'd that go over?'

'She didn't believe a word of it. Instead, she screams at Major Domo to produce his best warrior, so of course he shouts for Manduke.'

'Who's Manduke?' I can see I'm once again interrupting too much so I clamp my hands over my mouth.

'Manduke is my age, slightly bigger than me because he ordered armor two sizes too big. Handsome if you like slick GQ types. He likes Mally but she says he's a dolt. Anyway, the Major calls for Manduke and he comes prancin in like he's been waitin in the wings polishing his nails for just this moment.'

Benji looks at me giving me permission to speak. I can tell he's jealous of Manduke. Good thing Mally likes Benji better. Smart girl, just the kind we like.

'Then what happened?'

'Max beat the crap out of him.'

'Oh, that's grand!'

'Yeah, none of us saw it comin. I figured we'd be teaching Max how to fight, like we had to teach her how to fly, but she had Manduke lying on his back quicker than I can tell it. And you should have seen the look on Alonzo's face. Crikey, he whispers to me and Mally, Sir Max was never that good I can tell you. But all the stories, says Mally. Mostly made up, says Alonzo. Sir Max hired a publicist years ago. She's been cranking out the stories ever since.'

I wish Gran was here to hear this. I wish Darcy was here. I wish Billy was here.

'Then what?'

'Then Alfred comes galloping in. He's the one been searching the North. He says he's seen The Unseelie landing on the beach at Marble Hill. Everything goes deathly quiet and Queen C asks, how many? Alfred doesn't know what to say but finally he blurts out, you know that movie we saw last week?'

'You watch movies?' I can't believe it. I'm about to ask Benji what his favorite movie is when I see the look of disgust on his face. My hands fly to my mouth. Mmmmsorrymmmm.

'Queen C says, you mean *The Return of the King?* Alfred nods then he says, remember the Orcs? Queen C nods, her face turning the color of chalk dust. That many, says Alfred.'

I remember the Orcs. They went on forever.

'So, what are you gonna do?'

Grandad's got breakfast waiting for me. Two rashers of bacon (look it up!) and two of Mrs. Flynn's organic brown eggs, sunny side up, with Owl's Nest seven grain toast, Gran's yummy chili sauce, and a steaming mug of cowboy coffee. You can walk on the coffee but the egg yokes are runny the way I like 'em.

'You're on your own tonight and tomorrow,' Grandad says giving me that look that parents/grandparents have been giving teenagers since time began. The one that says: Do NOT Do Anything Colossally Stupid and

Keep Your Knickers On.

'Maybe you should have a sleepover?' Grandad suggests.

I was thinking that too but I decide not mentioning Billy at this particular moment might be clever of me.

'What about Kylie?' asks Grandad.

Kylie and I aren't talking at the moment but Grandad doesn't know that.

'I think I'll be busy working on my essay.'

'And what have you decided to write about?'

'I was thinkin about the effect the potato famine had on Irish culture.'

The look on Grandad's face. Kind of like a graphic *snort*.

'My that's a good idea.'

'I thought you'd like it.'

'How many words?'

'2000.'

'When's it due again?'

'Monday.'

I can see he's thinking of asking how many words I've written so far but he knows the answer.

'Make sure you research Jeanie Johnston.' *Jeanie Johnston* is the replica famine ship lives in Dublin harbor. Me and Gran and Grandad toured her last summer when we were there. 'No one knows where the name came from and get Feister looking like himself before Gran gets back.'

I find Billy in the school library. He's sitting at a table studying a football magazine probably dreaming of scoring the winning goal for Ireland in the World Cup. I sneak up behind him and put my hands over his eyes.

'Your lips are movin,' says me.

'I'm a ventriloquist.'

'Show me.'

Billy makes his hand into a face and as his thumb moves Homer Simpson says, 'They didn't have aspirin so I got you cigarettes.'

You're not supposed to bring food into the library but if you hide in the corner where the chesterfields are you can get away with it. I've got turkey sandwiches with cranberries and stuffing. Billy's not opening his lunch so we'll take it my turkey's more to his liking. I thought Billy might be different somehow after our time together but he's not. Billy's Billy and I like that about him.

I want to tell him he's now my best mate but I can see I don't need to say anything he already knows.

Billy says, 'We're the only ones on the memory card plus a rabbit or two.'

'They must be checkin it then. We'll have to get it back pronto.'

'It's already back.'

'My hero.'

Billy smiles at this.

'Have you got your essay done?' I ask.

'Yep."

'Wanker.'

'But I changed my topic.'

'What are you doin now?'

'The Irish at the Alamo.'

'What! There were Irish fighting with Davey Crockett?'

'There were a dozen Irish, probably more.'

Grandad Sky's gonna love this.

'You'll do well with that.'

'Dad's idea. Says the Davidsons will love it cos they spend their summers in Texas visiting their sister.'

Now that's smart. Don't research the topic; research your teacher.

'How's your dad know the D's?'

'Darts.'

Jesus and Mary! Billy's going to get 95% cos his dad plays darts.

'Do you know anything about the potato famine?'

Billy shakes his head, then he says, 'BFF.'

'What's BFF?'

'Before French Fries.'

That reminds me they're tryin to change BC, Before Christ, to BCE, Before the Common Era. Take that Popey and smoke it.

'I may need help. You may have to come over.'

Billy ain't bitin — there's probably some big football match on — so I flick my wrist again.

'Grandad's gone to Dublin to pick up Gran.'

Now he's got the fly in his mouth, figuratively speaking, but before I can reel him in it hits me. 'OMG! THAT'S IT!'

Billy's lookin at me like I've just noticed the chesterfield's on fire. 'What!?'

'At the funeral. Fungal was in his digger. He pulled his backpack up to get his lunch but it wasn't his.'

'What are you talking about?'

'I watched him. He rummaged around inside the backpack like nothing inside made sense to him. Then he put that backpack down and grabbed another.'

'So?'

'What if it was Darcy's backpack?'

'Why would...' Billy stops then says, 'Darcy's spyin on the guys digging the hole.'

'And it starts to rain.'

'A monsoon.'

'And he doesn't want Gran's book to get wet so...'

'He hides in Fungal's digger...'

'And leaves his pack in Fungal's cooler which is probably empty but he needs the book to say the spell...'

Billy shakes his head. 'Why does he need the book? Why didn't he just copy the spell onto your mobile and leave the book with you?'

'Because I told him the spell wouldn't work unless the book was close by.'

'Is that true?'

'I think so.'

'You think so?'

'It's just something Gran said years ago. Something about the book being enchanted.'

We stop here staring at each other knowing we're on the right track but still not making sense of things.

'I think you're right. Darcy would have copied the spell onto my iPhone and the spell that reverses the spell too.'

'But he doesn't know if your mobile's goin with him.'

'True.'

'Maybe he writes the spells on a piece of paper?'

'Once Darcy wrote something down, he said it was locked in his memory.'

Billy nods at this. 'So where does he say the spell?'

'I don't know,' I answer trying to picture it all. 'What are our choices?'

'In the digger.'

'It's dry there.'

'Wouldn't he be worried about whoever's drivin the digger comin back?'

'Maybe he thinks Fungal is there or maybe he thinks he'll only be gone a minute or two...'

'Or maybe he thinks the spell's not going to work so what does it matter?'

Now it's me shaking my head. 'No. If you don't believe in the spell it won't work.'

Now Billy's giving me the Inspector Mike *this-is-shite* look. Then he says, 'Maybe he went back to the tower and ran into Father McKenna and Ol' Man O'Reilly. They wouldn't like him knowing their secret.'

I think about this. They didn't seem to mind Billy and me knowing. Probably figured no one would believe us.

'That's a long way to go in a monsoon.'

'Maybe he went closer to the faery fort?' Billy says.

'I'm betting he stays in the digger figuring whoever's in the hole isn't comin out till the storm passes.'

'So, he says the spell and then what?'

'I don't know. I've never done it.'

'Why not?'

'Gran keeps the book hidden away. We'd look at it when I was little. She'd show me the pictures of the different faeries and tell me stories about them. But I outgrew it, I guess. Then Darcy says he's going to write about Irish faeries so I tell him about Gran's book and he got all excited so I showed it to him. That's when he found the spell to turn a human into a faery. This will make my essay, he says, especially if he can take a photo or two inside the faery fort with my iPhone. His mobile was busted of course cos he put it in the washer.'

I'm definitely babbling but Billy cuts through all the palaver and grabs truth by the throat and holds it up for me to see.

'You should have been with him.'

On the way out of the library I stop at Ms. Darling's desk. I know her outside school from taking some of Karen's evening yoga classes. Outside school her name's Janine and she's married to Rick, the sharpest solicitor between here and Sligo or so Gran says. She's also super nice and super smart.

'Do you by chance know who bought the bog down from the tower? There's No Trespassing signs that weren't there before.'

'As it happens, I do know because Rick was the solicitor on the deal.'

I put my hand up. 'Let me guess, Ol' Man O'Reilly?'

'He's the seller not the buyer.'

Now my brain's whizzing around trying different names on. Then one lights up.

'Adriana.' I can tell by the look of surprise on Janine's face I've struck gold.

'Now how did you figure that out?'

'Psychic.' I go into my third-eye-snake-charmer-belly-dance and Janine laughs.

'Okay smarty pants, so tell me why she bought it because Rick and I can't make sense of it.'

'Didn't Rick ask?'

'She said he'd have to wait and see.'

I know why, or at least I think I do, but I keep it to myself.

'Does she own the whole bog?' I'm thinking about the Faery Fort.

'I don't know but I can ask.'

'Yes, please.'

'It isn't Adriana herself buying; it's the corporation that owns the Inn. The money came from her father and I shouldn't be tellin you all this though if you went online for 40 Euros you can search the title.'

'I think your Rick's a pretty lucky fellow.'

'I keep telling him that.'

Now that I'm pretty sure I know what happened to Gran's book I'm all for skipping afternoon classes. I need to find Fungal and see if I'm right about Darcy's backpack. Billy says Fungal might still be dealing with Father McKenna's sewage backup but to be sure I call Fungal's mum, Deirdre.

'Hi Fiona. How you makin out?'

"Sad and mad.'

'That's what Fergus is feeling too.'

'Do you know where Fergus is workin today?'

'I forgot to ask. He left early before my brain woke up.'

'Did he finish at the manse?'

'He did but where he's going next, I'm not sure. But I can tell you where he'll be later. He'll be at the Parish Hall missing Darcy.'

Of course! Friday night. *Marauders.*

I ditch school and head home instead. This essay's sitting on my shoulders like the *Titanic*. I fire up the Dell and google Irish Potato Famine. Billy shows up after school and I tell him to come back at 19:00, that we're going to the Parish Hall to find Fungal.

Janine calls to say Adriana owns the west half of the bog, so not the faery fort. Who owns the east half? Janine shouts at Rick but he doesn't know. It'll be on file in Lifford.

Billy reappears at the appointed hour. I've got 1537 words most of them adjectives and adverbs. The trouble is the whole famine thing turns out to be awful/horrid/shameful but interesting too, like a window into the Irish soul, so I want to do it justice.

'Can you cook?' I ask Billy.

'Poundy.'

I love Billy!

'Go for it. Bandit will help.'

For sure Billy's eaten but he doesn't say a word just strikes off for the kitchen. By the time Billy shouts, 'Ready!' I'm typing my last sentence. 1906 words. I haven't found out where the name Jeanie Johnston came from so that will get me to 2000.

Billy's poundy — potato pancakes, better known as boxty if you're not from Donegal — are to die for and, as we're settling in, I start educating Billy about *an Gorta Mór,* which is Irish for The Great Hunger.

'The year's 1845 and in Ireland all the land is owned by wealthy landlords most of them English and most of them absent.

'The land's worked by poor Irish cottiers, farmers renting just enough land to feed themselves and their family, and there's only one crop and that's potatoes. A pathogen, *phytophthora infestans* — better known as potato blight — sweeps across North America and Europe turning the potato crop to mush. One day your crop's looking good and the next it's a stinking, rotting mess good for nothing. All the food you've been counting on to get you through the winter is lying at your feet as useless as dog shite.'

Billy's takin it all in like I'm a history professor and this is his first lecture.

'Soon everybody's starving and in that weakened state they're in no shape to fight off another disease sweeping the world, typhus. They think more than a million died in Ireland but at the same time as everyone's starving the English landlords are still exporting grain to England, not caring if their Catholic tenants die because they can then merge all the little holdings into bigger farms. Not all, mind you. Some landlords — usually the ones living here — went bankrupt trying to help their tenants.

'So those poor Irish not dying are desperate to get out of Ireland but all they can afford is berths on sailing ships so over-packed they're lying six to a bunk, three bunks high. Can you picture it Billy? You, me, your mum and dad, Crystal and Ben all lying together, the next bunk two feet above us with another six folks one of them moaning with fever. If it wasn't blowing you were allowed on deck for an hour a day the women using their time to cook the family's only meal, oats. Everybody shat in buckets.

'This was your life for at least six weeks, maybe longer if the weather was against you. So many people died onboard they started calling them coffin ships. They estimate over half a million emigrated during the famine most going to the United States and Canada. They were kept in quarantine when they arrived because so many were sick with typhus. Can you imagine? You make this journey through hell and end up dying within sight of the holy land.'

'We toured the famine ship in Dublin,' Billy says looking at me to supply the name.

'The *Jeanie Johnston*.'

'They was bragging the Captain and the doctor kept everybody alive.'

I nod at this because the *Jeannie Johnston* is in my essay as an example of what can happen when the people in charge care. Sixteen voyages the *Jeanie Johnston* made and no one died. In fact, a baby was born on the first trip, so they gained one.

'That's my tidbit,' says me. 'No one knows where the name Jeanie Johnston came from.'

'You figured it out?'

'Not yet,' I reply like it's not a problem. 'What's yours?'

'The last man alive at the Alamo, Robert Evans, was Irish. He was the

Master of Ordnance, meaning he was in charge of all the weapons and gunpowder.'

'That sounds important.'

Billy nods. 'He stored all the gunpowder in the church but then he got shot and, as he's crawling with his torch toward the powder, which would have blown the Alamo to smithereens, he gets shot again and dies.'

'Without setting off the powder?'

Billy nods again. 'Which was a good thing because all the women and children were hiding in the church.'

Well, it's certainly a tidbit, but maybe not as heroic as Billy would be wanting.

'I'd be changing that.'

'You can't be changing history.'

'Happens all the time. Ask Grandad.'

I can see Billy thinking about this.

'I could have him saving the church, not blowing it up.'

'Atta boy.'

FRIDAY

20:00

By the time me and Billy reach the Parish Hall it's almost eight. My essay still needs work but I'm pretty happy with it. Now if I can just lay my hands-on Gran's book all is right with the world or close enough given Darcy's gone and never coming back.

Billy rides by the stone steps at the front of the church and turns up the driveway heading for the rear. There's a plastic yellow sign glued to the front of the church that always makes me laugh: UNDER VIDEO SURVEILLANCE. Either God's not watching anymore or maybe he's too forgiving of his trespassers. Joke is the camera's a sham, which everybody knows, and, even if it was real, Father McKenna would still be locking the doors.

Billy stops outside the side door leading into the Parish Hall and I hop off.

'How come you're not a Marauder?' I ask.

'I tried,' he says, 'but I couldn't say Rapparee without laughing.'

Billy's being an eejit but I need to backtrack here so you know what he's going on about.

Rapparee is the name of a band of Irish raiders/bandits back in the 1600s. They claimed to be fighting for King James (Catholic) against William of Orange (Protestant) but really, they were just out for themselves, pillaging the countryside. And why did Darcy tell me all this? Because Rapparee is the name Fungal, Darcy and the others have chosen to call their band of Marauders.

'No, really,' says me, 'I would have thought you'd like this stuff.'

'I like games where you don't have to think much, you just blow stuff up.'

Darcy said the opposite. He liked being part of a gang plotting strategy then carrying it out. And Darcy liked that there were kids all over the world playing at the same time. Scotland has the Moss Troopers — isn't that a great name! — and the Border Reivers and The Cateran. Or you might be fighting the Red Bandits of Mawddwy in Wales, or Thugees in India, or The Innocents in America or the all-female Jackdaws of England. And Darcy said helping Fungal outmaneuver China's Madame Ching with over a hundred players/pirates made you proud to be Irish.

Most of all Darcy liked that there had to be at least five of you to be playing. He said it forced you out into the world interacting with your friends instead of holed up in your bedroom wanking off.

'Why weren't you playin?' Billy asks.

'There's enough fighting in the world.' *Just ask my mum and dad!*

I run up the stairs and pull on the door. It rattles but doesn't open. 'It's locked.'

Billy doesn't believe me so he pulls on it with the same result. The lights are on in the hall so Billy knocks hard on the door but nobody comes to open up.

We walk to the nearest window the bottom of which is above our heads. We both jump up but can't stay airborne long enough to see anything. I turn around and lean against the wall joining my hands together. Billy puts his right foot in my hands and his hands on my shoulders and pushes himself up. His belt buckle ends up in my eyebrows and I'm thinking of saying something rude but restrain myself. First Gran's book then...

'Sweetjeesus!'

'What?'

'They look dead.'

Billy jumps down and now it's me going up. Here's what I see. A long table with kids' bodies slumped on it but not comfortably like you might rest your head in your arms if you wanted to sleep sitting down, these are higgledy-piggledy like you fell asleep without warning, like there's a gas leak or something.

'Shite! They do look dead.' I push up on the window but it's locked too. I jump down. 'We gotta get in there.'

We try the next window. Locked. We race around back. There's one window in the rear wall but not for long. Billy picks up a stone and heaves it. *Crash!* I'm underneath the window with my hands out and Billy disappears inside. I run around to the door, which Billy opens and then relocks as I go by.

There's nine of them around the long table, seven boys and two girls, all of them lying face down. The table's covered in laptops and Marauders' paraphernalia. Sitting at the head of the table is Fungal, easily ten years older than everyone else, and in front of Fungal is Gran's *Book of Faery Spells* open with Fungal's head lying on the pages.

I'd be happy about finding Gran's book if it wasn't surrounded by nine dead human beings their eyes open but seeing nothing.

'They can't be dead.'

I'm checking for Fungal's pulse holding two fingers against his carotid artery like they do in the movies while Billy has his ear beside Rachel McSorley's mouth listening for breathing. I remember somebody in a book using a mirror to check for breath so I open Rachel's purse, pull out her compact and hand it to Billy.

'Hold the mirror under her nose.' I don't know how long to wait but I'm too impatient so I pull on Billy's arm. The mirror's not fogged or anything but when I run my finger along the surface it feels damp. I turn my phone into a torch and shine the light into Rachel's right eye. Her pupil contracts.

'She's alive.'

I shine the light in Fungal's eye and for sure his pupil gets smaller. That's when I see a piece of paper lying under Fungal's arm. I snatch it out and start reading. *Desperately need your help. Sí Dún depends on it. Max*

'Holy shite.' I hand the paper to Billy. Max has to be the female warrior Benji was talking about and Sí Dún is the faery fort.

'Hold Fungal's head up.' I pull Gran's book out from under and read the heading at the top of the page. *Spell for Becoming a Faery.* This is the same spell Darcy would have used. Underneath the heading is a picture of a faery not unlike Benji and at the bottom of the page the words, *Spell for Unbecoming a Faery,* with an asterisk stating that if there's a group of you one can say the spell and the others clap three times quickly and you'll all be transported to the same place.

'Shite Billy, what do we do?'

Billy's standing beside me reading the spell, mumbling the words out loud like he always does when he's reading. Then he's falling, landing on the floor in a heap. I drop down beside him shaking him. If Billy was Darcy he'd be playing a trick on me but I know right away he isn't. Billy's near dead like the others.

'Oh Billy, what have you done?'

Now there's nothin for it but to say the spell too but before I do that I slow myself down and think. There's paper on the table and pens. I write a note — *We're not dead. We've gone to Faeryland* — and lay it on top of Fungal's hands. Then I read the page in Gran's book three times trying to memorize every word. Then, using the pen, I print the *Spell for Unbecoming a Faery* on my left arm. I have no idea if that's going to stick with me so I say it over and over till I'm sure I won't forget it. Then I wonder if I'm going to be wearing clothes where I'm going but there's nothing I can do about that so I say the spell.

I'm not starkers; I'm wearing armor like Benji was wearing. What they call chainmail I think, thousands of little metal rings woven together, not shiny like chrome but dull like old silver. I'm bent over at the waist following other faeries dressed for battle. They're bent over too moving quickly and quietly like we're sneaking up on somebody. The armor stops at my legs and below that I've got on dark green leggings and suede, knee-high boots, honey-colored. The armor isn't heavy and I like the way it moves with my body. One of the faeries in front has a spear and a helmet but I don't. What I have is a long sword in my right hand and a short sword, a dagger really, tucked into a leather belt tied around my waist.

It's nighttime but I can see thanks to a Maxfield Parrish moon hanging in the sky like a theater prop. The faeries in front stop, crouching down. I stop too and hold the sword up to my face using it like a mirror. Hey, I'm still me.

The next question comes flying into my brain is: How big am I?

Benji's tiny when he's around me but maybe if I'm Benji size, and everyone else is too, maybe we're not small anymore. But there's no time to think about this because we're moving again.

We've been traveling through meadow with short grass and cowpats — a faery to my right found one the hard way — but now we're entering a forest. The trees are tall, looming over me like Dementors, and it's darker now that the moonlight falls in patches. There's no one behind so I speed up and come alongside the faery in front of me. It's Rachel McSorley!

'Rachel.'

'Fiona! What are you doin here?'

'We went to the Parish Hall. We saw your bodies. You looked dead.'

'I wondered about that. Who's we?'

'Me and Billy Ridout.' Rachel nods at this. 'What exactly are we doin?' I ask.

'We're sneakin up on The Unseelie. Max's comin from the other side. She's going to create a diversion and we're supposed to grab the princess.'

'Shhhhhh!' comes from the faery in front of us so the 300 questions I have die in my throat.

On and on we move through the trees a silent army following its orders. I stay near Rachel. How many of us are there? I count twelve in front of me but more to the sides. No way of knowing really. Then I wonder if I can fly like Benji but Rachel hasn't got wings that I can see and I'm pretty sure I don't either. So, what kind of faery am I?

I feel like a five-year-old full of questions with no one to answer. And here's another: Where's Billy?

Now I can see light ahead hugging the ground. As we get closer the light turns into flames from a thousand campfires so close together as to be one. We're comin to the edge of the woods and suddenly we're all together in a group hiding behind the last row of trees. Everybody's staring at the fires but me cos I'm checking out those around me. There's Ryan and Tyler and Helen from the Parish Hall. Then, hands on my shoulders, Billy glides in beside me. He's glad to see me that's clear and I know my face is sending the same message. Billy whispers in my ear, 'Fungal's in charge.'

Sure enough the guy in the lead turns to us and it's Fungal. He spies me and breaks into a grin.

'Okay, listen up,' Fungal says, not in his usual slow way, but quick like becoming a faery has changed him in other ways too. 'We're going to follow the woods around to where the camp's closest to the trees. There may be sentries out here so pay attention. When Max starts her diversion, we expect this side of the camp to move to where Max is. That's when we go in and snatch the princess. See that tall tent in the middle? That's where the princess will be. Okay, let's go.'

We're on the move again. Billy and I hang back till we're the last ones.

'Is everybody from the hall here?'

'I think so,' Billy answers, 'but there's lots I don't know and all different nationalities too.'

'Marauders,' says me and Billy nods.

I glance at the campfires. Now I can see the multitude of tents and the hundreds of silhouettes milling about. These must be The Unseelie Benji was talking about, the ones Alfred likened to Orcs.

I glance over at Billy. He's got his dagger out and he's pricking his finger with it. *What the?* He holds his finger up showing me the blood. You can die a thousand times in Warhammer or Call of Duty but this doesn't seem like that.

Fungal stops and the rest of us close up behind him. Fungal uses his hands to tell us to stay put. Then he rises up pulling back his arm and now it's pitching forward. His dagger cartwheels through the darkness and a shadow I hadn't seen goes rigid as the dagger sinks home. The body drops to the ground and Fungal hurries toward it waving us forward.

We surround the downed Unseelie. It's my first look at the enemy. This one's a she, taller than Fungal, wearing a short black tunic showing bare arms and legs taut with muscles, leather sandals with leather strips crisscrossing to her knees. She's got long black hair woven into a braid and her face is attractive but in a rough way like a diamond that hasn't been polished yet. Fungal's knife is lodged in her chest blood seeping around the wound. I want to look away but there's something making it unreal like I've fallen into the pages of a comic book.

Around her neck is a leather necklace with an amulet carved from what I think is bone. The amulet is faintly glowing on and off like it's tied to The Unseelie's heartbeat. Then the glow dies altogether making me believe it was her heartbeat I was seeing. Fungal pulls his knife from her chest and removes the necklace. He hands it to Rachel.

'Put this on.'

Rachel frowns but does as she's told and as the amulet lands on her chest there are suddenly ten more Rachels standing among us.

'Doppelgangers,' Fungal says. 'Clones, duplicates, replicates. They do what you do. The trouble is you can't kill them. The good thing is they can't kill you.'

'Fergus, how are you knowing this?' Helen asks.

'Alonzo. He said the old Sir Max was in a bar in Aberdeen when a fight broke out. It was eleven Unseelies against one Redcap. Sir Max was about to wade in when the Redcap tore the necklace from around one of The Unseelie's necks and the other ten Unseelies disappeared as if by magic.'

'Then what happened?'

'The Unseelie beat the crap out of the Redcap and Sir Max.'

'What about Alonzo?'

'He thought he'd check on the horses.'

We try to laugh but it comes out sounding high-pitched and nervous like Japanese schoolgirls giggling.

'Is she dead?' Rachel asks staring at The Unseelie. It's a dumb question but we all know what Rachel means. *Is she permanently dead?*

'Till she gets her amulet back,' Fungal answers. I'm pretty sure he's making this up cos he won't look at us but I figure he's doing it to keep our spirits up like it's just a game, nobody dies, so let's go.

Darcy loved this Dungeons & Dragons stuff but it's all too make-believe for me. Despite believing in faeries — and rightly so! — I like my feet on the ground but Darcy liked to fly, leaving constraints on the ground where they belong or so he said. We'd argue about which was better but finally agreed there was no winning just acceptance of the other person's point of view.

I'm all for grabbing Billy and getting the hell out of here but before I can make that happen a gigantic explosion rocks the far side of the encampment. We all stare mesmerized as blue/green flames shoot ten meters into the air. Fungal jumps to his feet. 'If you see an Unseelie wearing a necklace kill it, then grab the necklace and put it on. If it's not wearing a necklace it can't hurt you. C'mon!'

We're all sprinting now heading for the tents and the campfires. The good thing is it seems all The Unseelie are running too but away from us toward the explosion. Billy's beside me when we reach the first of the tents. The ground's littered with stuff like pots and packs, crates and garbage, so we're running but jumping and zigzagging too like it's a hurdle race through a landfill site. The good thing is there's no one to swing my sword at and no matter where you are you can see the tall tent in the middle. Then everything changes because — I learned this later — one of The Unseelie trips and falls and when he gets up, he's facing the wrong way and he sees us coming and sounds the alarm. Now there's no shortage of beings to swing your sword at.

Another of The Unseelie females appears around the corner of the closest tent just as I'm leaping a trunk. Her sword swishes right through me and I keep running paying more attention now. I catch up to an Unseelie male, limping badly, and as he turns to face me, I see his necklace and the sword plunging toward my waist. I block that just as Billy sinks his sword into the limper's side. There's a horrible sucking sound as Billy withdraws his blade red with blood. The Unseelie sinks to his knees then topples forward. I'm still trying to get my heart out of my throat when Billy throws me the necklace with the amulet. I put it on and now there are ten more Fionas staring at me waiting for instructions.

Billy takes off and I follow, my clones right behind. We meet four more Unseelies none of them wearing amulets. They hack at me with their swords but I ignore them. My clones aren't as lucky because clones can dispatch clones I learn as the Fiona beside me drops into a campfire sending up a tornado of sparks. There's a piece of me wonders what happens if one of the real Unseelies hides his amulet in his pocket or something but there's probably a rule about that. Darcy loved bizarre rules saying the game designers make them up sitting on the toilet.

To my right Rachel trips over a trunk and falls, which is fortunate because an Unseelie with a necklace has just swung at her. His sword passes over her head and she swings from her knees chopping his leg near off. Up she gets but either doesn't see the amulet he's wearing or can't be bothered to stop because The Unseelie is screaming and waving his sword around his head like he's covered in wasps, blood spurting from his stump like a horse peeing. I lop his sword hand off and remove his necklace. I catch up to Billy and hand it to him. Now there are ten more Billys to play with. He grins; I grin; we blunder on.

Billy runs through a tent that isn't there. Jesus, is there nothin real here? I come to a bench and rather than jump it I run through it but the next bench is real and sends me flying.

'How do you know if they're real?' I shout at Billy but he doesn't answer just taps his head. If I could punch him I would. So, ten out of eleven Unseelies are clones. It's probably the same for the tents, fires and benches. Then I'm thinking about the Orcs in *Lord of the Rings* and for sure they were computer generated (CGI) so how is this any different? Just means what seems to be an unbeatable number of Unseelies may not be that bad after all. All of which would be comforting if I weren't in a sword fight with a real Unseelie whose arms are the size of bridge cables.

Two of my clones jump at his head passing right through but it's enough of a distraction that I race on by and keep going.

We reach the tall tent. Ryan and Tyler are outside standing guard but worried/jittery cos they can see Unseelies coming from every direction. Billy and one of his clones — the rest have vanished — join Ryan and Tyler while I — no clones — dash inside. Two female Unseelies are lying on the ground on either side of an oval basket Fungal is reaching into. Up he comes holding a baby wrapped in a blanket. I'd been picturing a teenage princess but now I realize she's barely born. I move beside Fungal. The baby is beautiful, not dark-haired like The Unseelie, but blonde with fine lips, a button nose and sparkly blue eyes.

Fungal holds her out to me. I put my sword down and take her. The baby smiles at me. 'What's her name?' I ask.

'Isla'

'She's beautiful.'

Fungal nods. 'We need to get her back to Queen Caelia.'

I point my head at the two Unseelies lying on the ground. 'Hand me their amulets.'

As I watch Fungal removing the necklaces from the two downed Unseelies it occurs to me that this might not be the real princess. I put the baby back in its basket and pick the basket up. Sure enough, there's another basket hiding underneath. Inside is a baby wearing a baby-sized amulet. I pick up the real princess as Fungal pats me on the shoulder. 'Smart,' he says holding out the amulets.

'Put one around her neck and one around mine.'

Now there are ten more Fionas holding ten beautiful princesses.

'Can you hear me?' I say to the duplicates.

The ten clones nod.

'Good. We need to take the princess to Queen Caelia. We all need to take different routes. Got it?'

More nods.

Now there's loud fighting going on outside the tent flaps so Fungal slits the canvas at the rear of the tent and we all hurry through scattering into the night.

I'm following Fungal's back when suddenly he stops staring to his left. A swarm of Unseelies are rushing toward us trying to cut us off from reaching the woods.

'Go!' Fungal shouts. 'Go! Don't look back!'

I run as fast as my legs will carry me cradling the princess like she's four sticks of dynamite. I don't run in a straight line but keep zigzagging between tents hoping to confuse things.

When I reach the trees, I kneel down staring at the fighting going on around the campfires. I see one of my clones fighting with a male Unseelie. She's hampered trying to protect the baby and it only takes the Unseelie three swipes before his blade cuts her throat. Down she goes. The Unseelie picks up the baby then throws it into the fire.

Someone's crashing through the woods coming toward me. I put Isla on the ground and pull my dagger. Just before I plunge it into my attacker's leg, I realize it's Billy. Then I see the amulet and it really is Billy.

Billy drops down beside me staring at the baby.

'I thought she'd be older.'

'Me too.'

'What's her name?'

'Isla'

There's a ton to talk about but now's not the time. We can see the real Unseelies in the camp coming together yelling at each other. Their clones are standing still waiting for orders. Billy says, 'There aren't nearly as many as you think.'

'Still enough to do damage.'

Billy nods at this helping me to my feet. 'We need to get out of here.'

The trouble is Billy and I have no idea where we're supposed to be going. No, that's not right. We know we're supposed to bring Princess Isla to Queen Caelia we just have no idea how to find her.

We head in the direction we think will take us to the meadow where we started all this but after an hour we're still surrounded by trees and no longer pretending we have any idea where we are.

'We are more lost than D.B. Cooper,' Billy says trying to be funny.

'I don't think you can be *more* lost. You're either lost or not lost.'

Billy shakes his head. 'We are fecking lost is what we are.'

I perch myself on the nearest rock and lay Princess Isla on the moss beside me. She's sleeping probably from all the rocking my arms have been doing. My arms are aching but she's worth it.

'Will she be hungry when she wakes up?' Billy asks plopping down within reach.

'I would think so.'

Billy's real question is: what are we going to do then? I have no idea and Billy knows this.

'You'd think we would have seen one of the others by now,' says me.

'There were so many clones I have no idea what happened to anybody.'

That's how I feel too. I saw lots of Fungal's warriors go down but I have no idea if I was seeing clones or the real people.

'What do you think happens if you die here?' Billy asks.

'Want me to stab you and find out?'

Billy can hear how upset/tired/frustrated I am so he does the smart thing and shuts up. Feeling guilty I let my head fall on his shoulder.

I must have fallen asleep because the next thing I know Billy is jumping to his feet startling me awake. My eyes open just in time to see Billy plunge his sword into the waist of an Unseelie at the same time as the Unseelie buries his sword into Billy's chest. They fall to the ground together neither making a sound. Before I can react, Billy vanishes. One second he's there and the next he's not.

I'm trying really hard to believe it's a good thing Billy disappeared. Much better he's vanished than lying on the ground with a sword sticking in his gut that's for sure. But where has he gone? Back to the Parish Hall? I hope so. But there's some trick here of things being real and unreal at the same time — is that surreal? — that has me wondering if it's all a dream; that I'll be waking up trying to remember this weird fantasy I was having. Before I can think on that the downed Unseelie twitches and I have his amulet from around his neck quicker than you can say Manchester United.

The Unseelie goes back to being dead so I put my dagger away and take the time to study him. He's got the body of a bodybuilder and I can see it all but a few square feet below his belt, which is covered by a hunk of black material like a mini-skirt. His chest is huge and muscled like Arnie materializing nude in Terminator. Billy did well to stick him before he killed us all.

His face is ugly, rough like the female I described earlier, with every feature oversized like his nose, which is the size of my elbow, or his ears sticking out like wings. His bushy eyebrows would be moustaches on a normal person and his lips resemble skinny butt cheeks and all of these exaggerated features are linked together by a raw red scar running from his eye to his mouth. Over his shoulder I can see his black hair woven into a braid as thick as a ship's rope.

Billy's amulet is lying on the ground so I pick that up and tuck both necklaces in with the princess. We could put them on but the thought of ten clones following me around like puppies is more than I can handle. I lift Isla and we start walking again. Isla's awake now, but being good, not crying for milk or to have her nappy changed. She's too good really but I'm thankful for that.

'We need to get away from these trees,' I say to her and she smiles like, *yeah, they're driving me crazy.*

'No, really, we need to find some open ground so we can figure out where we are.' And better yet where we're going.

My arms are aching again and I can see Isla is trying her best not to cry. Me too, feeling sorry for myself, and wishing Billy was beside me to share things. It's still night the big moon bathing everything in blue light and we're still surrounded by trees and worse off really because now there are boulders as big as houses interlaced with knolls and ravines with streams full of water cold as ice. I've been trying to walk in a consistent direction hoping to hit a road or path or at least open ground but so far nothing.

Isla starts to whimper so I stop and open her blanket. She's wearing a cloth nappy (diaper) and its wet so I take it off figuring better nothing than stinky urine. We're beside a stream so I dip my hand in the water and let Isla suck the water from my fingers. 'You're such a good girl.' The irony of me carrying a baby, running away from the bad guys, isn't lost on me. This must be just like Angelina, the midwife, carrying me to safety. Is this irony intentional or some quirk of quantum physics? I have no answer for that.

I've never climbed a really tall tree before but it seems like this might be the time to see if I can do it. I tuck Isla between two rocks on a bed of moss. 'I'll be right back.'

'Okay Fiona, I'll just wait here,' are the words I'm sure Princess Isla would say if she could.

The first branch turns out to be the hardest. I have to jump from a boulder launching myself into space, then hook my hands over the lowest branch and swing myself up. It's a good thing I'm tall and strong — for a girl as Darcy would say — or I'd be doin a face plant on the boulder next door. After that it's just a matter of moving from branch to branch. I've heard of good climbing trees and this must be one of them. When I was reading about the coffin ships, I tried to picture myself scurrying up the rigging heading for the top of the mast not sure I could be doing that but here I am doing it and feeling good about myself. Mind you, the wind's not howling and the mast not swaying, but still...

Up and up I go until finally I emerge a meter or two above the surrounding trees. The moon and stars are shining above me but that's not what catches my attention, it's the two arcs of light. If the one arc is in the north, the other is in the south. I haven't a clue what direction anything is but you get the idea. I might be closer to the northern light but not by much. I figure the one is The Unseelie camp and I'm hoping the other is Sí Dún. The trouble is, which is which?

Finally, I decide the southern light is more solid than the northern light, not so flickery. If that sounds less than scientific, you're right. Really, it's a crapshoot, and the joke is I figure by the time I get back to the bottom I won't know north from Newtownabbey so what does it matter? Before I head down I use the moonlight to check my arm. The words to undo the faery spell are there. I shut my eyes and find I can say the words from memory, which is good. If it wasn't for Princess Isla I could get out of here but that isn't an option now. Whatever's happening here we're in it together.

Down I go concentrating on knowing where south is. When I reach the last limb I stop, my heart in my mouth, because something big and hairy is sniffing the princess. *'No!'* It raises its head when it hears me cry out and — Holy Shite! — it's a wolf, the color of coal and the size of a pony. Its yellow eyes are staring at me, its lips pulled back showing teeth. I'm frozen. After several seconds of staring at each other the wolf drops its head and goes back to sniffing Isla.

Slowly, I lower myself to the ground. The wolf raises its head staring at me again.

'Hi! I'm Fiona and that's my buddy, Princess Isla. I'd really appreciate it if you didn't eat her. I'm responsible for her, you see...' I take a step forward. 'I'm sure we could find you a tasty rabbit or something.'

Now it's the wolf that's walking toward me. I have no idea what to do so I drop to my knees. Now me and Wolfy are eye-to-eye. He/she keeps coming till his/her nose is an inch from mine. Sniff, sniff, sniff. I think about reaching out but I'm afraid to move in case Wolfy takes it the wrong way so I stay still.

Wolfy sits down.

I put my hand out and Wolfy raises his paw.

Me and Isla are following Wolfy. We seem to be on a path because we're not stumbling over things and I think we're headed south so I'm happy with the way things have worked out. Isla is quiet, not hollering for food like she understands the predicament we're in, so she's a real trooper as far as I'm concerned. Am I as brave as Angelina? I hope so.

Now I can see a clearing ahead full of moonlight and a dark shape that might be a house. Is that good or bad? Before I can make up my mind Wolfy lets out a howl that would wake the dead. A light pops on above a door, then the door swings inward. Standing in the light is a leprechaun.

'That you, Meatball?'

I do a doubletake. The leprechaun has a beard but the voice is definitely female. Meatball, aka Wolfy, runs into the house, disappears, then reappears sitting beside Ms. Leprechaun.

'And you've brought friends I see. Excellent. Come my Dear, you're just in time for tea.'

I've never liked leprechauns — the toy ones — the little green plastic bobbleheads that every dumbass tourist to Ireland buys to take home to little Jack or Emilia. They should be banned, like Lil Black Sambo in America, making us Irish look like ninnies with shamrocks shooting out our arses. Even Gran has trouble defending them saying it's not their fault — it's us have made them into the ridiculous creatures they're not.

'What are they then?' I'd growl and Gran would invariably change the subject.

'Come, come; I won't bite.'

I come because I'm so tired I can't think.

The house is tiny, made of woven sticks, the roof thatched. The door closes behind me and I find myself in a very pleasant kitchen not unlike the primitive kitchens in the Folk Lore Village in Donegal Town. Herbs are hanging from the rafters, the smell reminding me of turkey dressing, and there's a sturdy kitchen table with four chairs and as the leprechaun goes by, she pulls one out and says, 'Have a seat.' That's when I realize we're the same height or almost. I might be a smidgen taller. Then she goes to the fireplace where she blows on some coals adding twigs and the next thing you know there's a fire in the grate and a kettle hanging above it already whistling.

She's wearing the same Kelly-green clothes the stupid bobbleheads wear including the green stockings and upturned shoes. She's got fiery red hair falling past her shoulders thick enough to hide a bird's nest and the mandatory red beard hanging halfway down her chest. Mrs. Delgado at the grocery store has a moustache but I've never seen a female with a beard before. The only thing missing is the silly green top hat with black belt and gold buckle.

Ms. Leprechaun is studying me now so I try to hide my disdain for green plastic shamrock-stuffers because I've never met a real leprechaun before and so far, she's been nothing but kind giving me and Isla a roof over our heads and the likelihood of something to eat.

That's when she starts laughing and reaching up pulls off her beard. 'That's all right,' she says, 'I know exactly what you're thinking. Those hideous bobblehead dolls, right? How about the Vanishing Leprechaun? Can you still buy that?'

My vocal chords have quit because my jaw's dropped and why? Because the unbearded leprechaun is gorgeous! I mean she's not young but she's one of those females who get better looking with age — like Gran. When I look at photos of Gran as a young woman, I see a pretty girl but now when I look at Gran, I see someone whose beauty is directly connected to her soul.

'The look on your face!'

'I've never seen a female leprechaun before,' says me moving Princess Isla from my lap to the kitchen table, 'but if you're all wearing beards that may be why. Would you by chance have any milk for the baby?'

'Not yours then?' Ms. Leprechaun asks coming over for a better look.

'No.'

'May I?'

She picks Isla up and before I can react she pulls the shamrock pin from her lapel and sticks it into Isla's palm.

'No!'

Isla starts to cry and now the leprechaun is rocking her making soothing sounds. I'm on my feet, angry, but Wolfy — I refuse to call him Meatball — who was curled up by the fire is now between me and Ms. Leprechaun and there's no doubt whose side he's on.

'Just making sure she's not a changeling, Dear. They're usually pretty like this.'

Isla seems to be okay as the leprechaun hands her back to me. I'd forgotten about changelings, old faeries swapping themselves for human babies so they get looked after.

'What's her name?' the leprechaun asks.

'Isla'

'That's a good Scottish name. And you?'

'Fiona.'

'I'm Mairead but everybody calls me Peggy. Now you enjoy your tea and I'll get some goat's milk for our Miss Isla.'

A plate of shortbread cookies appears as if by magic and I'm too hungry to worry about poison or sleeping potions or good Scottish names. In no time I've eaten all the cookies and drunk all the tea. Peggy reappears with a leather cone full of milk, which she hands to me. At the bottom is a point that looks a bit like a nipple so I put that to Isla's mouth and she puts her two little hands up and begins sucking like this is the best thing since Pingu. I decide to forgive Peggy for sticking Isla with her pin.

'Do you live alone then?' I ask making conversation.

'I do. I'm what they call a solitaire.'

'What do you call the others?'

'Trooping faeries. Usually the shallow end of the gene pool and sticking together like sheep.'

I laugh at this. It sounds all too familiar.

'Why were you wearing that beard?'

Peggy makes a face at this.

'Don't get me going. Stupid males wouldn't be here without us and then they treat us like we're second-class and all because they're stronger than we are, like it isn't us giving them their muscles in the first place.'

Peggy's waiting for me to agree with this rant and I might if I wasn't so tired. She starts up again. 'Anyway, some male arses made a rule that we'll all be wearing beards when we go out in case there's a tourist happens to stumble into things. Makes you want to puke in their oatmeal, it does. Bullies really is what they are, except my son Kevin of course, he's an angel.' Peggy picks up the beard and puts it on me laughing. 'Though I will say it keeps the riffraff away.' Then she retrieves her hat from the coatrack in the corner and puts that on me too.

'A blonde leprechaun, now that would be something.'

The beard and hat fly into the corner and on the table another plate of shortbread appears. Peggy sits down and Wolfy buries his head in her lap.

'So, tell me, why are you wandering through the woods at night, wearing armor, and carrying a baby that isn't yours?'

I tell her everything. I'm not sure why other than she reminds me so much of Gran. When I finish, she says, 'That's quite a story.'

I don't know if she believes me or not, but if it was me I'd believe it because making it up would be too much work.

'So, you're a human who's become a faery, and Isla is an Unseelie princess, and you're to take her to Queen Caelia so that she can use the princess to bargain with Kade, the King of The Unseelie?'

I nod. That is what I think is happening.

'You and the princess need to sleep. When you wake, I'll have Kevin take you to Sí Dún, that's where Queen Caelia will be. How does that sound?'

'Wonderful.'

'We'll just send him a quick text.' I watch as Peggy writes a note and slips it inside a razorfish shell, which she puts in Wolfy's mouth. 'Téigh a Chaoimhín,' she says opening the door and Wolfy disappears. 'Now climb up into that loft and I'll hand you Isla.'

SATURDAY
09:00

It's not every morning you get woken by a kiss. My eyes open to find a cute, freckled-faced leprechaun kneeling beside me, a lopsided grin spread across his face.

'I shouldn't have done that, it's just that you looked so much like Sleeping Beauty I couldn't help myself.'

'You must be Kevin.'

'At your service.'

'Where's Isla?'

'Ma's got her. They're out in the garden making rainbows.'

'I need to pee.' You're probably hoping for more flirting and romance but not soaking your tights is important too. Kevin leads me to the outhouse hidden in the trees. I guess faeries have to relieve themselves as well but I don't remember reading about that in any of the books. All finished I return to the garden beside the house where I find Peggy holding Isla who's busy watching Kevin throwing a stoat into the air for Wolfy to chase. I'm pretty sure it's a toy weasel but probably better not to ask.

Peggy hands me a circle of material. It's all the colors of the forest and obviously woven by hand. 'Put that over your head onto your shoulder,' she says. I do that and she lowers Isla into the hammock/cradle the material's made at my waist. 'Your arms won't get so tired this way.'

Isla's wearing her blanket but I pretend to be fussing with it.

'Where are the two necklaces?'

'Oh, yes, right.' Peggy, looking guilty, pulls an amulet from each of her skirt pockets. 'What are these exactly?'

'If you put one on you suddenly have ten clones of yourself.'

'Ah, replicators. I've heard of these.'

'It allows The Unseelie to present a much larger force than they actually have.'

'They're a clever bunch for all their evil ways.'

Kevin reappears carrying a backpack slung over his shoulder and a stout walking stick that I figure is as much about defense as hiking.

'There's milk in the bag, more nappies and victuals.'

'How long will it take to reach Sí Dún?'

'Depends who you meet,' Peggy answers. 'Not too long if the way is clear.'

I give Peggy a hug. 'Thank you for all your help.'

'It's not every day you meet a human and a princess.'

My hand slides in beside Isla. Then I hold it out keeping my eyes on Peggy. She pulls the missing amulet from her pocket and hands it back.

'Force of habit,' she says laughing.

It's a beautiful morning, sunny and warm. We're walkin through trees their leaves rustling above us competing with the songbirds. For a second I wonder if it's morning back in Gloire Bay and if it is what my body's doing in the Parish Hall? Then I wonder if Billy ended up there and if so, is he coming back to find me? I know the answer to that one is yes but there's a lot of ifs in there. Grandad Sky says to worry about the things you can change not the things you can't.

Kevin's a talker so I let him prattle on only interrupting when I don't understand something like why he has *two* girlfriends.

'I get bored with only one.'

'Do they have more than one boyfriend?'

'Of course. I can be right boring too.'

So much for monogamy in Faeryland. I decide to change the subject.

'Why did your mum want an amulet?'

'She'd be fascinated by the spell. Or maybe she thought she could sell it. Things are a might tight at the moment what with The Unseelie and all.'

'How do The Unseelie affect your mum?'

'Everybody's scared so no one's travelin.'

'And?'

'No one's usin Airbnb.'

'You have Airbnb?'

'You stole the idea from us.'

Too funny. 'Your mum didn't ask me for money.'

'She knew you didn't have any.'

Now I feel bad about the amulet.

'I'll pay her back, I promise.'

'Do you like her?'

'I do, very much. She reminds me of my Gran.'

'Then you're a friend and friends don't pay, at least not with money.'

I like the sounds of that.

'Can I ask really daft questions?' asks me asking one.

'Of course. They're the best kind.'

'Why are you wearin a baseball hat with a bird on it?'

'You're not liking it?'

'I do like it, I'm just not understanding it.'

'Toronto Blue Jays. Go Jays go!'

I try to picture Kevin wearing the silly green top hat wondering if that would change everything which is daft when you think about it but true, like judging a book by its cover. I decide to move on to my next question.

'How did Meatball get his name?'

'My cousins from Italy were visiting and they brought a wolf puppy as a gift and Ma was making spaghetti for dinner so they'd feel at home and when she wasn't lookin the puppy ate all the meatballs.'

'What did Peggy do then?'

'Threw in prawns so we had seafood marinara instead.'

Not so different from home. Gran was going to serve cod cheeks one night and as she was sitting on the porch enjoying the sunset Bandit ate 'em. We had mac n' cheese instead.

'Where did faeries come from?'

Kevin's laughing now. 'You jump around, don't you?'

'Gran says I'm erratic.'

Kevin nods at this, then he says, 'Where did you come from?'

I get right away what Kevin is saying. We're all from the same cell that started all this so I might as well ask myself as Kevin. 'No, I mean how did you end up a faery instead of a human?'

'I'm not sure. Ma says we're descended from the Celtic gods and goddesses of old before Christianity put a stop to anything but its own mythology.'

Grandad says one of the problems with Christianity and Islam is that they don't allow for other beliefs. It's our way or the highway whereas most Asian religions like Hindu and Buddhism are happy to share with all.

'But why are you little and living underground?'

'I'm as tall as you!'

'I think I'm normally much taller than this.' Kevin raises his eyebrows like what magic mushrooms have you been eating? 'I don't mean to be insulting, I'm just trying to understand.'

'Do you live underground?' Kevin asks letting the height thing go.

'No.'

'How do you know?'

'I've seen photos from space. My sky has nothing above it but stars.'

Kevin points up. I look at the blue sky that seems to go on forever just like my sky. 'But...'

'If ifs and buts were candy and nuts–'

'But when I walk out to the bog there's a mound stickin up in the peat and everybody says that's a faery fort, that's where the little folk live.'

'And you believe them?'

'I want to believe them.'

'Do you feel like you're in a mound here?'

'No.'

'So maybe we live together but in a way that we can't easily see each other.'

'Like an owl at night? I rarely see one but I know they're there.'

I can see Kevin thinking about this. Finally, he says, 'I don't know how it works exactly, but Ma says Big Magic — that's the stuff of legend — expands and contracts depending on how many people believe in it. She says The Church diminished Big Magic something awful and then The Hunger just about finished it off but now it's comin back because folks are opening their minds again to the wonders around them.'

'I'm writing an essay on The Great Potato Famine. Grandad says it was genocide. That the English could have saved everyone if they'd wanted to.'

'We call it The Hunger. Some folks blame the Fear Liath saying they saw fighting in the night sky, then a thick blue fog settled on the potatoes, and in the morning all that was left was black mush.'

'Who's Fear Liath?'

'Graymen, more ghosts than faeries.'

I've never heard of Fear Liath but I understand the need to be blaming someone or something for your world ending. Before I can say that Kevin says, 'Ma says it's hard to believe in magic when your child's dying in your arms.'

I'm about to ask more about The Hunger — it'll make my essay! — when Kevin pulls me down and we crouch hidden by a bush and shadows. There's a body moving slowly through the trees searching for something. All at once I know who it is.

'Rachel!'

I stand and Rachel comes hurrying toward me. She's wearing an amulet.

'Fiona. Everybody's looking for you.'

'For me or the princess?'

'Both.'

I thought Rachel would give me a hug but she stops a step away staring at Kevin standing up beside me. I don't think she realized he was there and she's not looking happy about it.

'This is my friend Kevin. Kevin, this is Rachel.'

Rachel isn't sure what to do about Kevin and that doesn't feel right to me. She's not carrying a sword but I can see her right hand making sure her dagger is where it's supposed to be. So is mine.

'He's taking me to Sí Dún.'

Rachel points back the way we've come.

'But it's that way.'

Now I can feel Kevin bristling.

'Rachel, what's the name of our principal?'

A flash of annoyance whips across Rachel's face and then her hand goes for her dagger. Kevin is quicker. Wham bam thank you ma'am Rachel is lying face down on the ground Kevin pinning her dagger hand high up on her back. As he wrenches the dagger from her hand Rachel starts screaming. I drop to my knees and shove a handful of dirt into her mouth. She's spittin that out when the handle of the dagger crashes into the back of her head and she lies still. I pull the necklace from around Rachel's neck and hand it to Kevin. 'Give that to your mum.'

Rachel's disappearing just like Billy did, but unlike Billy who left nothing but his sword behind, Rachel is turning into something else and that something else is a female Unseelie, twin of the one Fungal took down in the forest.

'Shape shifter,' Kevin says looking surprised. 'It's not a power The Unseelie have.'

'Big magic's comin back, remember?'

'We need to get out of here.'

Kevin's advice is good it's just too late. Already we can hear bodies crashing through the underbrush rushing toward us close enough that they must have heard Rachel screaming.

'C'mon,' Kevin says pulling on my arm; both of us running now crouched over like my introduction to Faeryland. We scoot around one of the giant boulders that suddenly seem to be everywhere, like mama dinosaurs have stopped every fifty meters to lay a petrified egg. I'm petrified so maybe I'm making them up, another quirk of quantum physics.

Kevin makes a hard right turn and now we're between two of the giant boulders — so close together I could touch them both if my arms weren't cradling Isla — on a mossy path that is headed down at such a steep angle I couldn't stop running if I wanted to. As my head drops below the surface, I look back in time to see Unseelie hurtling past not seeing us.

We're racing downwards so fast I pull Isla to my chest. She must be thinking *what the heck is going on here?* I know if I lose my footing I've got to land on my shoulder otherwise Isla is going to be flattened. Fortunately, the path soon levels out and I come to a stop by crashing into Kevin who catches me in his arms Isla safe between us. Then he leans forward and kisses me. As far as I'm concerned this kiss can last forever but too quickly Kevin pulls back and says, 'Welcome to Hotel California.'

Too funny, right? Except it's not because according to Kevin we're in a cave system where two groups of faeries live — the Grogoch and the Pooka — except they don't coexist like, this is your half, this is mine — instead they beat the crap out of each other every chance they get.

'How do they feel about strangers?'

'They torture leprechauns. Strangers they probably eat.'

That's comforting coming from your male protector.

We're in a tunnel not much taller than we are and we can see a little thanks to dim phosphorescent green light coming from mold/lichen/moss clinging to the walls and ceiling. So far we haven't met a Grogoch — Kevin says they're our size, covered in long reddish-brown hair, with big bellies and bare feet and swept back hair stiff like porcupine quills — or a Pooka who are shape shifters so there's no telling what they'll look like till we meet one.

'Will these tunnels take us to Queen Caelia?'

Kevin shakes his head. 'But they should get us past The Unseelie.'

Kevin explains that if we make it through the tunnels we'll be on the other side of the forest and it's unlikely The Unseelie will be in the open meadow surrounding Sí Dún, unless they've moved camp, in which case we're in real trouble, which we're obviously already in, but Kevin doesn't want to say this.

Right now the tunnel is so tiny I don't see how either the Grogoch or the Pooka could live here but then I see real light ahead as the tunnel expands like a reverse funnel. Kevin slows and we crouch down. We're high up looking downward into a bowl as big as a football stadium. There's a little lake in the middle surrounded by mud huts with chimneys leaking smoke that rises to the roof of the cave where it disappears out a hole big enough to light the place.

'Grogochs,' Kevin says pointing at a female hairball standing in a doorway scratching her belly. As we're watching two little hairballs come running out of the hut whacking each other with sticks. I'm thinking an alternative route might be a good idea but I don't see one.

'Maybe we could go back. Maybe The Unseelie are gone by now?'

Kevin gives me his *when pigs can fly* look.

'Okay, so how do we get by the hairballs?'

'Is Isla hungry?'

Isla gives me one of her cute little smiles like *I'm really happy being here with you.* I give her a kiss.

'She's good. You're tryin to buy time, right? Cos you haven't got a clue how to get us to the other side.'

'I don't hear any suggestions coming from the female side of the team.'

Ouch!

'Kiss me again.'

That doesn't get us any closer to a solution but I feel better.

'Look!'

Instead of looking down Kevin is staring across at the tunnel on the far side of the bowl, the one we'll be taking if we can get there. Now I see what Kevin sees, three heads sticking up. Human heads looking Native American with Mohawk haircuts and streaks of black war paint under their eyes.

'Pookas. Young ones. Probably trying to steal locks of Grogoch hair.'

'Prove your...' I'm about to say 'manhood' but my feminist upbringing rears up and swats the word away and before I can say *courage* Kevin finishes the sentence with: '*stupidity.*'

We watch as the three Pookas make their way slowly down the pathway sliding from rock to rock. Kevin pulls my hand and we start down our path. We're about halfway to the bottom when I hear a noise behind me. Unseelies! There's a bunch of them standing at the mouth of the tunnel staring into the bowl until one of them spies me and Kevin crouched on the path. He shouts and now The Unseelie are stampeding toward us but not as fast as me and Kevin are stampeding because we're running for our lives and that motivates you like nothing else can.

The Grogoch out in the open have stopped what they're doing, all of them eyeing us probably wondering, *what's going on here?* I look for the three teenage Pookas on the other side. They've stopped and are watching us too.

'Unseelies! Unseelies!' I scream and that brings the rest of the Grogochs lumbering out of their dwellings. Kevin and I reach the bottom of the bowl still hoofing it for the far side. This is the moment of truth. The Grogochs can stop us easily or they can let us go by. Then they can fight The Unseelie or run for their lives like the rest of us. I look over my shoulder. The path comin down the hill is solid with Unseelies. How many are clones is academic. The Grogoch are huddled together trying to decide what to do. Kevin and I race by. The three young Pooka start hightailing it up their trail. I can hear them from here. *Let's get that Grogoch hair another day. Whaddya say?*

The Unseelie are still comin out of the tunnel. It's obvious there are too many for the Grogoch to deal with so they're waddling up the path behind us. Their legs are so short they're lousy runners so Kevin and I don't have to worry about being overrun. We race up the hill and enter the other tunnel. I can see the three young Pookas ahead of us. Suddenly they stop. Two of them change into hares, hightailing it down the tunnel like their tails are on fire. The third Pooka isn't as lucky. He turns into a three-legged piglet, then a two-legged goat dragging his back end, and finally a one-winged barn owl flapping around unable to fly. Kevin scoops up the owl as we run by. The owl starts pecking at his hands and Kevin shouts something in Irish that I don't understand. Whatever it is the Pooka gets it because he stops pecking. But he doesn't stop trying to be something else. In rapid succession Kevin is carrying a two-headed badger, a no-headed lizard, two whippets glued together, finally a pony with no legs. The pony's so heavy Kevin crashes to the ground.

Kevin, obviously disgusted, yells something at the pony. Next thing you know the young Pooka with the Mohawk is back and we're all running again. Behind us in the distance I can see Grogochs being bowled over as The Unseelie force their way to the front of the pack.

'They're gaining!'

Kevin and the Pooka look back and now they're conversing with each other, which isn't easy when you're sprinting, your breath labored like it's the Olympics and the finish line is nowhere in sight. We come to a curve in the tunnel and now there are two more tunnels forking left and right off the main tunnel. The Pooka points right but heads left. Kevin yells something at him and the Pooka shouts back, 'Adh mor!' That I know. It means, 'Good luck!'

Kevin pushes me into the right-hand tunnel and we're racing again but not as fast because my legs are filling up with concrete or at least that's how it feels.

'Prince says this will take us to the meadow.'

'Prince?'

'That's his name.'

We go around another curve and Kevin slows to a walk.

'Walk quietly. They'll be listening to figure out which way we've gone.'

I don't argue because my legs are alternating between concrete and jelly but if it was me, and I had all those guys, I'd split up and race down all three tunnels. And I want to ask Kevin why he trusts Prince but we're committed to Tunnel Number Three so I guess it doesn't really matter...

No one seems to be following so Kevin was right about that. The trouble is we've come to another split in the tunnel. We have four choices this time. Because we've stopped altogether Isla gives a little cry and I realize she's been waiting for this moment to remind me she's here.

'You are such a good girl.' I give her a kiss. That's when my nose wrinkles. 'We need to change her nappy.'

I can see Kevin — the male side of the team — isn't buying the *we* bit — wanker! — except he's willing to put his pack down and hand me a nappy. I use the dirty nappy to clean her bum and wrap her in the new one.

'What do I do with this?'

'I'm for leaving it behind.'

This goes against my ecological upbringing but I stuff the stinky nappy into a crack in the rocks. If The Unseelie are like Wolfy, good at sniffing, this should help.

'Does she need a drink?' Kevin asks.

'Might as well. Did Prince say which way to go?'

Kevin shakes his head and I feel sorry for him. He's put himself in charge and now he's in danger of screwing up.

'Why couldn't Prince change into a hare like the others?'

'He hasn't mastered shape shifting yet. He says he pictures a pony and turns into a hedgehog.'

I laugh at this, sympathizing. 'It's tough growing up.'

Isla is chugging away so I watch Kevin moving from tunnel mouth to tunnel mouth. He stops in the middle right one and says, 'The air's different here. Fresher.'

'Then that's the way we'll go.'

Five minutes later we walk out onto a meadow drenched in sunlight and in the distance I can see a city tipped in gold that has to be Sí Dún. I turn to give Kevin a kiss — my hero! — but his eyes are saying something different. I spin around to find a dozen Unseelies standing up in the grass, staring at us, licking their lips like *did you really think you were free of us?*

There's eleven of them actually but only three are wearing amulets. They're all male, all ugly, all carrying spears and wearing daggers except the closest one who's two sizes larger than the rest and obviously feels his size is weapon enough. It suddenly seems odd to me that no one in Faeryland has a smartphone or an AK-47. Strictly medieval which I guess is good unless it's me carrying the AK-47. Then I remember Benji using his bow and arrows to turn Rufus and Rory into potbellied pigs.

I ask Kevin, 'Why is it I'm not seeing any bows and arrows here?'

'The Queen forbade them. Someone hit her by mistake. In the buttock. Changed her into a star-nosed mole.'

If The Unseelie weren't getting closer with every step I'd be laughing at this thinking it probably wasn't a mistake but a well-aimed arrow.

'Only the ones wearin necklaces are real,' says me as Kevin brings his walking stick to his chest holding it with both hands.

The Unseelie spread out around us. Two clones move behind us blocking the tunnel entrance but I've had enough of tunnels so I ignore them.

'Can we take three of them?' asks me cradling a baby.

'They probably don't care about us but they'll want the princess alive.'

I think about holding my dagger to Isla's throat but they'll know I can't do it.

The oversized Unseelie steps forward and says something.

'Is that Irish?'

'An old version. He says if you hand him the baby he'll let us go.'

'Do you believe him?'

'No. These guys like to kill. They think it makes them strong like your life force joins with theirs.'

'I don't think I can die here.'

'I can.'

That's when we hear a noise growing in the tunnel like a herd of buffalo running for their lives. Before that makes sense a horn sounds from across the meadow and all eyes turn to see a dozen furry things galloping toward us carrying riders with swords glinting in the sunlight and banners as big as beach towels. The big Unseelie lunges at me but I turn my back. He wraps his arms around me lifting me off my feet but Kevin whacks him on the back of the knee and the big oaf pushes me away switching his attention to Kevin.

The noise coming from the tunnel is deafening. I turn to see black horses erupting from the tunnel changing midair into Pookas looking like angry Irish potato farmers swinging pitchforks and scythes. The Unseelie run for it but they don't get far. The three with amulets are soon lying still in the grass. A puffin with four legs and no head waddles up beside me then morphs into Prince. 'Take their necklaces,' says me, 'or they'll come alive again.' Prince looks to Kevin for a translation.

The riders from Sí Dún are still coming hell bent for leather and when I finally figure out what they're sitting on I start chuckling. Corgis! You know the funny little dogs Queen Elizabeth liked? The ones look like furry skateboards?

Release the hounds! Ha ha, too funny.

The corgis brake to a stop their riders obviously disappointed there are no Unseelies to vanquish. The lead rider is a young woman as striking as any female I've ever seen. She's wearing gold armor decorated with a magnificent, chrome-silver, open-mouthed dragon curving over her shoulder onto her chest. Her hair is dark brown, almost black, cut short like a man's. I suddenly think of Joan of Arc leading her people against the hated English. Her right hand holds the reins of her corgi, her left hand a blazing silver sword with a braided gold handle and words inscribed on the blade too far away for me to read. Her tunic and tights are sky blue in color, her leather boots sunset yellow.

She stares at me, then Kevin, then the Pookas spread out around us and the three lifeless Unseelies. Her eyes come back to me.

'You must be Fiona.'

'You must be Max.'

That's when one of the riders behind Max advances.

'Benji!'

Benji slides off his corgi and we hug awkwardly trying not to suffocate Isla. I turn back to Max and say, 'This is Princess Isla and this is Kevin. He saved our lives. And this is Prince. He saved us too.'

Kevin translates and Prince grins making sure all the other Pookas can see what a big hero he is. *I may not be able to shape shift worth shite but look out!*

A conversation ensues between Max and the head Pooka, who I think is Prince's father, the result of which is the Pookas hand over the three amulets in exchange for a bag of gold coins. After much bowing and waving the Pookas head back into the tunnel and Benji calls for a corgi for me to ride.

'What about Kevin?'

Benji stares at Kevin and I get the feeling leprechauns are looked down upon by the inhabitants of Sí Dún. Because I might have been guilty of that same racist crud — before I met Kevin and his mum — my back goes up like feck you Trump. The corgi arrives — the markings on its side looking like a saddle — and Benji helps me and Isla up. Then I hold my hand out to Kevin. He comes close so we can whisper.

'C'mon Kevin, there's room for three.'

'I don't think they want me.'

'We want you!'

Kevin nods and pulls himself up behind me. I glance over at Max. She's grinning at me like I've just passed some test only kickass females know about.

Sí Dún is just the way Benji described it and everything a faery city should be except Benji's left out the most important bit: it moves.

'This is just like the model we found someone building under the bog except that one wasn't lurchin from side to side.'

'What model? What bog?'

I tell Kevin about finding the faery city made of silver and gold and by the time I've finished we've reached the outskirts of Sí Dún. When I read novels, I usually skip paragraphs of description — get on with it! — but I'm breaking my own rule here so you can see it. Spread out in front of me is a city/town looking like any place with buildings and streets, and folks and dogs moving about except firstly, everything's strictly medieval like watching *Shakespeare in Love,* and secondly, the town's made of silver and gold instead of black beams and white plaster. Are you seeing it so far?

What's making me pause is the castle made of crystal jumping up and down in the middle like a kid on a trampoline. Up the castle comes but before I can take it in it disappears only to jump up again. I'm about to ask Kevin what's going on but decide to wait a bit, that maybe things will become clear on their own.

We enter the village through open gates that there's no point in closing because you could just walk around them. But as soon as we're through my senses are assaulted by sounds and smells, most of them good — laughter and cinnamon — but some of them bad — screams and shite — so maybe the gates are doing something after all like there's an enchanted wall that I can't see. High Street, the one we're riding our corgis up, is made of orange bricks and the bricks are getting a workout because High Street is bustling with faeries of all kinds. I see goblins, elves, sprites, brownies, clurichuans, gnomes and just as many others I have no names for. If you're a Harry Potter fan think Diagon Alley.

Folks are going in and out of the shops carrying baguettes and brooms and spider webs. Others are sitting at tables in front of cafes and tearooms chatting to their buddies. The Unseelie may be on the horizon, and there's a crystal castle jumping up and down in the middle of town, but here in

High Street it's business as usual until we go riding by becoming the topic of everybody's conversation.

The funny part is the street isn't level it's swinging like a hammock first going up to the left then slowly changing till it's up on the right. The legs of everybody on High Street including the corgis keep changing length to accommodate the angle so even though the road may be swaying no one seems to notice. Even the table legs compensate so your teacup doesn't go flying every time the road swings. It's only the buildings don't seem to care leaning this way and that like a bunch of drunks on St. Paddy's Day. Now the model Billy and I found makes sense. It was wonky like someone took a photo of Sí Dún freezing it at its worst.

'Why is everything moving?' I ask my curiosity getting the upper hand. 'And why is there a castle jumpin up and down?'

'The Queen must be agitated,' says Kevin.

'What?' This makes no sense.

'Gùne Banrion,' Kevin answers like that explains it.

From Irish class I know Gune means dress, and Banrion means Queen, so Queen's dress. I look at Kevin like I'm no further ahead.

'The Queen controls her environment like it's a dress she's wearing.'

'So, she's dreaming all this?'

'No, it's actually her. Sí Dún becomes part of Queen Caelia.'

'And it's heaving this way and that because the Queen is agitated?'

'That's it.'

'So, if she's having a good day everything is calm?'

'Yep, levelheaded.'

'What about the castle?'

Kevin has to think about this.

'The castle's her brain.'

Now who's on magic mushrooms?

Before I can say anything the castle — the Queen's brain! — jumps up and does a somersault. I'm not kidding! The castle just did a somersault! For sure any folks inside are ass over teakettle! I look back at Kevin a question mark screwing up my face but he just shrugs.

As we get closer to the center of town more and more of the faeries are dressed as soldiers. The stores and cafes disappear replaced by armor works and blacksmiths banging out swords and pikestaffs, daggers and shields. Queen Caelia is getting ready for war.

Five minutes later we reach the castle, which has stopped jumping and is now floating above us like a transparent cloud. Before I can ask how we're getting inside a glass drawbridge comes hurtling out of the sky, like a giant deck of cards unraveling, the last card striking the bricks in front of us with a noise like thunder. Our corgis charge forward, before Queen Caelia changes her mind, or at least that's what I'm thinking. Up the glass pathway we race until we pass through crystal-latticed gates into a huge courtyard where we dismount. Most of the riders stay put tending to the corgis but one of the female warriors and Benji usher me and Kevin forward all of us following Max as she strides her way into the castle itself. Broad stairs lead to a long, upward sloping hallway flanked on either side by portraits of Queen C's ancestors I'm betting and in between each painting stands an armed guard — one leg longer than the other! — spear at the ready.

At the end of the hallway gigantic double doors wait and standing in front of them is a tall, aristocratic guy, silver-haired, wearing a uniform covered in medals. If he's trying to hide his anxiety, he's not doing a good job.

'Is the Queen all right?' Max asks.

'Yes. She took a tumble but fortunately she landed on Dixie.'

Max and the old guy chuckle at this and I find out later Dixie is the Queen's pet hedgehog and favorite cushion.

'Did you find the princess?' the old guy asks.

Max waves me forward.

'Fiona, this is Major Domo, Queen Caelia's Aide-de-Camp.'

The Major bows to me and I bow back. Then he bends over Isla and she gives him one of her cute smiles.

'The Queen will be pleased.'

The double doors swing inward, with no one making it happen that I can see, and inside faerie folk dressed like a royal court are scrambling around trying to look organized like they knew we were coming. Up by the throne I catch sight of Queen Caelia straightening her blonde wig as she sits down waving away her attendees like, *I'm fine, I'm fine.* I'm expecting tall and regal, but Queen Caelia is plump and plain and scary, my idea of Queen Victoria. *I may look like a Chinese dumpling but mess with me at your peril!*

Max strides to the first of three steps and drops to one knee, head bowed. The rest of us stop waiting for some cue.

'Rise,' says the Queen.

'Your Majesty, may I present Fiona O'Hara.'

I step forward and curtsy. I didn't know I could curtsy but it must be in my DNA left over from some ancestral lady-in-waiting.

'Is that the princess?' Queen C waves me forward. I walk up the three steps and take Isla from her hammock. That's when I see the two amulets I'd forgotten about lying underneath her. The Queen puts her hands out and I hand Isla to her. "She's beautiful,' the Queen says in a way that makes me wonder about her children.

'Much too beautiful to be an Unseelie,' says me wanting to say something.

'Unseelie?' Queen Caelia looks at me like my brain was damaged at birth. 'This is the daughter of Hebrides, Queen of The Seelie.'

TUESDAY
10:30

Who knew, right? Me and Kevin are sitting in a window of the castle overlooking High Street. The street's not moving so Queen C must be calm or happy or eatin pot gummies. We can see forever including the woods where I met Kevin's mum, Peggy. Kevin would like to be back in those woods I can see it in his face.

I lean over and kiss him. 'Thanks for staying with me. It means a lot.' Then I ask, 'Why are the others so mean to you?'

We were in the castle cafeteria getting a late lunch and the servers all but snubbed Kevin and then as we're finding a table some of the faeries at other tables made rude noises. Kevin ignored them which is all you can do, right?

'They don't like leprechauns because we get all the attention, but instead of helping people believe in faeries, they think we make faeries look like ninnies. We're like the pariah of faeries.'

This is sounding way too much like what I was thinking seeing Peggy standing in her doorway.

'So, really, the others are jealous of you?'

'They don't think that. They think they're authentic and we're not.'

'In Ireland what could be more authentic than a leprechaun?'

Kevin moves his head side-to-side like's he's a bobblehead doll. 'It might help if their bottoms weren't stamped *Made in China*.'

Honestly, I bet every world in the universe is fecked one way or another. I lean forward and give Kevin another kiss so he knows I think he's the cat's pajamas, whatever they are.

'I miss Isla,' says me meaning it.

'Me too; she's special.'

I ask, still feeling stupid and not liking it, 'Did you know she was a Seelie princess?'

'No, but it didn't seem right. She's too adorable to be an Unseelie.'

'I'm trying to remember if someone told me she was an Unseelie princess or if I just assumed that.'

Queen Caelia explained it to me. Queen Hebrides had finally had enough of The Unseelie disrupting everything so she summoned King Kade and told him to gather his tribe of degenerates and leave Scotland forever. Kade told her *to feck off* so they went to war and The Seelie won — no one's sure how — except an Unseelie female managed to impersonate one of Queen Hebrides's wet-nurses — shape-shifting for sure! — and stole Princess Isla. She made her way to The Unseelie camp but by then they were loading onto ships heading for Ireland and it was only when they landed here that King Kade realized what he had: a bargaining chip the size of Ben Nevis. But before he could play it Queen Caelia heard about the kidnapped princess and sent Max to rescue Isla. That's where I came in which reminds me...

'Is time the same here as in my world?' I ask Kevin because I keep wondering what's happening at home? If it's Saturday afternoon in Gloire Bay I've been gone over sixteen hours. I could say the spell that will take me home but something's holding me here. Princess Isla or Kevin I guess, take your pick.

'I don't know but I assume so.'

'Dumb question.'

'I have one of those.'

'Yes?'

'Do you have a boyfriend?'

'Two,' says me laughing.

'Tell me about the other one.'

So I tell him about Darcy going over the cliff and how we were best mates but not b.f./g.f. because Darcy was gay and how I've been hanging out with Billy since then and how much he's come to mean to me. 'Billy came here with me but an Unseelie stabbed him and then he just faded away so I'm hoping he's back in my world.'

'He'll come back for you.'

'That's what I think too.' Then I ask Kevin about his two girlfriends and he tells me everything and he's so funny about it. First there's Bridget who's the barkeep at The Spark & Fire. She works all night and sleeps all day, which is handy because Kevin's other g.f. is Miriam and she's a nurse, works all day and sleeps all night. Too funny.

'And what is it you're doin while the girlfriends are workin and sleepin?'

'I work shifts at the hat factory.'

'Not the green top hats with the gold buckles?'

'The very same,' Kevin answers looking sheepish.

Before I can blurt out, 'But you're not wearin one!' I hear footsteps coming behind me and turn to find Benji grinning at me. Beside him is the female who went with us into the castle and she's grinning too. 'Fiona, Kevin, this is Mally, my best friend.'

Mally is lovely, tall, athletic, and I can see intelligence dancing in her eyes. Before I can react Mally gives me a hug and Kevin too and then she's back beside Benji and I can see the love they feel for each other puffing them up making them invincible.

Benji says, 'We're taking Princess Isla to the beach at Ballyhillin to meet up with Queen Hebrides. Max wants you to come.'

'Kevin too?'

'Of course. In fact, I'm trusting Kevin to carry our bag of amulets.'

Kevin nods obviously pleased to be included/trusted and off we go following Benji and Mally through the castle and out the back into another courtyard this one with open stables along one side. Max is there with a wiry old boggart I figure has to be Alonzo — Sir Max's companion

— and he's busy saddling what has to be one of the pterippi, the horses with wings. Watching is Queen Caelia cradling Isla in her arms. She waves me over.

'She's a dear, isn't she?'

Isla lights up when she sees me.

'She's the sweetest baby ever.'

Queen Caelia sighs. 'I tried to have a baby. Three husbands and not a baby-maker among them. Maybe just as well, they were all thick as bricks.'

The Queen hands me Isla and I slip her into her hammock.

'We give Queen Hebrides her baby back and she helps us send King Kade and his ugly crew packing. You leave now on the pterippi while Major Domo prepares the army. Ádh mór!'

I've been in planes before — Texas, Paris, London — but that kind of flying isn't really flying, it's just fast transportation, a bus with wings. Sitting on the back of a pterippus making your own wind that sets your hair streaming and your eyes blurring, now that's flying!

I glance over at Kevin. He looks like Hiccup from *How To Train Your Dragon* riding Toothless. Kevin the Flying Leprechaun! Now there's a bobblehead doll I'd be buying. Kevin waves and I wave back.

Isla has no idea what's going on so I sit her up in my lap my left arm holding her tight. Next thing I know she's waving her arms around and gurgling. She's scared I think, but loving it too, like terrifying yourself on a rollercoaster.

'We're riding Marta' — that's the name of our pterippus — 'and Kevin's riding Dieter.' I'm not sure what Isla thinks I'm going on about but she waves her arms extra fast so we'll take her reply as, *let's go, let's go!*

We're flying not too high off the ground and far ahead I can see the blue of the ocean. It reminds me of the blue Max is wearing. She's leading the way, strong and confident, and it makes me happy that she's female and not some narcissistic (self-important) male pretending he's stronger and smarter. The silver dragon — wings and tail — on the back of Max's armor is glinting in the sun and it makes me wonder if they read books in Faeryland? Could Max have read *The Girl With the Dragon Tattoo?* The girl's name is Lisbeth Salander and there's a kickass female if ever there was one. Darcy gave me that book for my thirteenth birthday. Darcy would have loved this and suddenly I'm wishing he was here with me living this.

Now we're gliding down. I can see five ships anchored in the water — they look like Viking ships with the heads of sea monsters sticking up at the front. Their sails are down. Behind one is a raft carrying a giant wooden crate with round air holes in the sides. Now I can see the beach and the folks gathered on it staring up at us. Pulled up on the beach are two more of the Viking craft and another raft but this time, instead of a crate, there's a huge cube covered in a red tarpaulin tied down with ropes. We follow Max as she circles the beach doing reconnaissance making sure there are no surprises. That makes me think she doesn't altogether trust Queen Hebrides.

After Benji's talk of Seelies/Unseelies I googled Faery Courts and found the following information. There are six in all; three good like the Elven Court and three evil including The Slaugh Court — the restless dead — The Seelie Court and The Unseelie Court. The Unseelie are the worst of all but The Seelie aren't good guys by any means, they're just a shade less evil than The Unseelie.

I figure we'll land on the beach but Max surprises me by landing on the high bluff overlooking the ocean.

'I don't trust Queen Hebrides not to steal our pterippi,' she says dismounting. 'Okay, listen up! I'm going to parlay with the Queen. The rest of you stay here. And watch your back. The Unseelie may be lurking nearby.'

Benji says to Max, 'That's not a big enough force to help us defeat King Kade.'

'That's what I'm going to talk to the Queen about. If she makes sense of it I'll wave my sword. Fiona, you come then with the princess. If I don't like it, I'll tell the Queen I'm going to fetch Isla. I'll come back here and we'll take off. Either way, be ready. If they try to detain me, dive-bomb the bastards till I can escape. Got it?'

We all nod and Max starts down the hill everybody on the beach staring at her. The faery beside me asks, 'What do you think is under the tarp?' Nobody knows but everybody starts guessing — luggage (boring), secret weapon (maybe), something The Unseelie are allergic to (how bout Goodness & Mercy?)

Max reaches the Queen, drops to one knee and the Queen waves her to her feet. They talk for several minutes then the Queen leads Max to the raft pulled up on the beach. Two of her sailors have loosened the ropes and with a nod from the Queen they yank the tarpaulin off exposing the cage underneath. From all of us gathered on the bluff there's a collective *gasp.*

'What is that thing?' Mally asks her voice incredulous.

Alonzo answers, 'That, I think, is a Nuckelavee, half human, half horse. I've never seen one before but I've heard tales about them from ancient times. I thought they were something invented to scare Scottish children but obviously I was mistaken.'

We're all staring at the monster in its cage. To say I've never seen anything like it is a good place to start. To begin with it's huge — think Hagrid taking growth hormones — its ogre head as wide as a basketball hoop, completely hairless with lips like a folded-over inner tube, and ears sticking out like Yoda. Its chest is as round as a whiskey barrel and its steel-cable arms so long they reach almost to the ground. Unlike a centaur, the human/horse from Greek mythology (and Harry Potter,) the two halves of the Nuckelavee don't flow together but look totally botched like two pipes joined side-by-side, not end-to-end, like the welder/surgeon was either drunk or blind or both.

But none of that is the truly creepy thing. The Nuckelavee has no skin! I can see muscles and ligaments, bones and flesh, blood flowing in its veins and arteries, all of it looking like it's held together by slimy plastic wrap.

'It's like he's been skinned alive.'

'Can you imagine trying to fight that thing?'

'That must be how The Seelie beat The Unseelie.'

As the rest chatter about the Nuckelavee I pull Kevin away. There's something about the two rafts is bothering me.

'Fiona! Max just waved her sword in the air.'

'Be right there!'

That buys me another few seconds and that's enough. I head down the bluff my feet sliding in the sand. Everybody on the beach is watching me giving me the same feeling as arriving late at Darcy's funeral. Most on the beach are Seelie sailors armed to the teeth like pirates. Queen Hebrides is tall and slim — the antithesis of Queen Caelia — her figure set off by wearing a long, tightfitting dress made of a dozen gossamer layers shimmering with all the colors of the sea. If she has wings, they're concealed, unlike Queen Caelia's that flop around her like windblown sheets. Queen Hebrides' hair is the color of wheat — just like Isla's — falling in a braid almost to her waist and on top a diamond tiara sparkles in the sunlight making her look every bit a queen. On either side, but back a pace, stand two female attendants trying to look bored like meeting strangers on a beach is an everyday occurrence.

Max is smiling at me willing me not to be nervous. I arrive in front of Queen Hebrides and curtsy. She reaches out her hands and I take Isla from her hammock and hand her to the Queen but not before I make a show of giving Isla a kiss and a whispered, 'I love you.'

'I didn't think I'd ever see her again,' the Queen says signaling one of the attendants to take Isla. 'She probably needs milk and she certainly needs her nappy changed.' This makes me smile as I watch the two ladies-in-waiting — one carrying Isla — hoist up their skirts and wade into the water heading for the nearest ship.

'You can thank Fiona,' Max says. 'She's the one who rescued the princess from King Kade's tent.'

'Thank you, Fiona.' The Queen is staring at me trying to make sense of what she sees.

'What kind of faery are you?'

Oh boy, what do I say? I look at Max who nods.

'I'm human.'

'Human?'

'My grandmother has a book of faery spells. There's one to change a human into a faery.'

'What about faery to human? Is that possible?'

'I don't know. I don't remember seeing that but it's a large book.'

'How do you go back to being human?'

'I say a spell.'

'What is it?'

I can't say it out loud obviously so I hold out my arm and show the Queen the words written there.

'Ad mutare mei pristine sui,' reads the Queen in a loud voice but nothing happens. 'Pity. I'd like to try being human for a while. I have a feeling I might be a sensation.'

Any further conversation is impossible because from both ends of the beach come the shouts/shrieks of a thousand Unseelies making more noise than a Manowar concert. Max looks at me and then the Nuckelavee locked in his cage.

'THE KEY!' Max screams at the Queen who's already splashing through the water hurrying to her ship. The Queen removes, from around her wrist, a bracelet with a brass key fastened by a ring and flings it at Max. It lands in the sand at her feet and Max picks it up. 'HOW DO I CONTROL IT?'

'TELL HIM YOU LOVE HIM!'

'Sweetjeesus.' Max turns to me with a look on her face that says, *We're going to die! Here! Now!*

I look at The Unseelie charging toward us and shove Max toward the cage. 'Let it out! Things can't get any worse!'

Max pushes the key into the padlock and turns. The Nuckelavee is staring at us — its eyes yellow, the size of billiard balls — like who should I devour first?

'I LOVE YOU!' Max shouts annunciating every word like she means it, 'and if you can hold The Unseelie off till we get out of here, *I really will love you!*'

Max yanks open the door. This is it. Live or die. Which will it be?

But the Nuckelavee, instead of rushing out, pushes back into his corner.

What the...

A loud thumping noise makes me spin around. The Seelie sailors are back in their ships, anchors up, the sails rising. Over by the raft carrying the crate Queen Hebrides is hovering in the air like a hummingbird. What I thought was the Queen's gossamer dress turns out to be her wings and underneath she's wearing a skin-tight bodysuit, smooth and shiny like chrome. She's yelling instructions to a sailor balancing on the edge of the raft. In one hand he holds a long pole with a hook at the end while his other hand is gripping one of the crate's air holes. He's holding on for dear life because something large inside the crate is charging from side-to-side turning the raft into a wave machine. The Queen puts her fingers in her mouth and whistles. Whatever's in the crate stops moving and the raft settles down. The sailor sticks his pole into one of the air holes while looking through another. The Queen flies to the largest of her ships and lands in the rear facing our way. She finds me staring at her and waves. Is she laughing? Yes, she is. Whatever happens on the beach she's free of it. And she's not even in the same ship as poor Isla. So much for motherly love.

Max gives a cry and I spin around. The Nuckelavee is out of his cage and holding Max up in the air her arms pinned to her sides. I'm frantically trying to pull my dagger free when the Nuckelavee pulls Max's face to his mouth and gives her a toilet-plunger kiss. OMG, the look of utter surprise/disgust on Max's slime-covered face will be etched on my brain cells forever. Then the Nuckelavee drops Max butt first into the sand and turns his attention to the task at hand. Beat the crap out of The Unseelie.

Max and I take off for the bluff. It's hard running up in the soft sand and beyond tiring. The Nuckelavee is behind us, not fighting yet but covering our backs. Benji and some of the others are clambering down the hill their swords out. We're halfway up the hill when The Unseelie arrive at the bottom. The Nuckelavee is fighting now tearing the lead Unseelie apart like a dog with a rag doll. The next Unseelie tries to use his spear but the Nuckelavee grabs it and twists. The Unseelie does a somersault and somehow ends up suspended in the air, his spear sticking out of his stomach like the shaft of a beach umbrella. The rest of The Unseelie put on the brakes not wanting to be next.

That's when the Nuckelavee vanishes!

We're for it now. My muscles are screaming, my lungs are on fire, but I can see the pterippi waiting at the top of the hill so I keep scrambling up the loose sand using my legs and arms like a crab running for its life. I can hear the Unseelie behind their screams getting louder. Finally, I stagger to the top and Kevin, flying on Dieter, lands beside me.

'Hop on!'

'What about Marta?'

'Mally's got her!' Kevin points and I see Mally on Marta rocketing down the hill. Kevin pulls me up behind him then carefully hands me the bag of amulets. We take off, staying low, heading down the bluff right for The Unseelie. Benji and Max are fighting a rearguard action holding The Unseelie back so the others can regain the top. Kevin swoops in front of Max. Dieter's hooves are kicking like pistons and they connect with the nearest Unseelie dropping him in his tracks.

Max and Benji lumber up the hill as the rest of the pterippi take their turn dive-bombing the enemy. Then we're all in the air and cheering like mad!

There's a big surprise waiting for us when we arrive back at Sí Dún. Two surprises actually, but the second comes later.

To start with Billy is there, grinning at me, each of us hugging the other happy our adventure has brought us back together again.

'Are you alright?' I ask. I don't say how afraid I was that dying in Faeryland might be permanent. 'I thought it was a good thing you vanished.'

'Woke up in the Parish Hall my stomach on fire. Seems fine now.'

'I'm glad you're back.'

'Me too.'

Billy's not alone, he's come with Fungal and Rachel and the rest of the Marauders except Flynn. 'He's always late,' Rachel blurts out. 'The only way his mum gets him to school on time is dumpin water on his head.'

'Tell me what happened?' I say and Fungal starts in.

'Every time one of us died we'd wake up in the Hall. Soon we were all there but you and Billy. It was late so everybody headed home except Rachel and Helen who volunteered to stay with your bodies.'

Rachel: 'My mum thought I was havin a sleepover at Helen's.'

Helen: 'And mine thought we were sleepin at Rachel's.'

Fungal: 'We agreed to meet back at the hall next morning at ten.'

Ryan: 'We figured any earlier and our parents would know something was going on.'

Rachel: 'Then Billy showed up and told us about you carrying the princess and him getting stabbed by an Unseelie. Billy's all for going right back but we talked him out of it by arguing if you died you'd end up in the Hall and he'd better get home or his parents would be sounding the alarm. Billy's not happy...' (Rachel stops here letting Billy make an angry/sad face makes us all laugh.) '... but he heads home and me and Helen lay down on the rug and we're still out cold when Big Mouth and Wide Arse come barging in, demanding to know what the hell we're doin sleeping in the Hall?'

Helen: 'The Women's Aux had the Hall booked for ten.'

Rachel: 'Then Wide Arse saw the broken window and stormed out looking for Father McKenna.'

Helen: 'You looked dead of course so Rachel and I pulled you up between us and staggered out.'

Rachel: 'I told Big Mouth you were passed out and she said it wouldn't be the first time.'

Everybody laughs at this so I chuckle too, horrified, thinking wait till Gran hears about this. 'What about Gran's book?'

Fungal: 'I took it home with me.'

Rachel: 'We get you outside and go around back, hidin. Helen texts Fungal. He shows up drivin the digger so we put your body in the bucket and drive to Stonehaven knowin it's empty.'

I look at Billy who nods.

Fungal: 'And here we are.'

They're all grinning at me like, *what a time we're having!*

I turn to Fungal. 'Where's Gran's book now?'

'Stonehaven. We left it out in case Flynn shows up.'

That's when Queen Caelia appears wanting to know all about our meeting with Queen Hebrides. Max starts telling her and when she hears about the Nuckelavee her eyes go wide. 'A Nuckelavee? Well, I'll be. I thought they were just the stuff of legend. Was it as horrible as they say?'

'Worse,' Max says meaning it.

'That will be how Queen Hebrides defeated King Kade. I wondered about that. She must have *just* found it or she would have used it before. There was talk she'd traveled to Iceland. Perhaps she found it trapped in the ice...'

Queen Caelia pauses trying to put the pieces together, the major mystery being why did our Nuckelavee disappear?

'So, Hebrides had the real Nuckelavee in a crate behind one of her ships?'

'I assumed it was another Nuckelavee,' Max says, 'but I figured it was like a breeding pair or something. My mind didn't go to clones.'

'And at the worst possible moment,' Queen Caelia says, picturing it, 'she removed the amulet from around its neck.'

'And our Nuckelavee vanished leaving us surrounded by Unseelies.'

You didn't need to be a mind reader to see Max was upset with herself for not foreseeing that possibility.

'Queen Hebrides didn't think we knew about the amulets. She told me The Unseelie had a trick that made it look like they had a much bigger force than they actually had. When I asked her what the trick was, she said, *you'll figure it out.*'

'So, she had no intention of helping us she just wanted her daughter back?'

'She doesn't want The Unseelie returning to Scotland.'

Queen Caelia nods at this. 'So now that she's got Princess Isla back...'

I've been standing in the rear with Fungal, Billy and Kevin, running a dozen different scenarios through my brain trying to get the outcome I want, but then I remember Queen Hebrides saying the unfaery spell without result and I realize there's nothing I can do right now so I say in a loud voice, 'Actually, she doesn't have her daughter back.'

Now everybody's staring at me most with their mouths hanging open.

Kevin's holding Benji's amulet bag, cradling it like it's heavy. I reach inside and lift out Isla. She rubs the sleep from her eyes then smiles at me and my heart is breaking because more than anything in the world I want to take her home to Stonehaven but for the life of me I can't figure out how to do it. I walk forward and hand her to Queen Caelia. A tear comes spilling down my right cheek and I wipe it away.

Queen Caelia stares at Isla love in her eyes, then she stares at me.

'You gave a clone to Queen Hebrides?'

'Yes.' It seemed obvious to me what was going to happen but I don't want to say that. Max feels bad enough already.

'Will she know?'

'The amulets only work for a certain distance,' Benji answers. 'I imagine her daughter has already disappeared.'

I can see the Queen thinking there's some justice in that given Queen Hebrides's double-dealing.

'So, she'll be coming back.'

'With the real Nuckelavee.'

Queen Caelia, Max, Benji, Mally and Major Domo go off to discuss things — a Council of War you might say — leaving the rest of us on our own. I introduce Kevin to Billy and I can see them eyeing each other like rivals for my affection. And what am I thinking? I'm thinking this two-boyfriend idea may catch on.

I send Kevin off to find us tea or something. I kiss Billy.

'I missed you.'

'You sure?' Billy says smiling.

'Not too much, but...' We're both grinning now.

'He seems like a good guy.'

'He is, just like you.' We kiss again. 'What time did you get here?'

'OMG, what a right smash-up,' Billy says, laughing. 'We say the spell together and appear right in the middle of a leprechaun stampede. You'd have thought it was St. Paddy's Day at St. Brendan's.' (St. Brendan's is the old Insane Asylum in Dublin.)

'That's hilarious.'

'Yeah, except the reason they're stampeding is The Unseelie are chasing them.'

'Why?"

'The leprechauns were making off with The Unseelie's stash of amulets.'

Now there's a quick way to even the sides.

'And how did they manage that?'

'There were two of them — Ginger and Shirty, teenagers on a dare apparently — snuck into King Kade's tent looking for something that would prove they'd been there. So, don't they find this wooden chest wearing a padlock they can't open and the chest is heavy so Ginger says to Shirty, *It's bloody pirate treasure! We'll be rich!* So they take the chest between them sneaking back the way they came.'

Billy's enjoying telling me the story — it's usually me doing all the talking, exaggerating and embellishing — so I'm quiet giving him my rapt attention.

'But just as they're leaving the camp doesn't Shirty trip over a tent peg and land on a sleeping dog who doesn't appreciate being smucked with a heavy treasure chest so he starts barking making so much noise the camp wakes up.

'Now the two thieves are running for their lives, the chest between them, but the ruddy thing is heavy so they're tiring fast. Ginger's all for ditching the chest but Shirty says let's at least see what's inside. They climb up on one of the big boulders and throw the chest over and it explodes leavin the ground covered in amulets. Ginger's disappointed but Shirty puts one on and as it lands on his chest ten more leprechauns appear. *Would you look at that!* Shirty cries admiring himself ten times over. Ginger thinks that's so cool he puts on an amulet and now there's ten more Gingers starin at them.

'Next thing you know Ginger and Shirty are each wearing ten amulets so there are two hundred and two leprechauns stampeding through the woods being chased by twenty Unseelie with sharp spears.'

I grin picturing it. 'Then what happened?'

'We appear in the middle of the stampede.'

'You must have wondered what was goin on?'

'Fungal figured it out right away.' Billy stops here remembering. 'Fungal's amazing, y'know.'

'Darcy always said that. If you think Fungal's slow you haven't seen him outmaneuver the Moss Troopers. Then what happened?'

'Fungal stops Ginger and takes his amulets off. Half the little green men disappear. Then Shirty comes to Fungal and he takes Shirty's amulets off and now it's just us and two leprechauns with twenty angry Unseelies hurtling toward us screaming something like *we want your guts for sausage casings!* I figure we'll be back in the Hall before you know it but doesn't Fungal drop one of the amulets over a blackthorn bush and now there're ten more bushes with their spikes out and the rest of us are picking up amulets tossing them onto the bushes and before you know it there's a twenty-meter barricade of thorns with The Unseelie thrashing about in the middle and clearly not happy about it.'

I'm about to say how clever that was when Kevin reappears carrying a tray of teacups with Flynn following behind with a platter loaded with biscuits minus the one he's munching on.

'Where have you been?' Billy says to Flynn.

'It's not my fault. Me mum wouldn't let me go till I cleaned my room.'

'I've seen your room. What did you use, a flamethrower?'

'Pushed everything into me wardrobe.'

'Good thing she didn't open it.'

'She did. That's when I ran for it.'

We all laugh imagining Flynn's mum buried under an avalanche of dirty underwear and X-Box cartridges.

'You guys weren't at the Hall, so I asked Mrs. McLeish where you were, and she said you'd gone to Fiona's, so I went there but you'd already said the spell.'

'Was Father McKenna at the Hall?' I ask.

'Yeah, he wasn't happy about the broken window. I said we'd look after it as soon as we got back from Faeryland.'

'You didn't!'

Flynn can't understand why I'm upset. 'He just thinks it was us getting carried away with our silly game,' Flynn says taking another biscuit.

The world could be coming to an end and Flynn would still be focused on tea and biscuits!

My brain's whirling with the possibility of Father McKenna going to Stonehaven and stealing Gran's book when Queen Caelia reappears holding Isla in her arms. She starts addressing everyone like we're an audience — the way Queens do — but she's mainly talking to me.

'I have decided to keep Princess Isla. After Queen Hebrides's treachery I feel Princess Isla is a *spoil of war* and I intend to spoil her.' Queen C looks around seeking everyone's approval but we're all shaking our heads like *are you serious? Are you not thinking Queen Hebrides may have something to say about this?*

'I'm sending Max to negotiate with King Kade. If we can get The Unseelie on our side we have a chance.'

'What about the Nuckelavee?'

'The Nuckelavee is a problem. I'm hoping King Kade has some ideas.'

King Kade is the one who hightailed it out of Scotland, remember?

Before any of us can bring this little detail to the Queen's attention an old brownie, with a limp, hurries in bowing. 'Your majesty, Manduke just arrived. He's in the washroom.'

'Did he find King Kade?'

'He wouldn't say.'

'What's he doing in the washroom?'

'Grooming his hair, I believe. Also, there's a very strange delegation wishing to see you.'

'Is it anything to do with King Kade or Queen Hebrides?'

'No. Something else I believe. A business proposition.'

'That can wait. Have Esmeralda take them on a tour of the city. Tell her to bring them back at teatime.'

'As you wish.'

The brownie scurries out only to be replaced by Manduke, aka Full-of-Himself.

'What news of King Kade?'

'After many trials and tribulations, some life-threatening, I have ascertained the whereabouts of said enemy warrior.'

'Yes Manduke, you can tell me all about it later. Now, cut to the chase.'

'Pardon?'

'Where is King Kade?'

We can all see Manduke is dying to elaborate on his Life-Threatening

Trials & Tribulations but is just smart enough to see the floor he's standing on is beginning to quiver a sure sign the Queen is growing impatient.

'He's in the Unenchanted Forest.'

'What's he doing there?'

'He's visiting a leprechaun.'

'Who?'

Manduke points at Kevin. 'His mother, I believe.'

My plan had been to go home to rescue Gran's book. Now that Queen C has adopted Isla — I'm okay with that! — I felt I was free to leave. The others could battle the Nuckelavee if they wanted, but King Kade being at Peggy's house changes everything. Within twenty minutes the pterippi deposit us at the edge of the Unenchanted Forest — Kevin says don't believe a word of it! — and in we charge Kevin leading the way. We haven't taken three steps when I feel electricity all around me, my skin prickling, my scalp tingling, the hairs on my arms bristling like there's a lightning bolt getting ready to strike.

'It wasn't like this before,' I whisper to Billy but he just shrugs.

We're trying to be quiet, not alerting the enemy, but Kevin — worried sick about his mum — is in too big a hurry so despite our best efforts we sound like elephants in Doc Martens.

It's only as we approach Peggy's house that we actually resemble something close to stealth-like — elephants wearing ballet slippers maybe, dodging from tree to tree trying to be invisible. The trouble is we can't see any Unseelies; in fact, it's suddenly so dark out we can barely see ourselves. Max says she can feel The Unseelie around us but that's as close as we get to actually seeing one and when I ask Benji why it's suddenly pitch black out he says things are *different* in the Unenchanted Forest. That's when the young aspen tree I'm trying to hide behind asks me my name.

'Fiona.'

'Duggan. Nice to meet you.'

Gran's reading *The Secret Life of Trees* so she's going to love this, but before I can ask Duggan any questions Kevin puts his fingers in his mouth and whistles. Inside the house Wolfy barks. Then the door opens, light pouring out, and Peggy (beardless) is standing in the doorway waving to us while Wolfy bounds across the open space jumping up on Kevin.

'It's okay,' Peggy shouts. "Come in."

Max orders everyone but Kevin and me to surround the house. Billy doesn't look my way just trundles off behind Fungal. We go inside to find a larger-than-life Unseelie sitting at Peggy's table a mug of tea in his hand and a grin on his face. He's big enough to remind me of Grandad Sky trying to have tea with me when I was five; Grandad sitting on a little kid's chair so low to the ground his knees were rubbing his moustache.

'This is King Kade,' Peggy says. "King Kade, this is my son, Kevin, and Fiona and...'

'Max,' Max says sticking her hand out and the next thing you know we're all shaking hands even Kevin and his mum making a game of it.

'I'd get up,' the King says, 'but I caught my foot in a leg-hold trap so rusted I'm surprised it worked. Hurts like hell.'

We all stare at the King's ankle, which is red, swollen, and showing the nasty wounds the teeth of the trap have left. This is so different than I thought it would be. This is The Unseelie King, King Kade, the Nastiest of Nasties, the Ultimate Evil, and here I am feeling sorry for him.

'We set traps for the Torc Triath,' Peggy says which means nothing to me till Kevin whispers in my ear, 'The Wild Boar.'

'Ah, and did you catch it?' King Kade asks.

'We did but not before he had his fill.'

'I almost had him near Tintagel,' King Kade says. 'Struck him with my spear but it glanced off and he escaped. Some said he swam to Ireland but I didn't believe them.' The King reaches down and pokes his leg puffed up like a pillow. 'Now he's had his revenge even if he knows nothing about it.' The King raises his head and stares at each of us in turn.

'And which of you had the bright idea to throw the amulets onto the thorn bushes?'

My eyes leave his face and go to his massive bare chest, which I now see, is a crisscross of scratches. He must have got caught in the brambles with his men and not seen the trap at his feet.

'That was my friend Fungal's doin,' I answer. 'He's clever that way.'

The King nods at this as Peggy kneels down beside him holding a pot of something that looks like stewed seaweed and smells worse. She starts wrapping the seaweed around the King's ankle and he wrinkles his nose.

'That should kill everything, me included,' he says grinning at us.

I don't want to like the King but I do. He's one of those enormous blokes you want on your side not against you. Like Lebron James of the LA Lakers — Grandad Sky loves basketball! — or the Rock, Dwayne Johnson. And unlike the other Unseelies his hair is cut short and he's clean-shaven which is a far cry from the others I've seen who have long greasy hair and beards cut this way and that. The King's eyes keep returning to Peggy and I start feeling male/female vibes. Then he lets Peggy go and stares at Max as if trying to read her mind.

'Peggy said you'd come bringing a message from Queen Caelia.'

Max tells the King about meeting Queen Hebrides on the beach and her offer to give us a Nuckelavee in exchange for Princess Isla.

'And what did you think of the Nuckelavee?' King Kade asks.

'Unstoppable,' Max replies and King Kade nods at this.

'We haven't figured out how to defeat it. That's why we had to leave Scotland before it killed us all.'

Peggy wraps a piece of netting around the King's ankle trapping the seaweed and uses pieces of cloth to secure it.

'Thank you.'

'You're welcome.'

Peggy smiles at the King and he smiles back and I feel those male/female signals again washing over me like a wave. Then King Kade turns to Max and says, 'So Queen Hebrides is gone and you're stuck with me.'

'Not exactly,' Max replies telling the King the rest of the story.

Now the King's staring at me as the one who decided, on her own, to keep Princess Isla. 'I'm not sure that was very clever.'

'It seemed right at the time.'

'But now you have two enemies to fight, one with an unbeatable monster.'

'We're rather hoping to form an alliance with you,' Max says but no sooner are the words spoken then outside the house all hell breaks loose. The King hobbles to the door and like a disgruntled parent screams, 'Enough!'

That works. The two hundred Unseelies surrounding the house — waving their spears and screaming — fall silent and Benji, Billy and the rest, swords in the air, stare at King Kade towering above them like, *okay boss, whatever you say.*

'What do I get?' the King asks sitting back down.

'Scotland,' answers Max.

'I'm feeling unloved and unwanted but I understand. I wouldn't want me for a neighbor either. So is Queen Caelia willing to give the princess back?'

'No,' Max answers. 'She's going to adopt her and make the princess her heir.'

King Kade whistles at this.

'Does Queen H know?'

'Not yet.'

'She'll be livid.'

'She has other children.'

'You're obviously not a parent.'

We know King Kade is right we just don't want to admit it.

'So that brings us back to the Nuckelavee,' King Kade says. 'One is bad enough but when he wears his amulet there are ten more to deal with.'

I ask, 'Were the amulets your idea or Queen Hebrides?'

'Mine. I read about replicators and set out to find one. The irony is I told everyone I was going to find a Nuckelavee thinking that a fine joke but Queen H heard the rumors and went looking for her own monster.'

It's quiet in the wee house. I can hear Wolfy whimpering in his sleep. The rest are thinking about how to defeat the Nuckelavee but I'm stuck on giving up Isla and how my mum Fallon had to give me up.

Finally, Peggy says, 'There's one who can defeat the Nuckelavee.'

Every eye in the room goes to Peggy who's standing near her stove stirring something in a small pot that smells much better than seaweed. She pulls her spoon out and tastes whatever it is she's cooking. Then she takes a spoonful to the King who blows on it then opens his mouth. 'Delicious.'

'You'll be staying for dinner, I trust.'

Now the yin/yang vibes aren't vibrations they're tremors.

'Yes, I'd like that.'

Peggy smiles at the rest of us like, *time for you to go!* Even Kevin is shaking his head like, *that's me ma.*

'So, have we got a deal?' Max asks.

'Yes,' replies King Kade sticking his hand out to shake on it. 'I help you defeat The Seelie and get Scotland in return. And where will we send Queen Hebrides?'

'Boston.'

King Kade bursts out laughing his laughter so loud and infectious soon we're all laughing. 'Perfect, the Celtics will love her. Now, good Peggy, please tell us which of us has the power to defeat the Nuckelavee?'

Peggy looks at each of us in turn until finally her gaze returns to the King.

'It's not necessary to know who, only that the Nuckelavee is not invincible.'

We arrive at the castle to hear the news that Queen Hebrides is back, camped on the beach at Ballyhillin.

'What's she waitin for?' Benji asks.

'Her army,' Max answers.

'I wonder how many amulets she has?'

'She only needs one and we know she has that.'

'What if she puts two on the Nuckelavee?' Mally asks. 'Will there be twenty of them?'

I pull the two amulets from my pocket and slip them over my head. Now there are twenty Fionas staring back at me. Ugh! I take the amulets off and hand them to Benji. Two more for his collection.

That's when Flynn comes bursting into the room waving his arms like his armpits are on fire.

'Father McKenna is here!'

'What!'

'That's the delegation wanted to see the Queen. Father McKenna, Ol' Man O'Reilly, Adriana and some bloke I've never seen before looks like Adriana.'

'Show me!'

While the rest of us were concerned with saving the planet Flynn trundled off to the kitchen looking for more tea and biscuits and returns with bigger news than anything we've come up with. This should be a lesson to us all, thinks me, as Flynn hustles me through the kitchen to a door with a porthole window. On the other side is a dining room and seated around the table are Queen C, Major Domo, Father McKenna, Ol' Man O'Reilly, Adriana and her twin brother, Alessandro.

I know exactly what they're talking about. 'We want to open Faeryland under the bog. We want you, Queen C, to staff it with faeries. We'll make a mountain of money — to say nothing of filling the Inn — and you Queen will return to your former glory with millions of new believers.'

I hurry back to the others. 'I have to go home. Now! They've got Gran's book.'

Fungal, Billy and the others jump to their feet. 'We're coming too.'

Kevin is standing between Benji and Max looking lost, like his best friend has just announced he's moving to Australia. I hurry to him, give him a hug and whisper in his ear, 'I'll be back, promise.'

'I know you will. And bring Billy, I like him.'

I nod to Max and Benji giving them a look. Benji gets my meaning right away and puts his arm around Kevin. 'Don't worry Fiona, Kevin's one of us.'

Kevin will be okay; Princess Isla will be okay; and I'll be okay if I can rescue Gran's book.

'All right everybody. Stand in a circle. I'm going to say a few words. When I nod clap your hands three times fast like this.'

We wake up in Stonehaven. It takes me a few seconds to realize the furry thing rubbing against my forehead isn't another hangover but Bandit trying to wake me. I sit up watching as the others slowly figure out where they are. Just like last time everything that happened in Faeryland is out of focus like a drunken dream. There, but not there. 'Is that my head pounding?' Fungal asks and that's when I realize someone is hammering on the door.

It's Rachel's mum and Helen's mum. Rachel's mum phoned Helen's lookin for Rachel and that's when they realized their daughters weren't at either house. Thinking the worse — snogging, booze, drugs, sex! — they'd gone looking finally ending up at Stonehaven thanks to Big Mouth and Wide Arse implying the worst.

'Rachel McSorley, you are grounded forever. Say goodbye to your friends. You won't see them again till you're twenty-five!'

Rachel snorts at this. 'Sounds like an idle threat to me,' she says waving to the rest of us as she follows her mum out the door.

Helen's mother is more curious. 'What were you doing here all collapsed over like that?'

'It's part of Marauders, Mum. Role playin.'

'What were you playin? Comatose?'

Helen waves and she's gone too.

'Who else needs to go home?'

'What time is it?'

'Almost 22:00.'

'Shite. I need to go,' Ryan says.

'Me too,' echoes Flynn. 'Sorry.'

'Don't be sorry. I totally understand. Billy?'

'I'm okay. Mum thinks I'm at Tyler's.'

'Fungal?'

Fungal answers, 'Let's find 'em,' meaning Father McKenna and the others who've obviously taken Gran's *Book of Faery Spells* somewhere they consider safe.

'Where do you think they are?'

'Manse or the Inn.'

'What about Ol' Man O'Reilly's?'

'Too far out.'

'Tower?'

'Same.'

We ride Fungal's digger to the Inn. The place is quiet, the only person around Gail Murphy standing behind the granite counter at the front desk thinking we're late arrivals but then seeing it's just three locals but then double-clutching again because the tall one bringing up the rear is Fungal. Gail lights up.

'Fergus, what are you doin here?'

'Hey Gail, is Adriana around?'

Those male/female vibes are back flashing between Fungal and Gail like minnows caught in the moonlight.

'Yes, she's in her office with Father McKenna and Mr. O'Reilly.'

And her twin brother Alessandro but you probably don't know that.

'They've been in there forever. I knocked on the door offering to bring them refreshments but no one answered. Then I put a call through from Adriana's dad but she didn't pick up.'

'You thought it strange?'

Gail nods at me. 'I did, but I figured she wanted her privacy so...'

'We need to get into that room,' Fungal says. 'Father McKenna has stolen Fiona's Gran's book and we need to get it back.'

Gail has the same look Kevin had back at the castle. She's bewildered not knowing what to do.

'It'll be my job.'

'Then we're going to kick the door down,' says me out of patience, striding down the hall like I own the place.

'No, wait!' Gail cries trying to catch up. 'We need to knock first.'

'Sure.' *Knock yourself out.*

Gail knocks and no one answers. She knocks again harder this time. Fungal takes the passkey from her.

'Go back to reception, Gail. If there's any trouble, I'll say I stole it.'

Gail shakes her head. She likes Fergus too much to leave.

'I'll just say I thought there was a gas leak or something.'

Fungal opens the door. The office is empty but the apartment behind isn't. Father McKenna, Ol' Man O'Reilly, Adriana and her brother are slumped over around the dining room table.

'Who's that?' Gail asks.

'Alessandro, Adriana's twin brother.'

I can see Gail thinking *why haven't I seen him before?*

'They're not dead, are they?'

'Sleeping. Self-hypnosis. That's what my Gran's book is about.' I pick up Gran's book and tuck it under my arm.

'Can you two find your way home?' Fungal asks meaning he's staying with Gail. Then he tries to wink and it comes off looking like a five-year-old practicing.

'You might want to break a window from the outside. Make it look like someone broke in.'

Fungal gives me a grin like if he was a kindergarten teacher, I'd be getting a gold star.

SUNDAY
OO:45

By the time Billy and I stumble back into Stonehaven it's well after midnight. On the way we're talking about all the things we could have done to Father Wanker and the others if Gail hadn't been there. It's me with all the lewd suggestions Billy just hooting when he likes one.

'Why is Adriana's brother hidin out?' he asks.

'Yeah, not sure about that.'

'Hiding from his father maybe?'

'Hidin from somebody. But it came in handy when he was out in the boat. I told Inspector Mike it was Adriana and she could prove it wasn't. Made me look a right eejit.'

Billy makes a grunting noise like that wouldn't be hard and I'm forced to kiss him into submission. I lock all the doors, something that never happens, then I lead Billy upstairs.

The rest you can be exercising your imagination. Just make it happy and good, like Irish immigrants seeing the Statue of Liberty for the first time.

Billy heads home about ten but not before I try to make him Eggs Benedict. Eggs Taste Like Shite is what he gets but Billy does the boy thing and says they're outstanding. Grandad Sky says males have a lot to learn about females, things like being wrong when they're right. I have no sympathy. In my experience dealing with males is like trying to make sense of a plugged toilet. It should work it just doesn't. As Billy's waving goodbye to me we hear church bells and we grin wondering if Father

McKenna will be there to deliver his sermon.

Gran sends me a text. Dale, Grandad Sky's 1966 Chevy pickup, has a broken tie rod. The part has to come from America so they're renting a car and probably won't be home till very late. This is good news cos it gives me more time to tidy up.

I'm putting Gran's book back in the Secret Hiding Place when I remember Feister the Horned Toad. I find the piece of paper with the spell and take it outside.

'Feister? Feister?' I find him under a rock. I can't tell if he's disgruntled but when you're that ugly you'd have to be, right?' Like Miss Carmichael down at the Post Office. Grandad says she so plain she looks like *a tray of frogs,* an American expression I now get. Gran says Grandad is being unkind but he says he's just trying to account for why she's so disagreeable.

'Bunaidh a thabhait duit,' says me and Feister turns back into himself, which means he's just as ugly as the Horned Toad just in a different way.

'Hi Feister, glad you're back. The parental unit will be arrivin late tonight and I need your help cleanin the house.'

Feister, obviously not the kind to forgive and forget, spins around and moons me, meaning *I am going to do everything I can to make your life miserable!* I turn him back into a Horned Toad.

Two hours later the house looks presentable. I remember Flynn's wardrobe landing on his mother and figure I've done better than that. Billy texts. Like Rachel he's grounded forever cos his mum called Tyler's and found out he wasn't there. Where were you then? Fiona's I bet and overnight too. What about Darcy? Have you two no feelings?

I know what happened to Darcy now. The conspirators at the dig site found Darcy's body in Fungal's digger. They thought he was dead — how he died must have perplexed 'em — so they tossed him over the cliff so he wouldn't be found near the bog. Does that make it murder or a tragic accident? Or both? And deciding that won't change things; won't bring poor Darcy back.

Of course, I'm worried about everything going on in Faeryland — Seelies, Unseelies, Nuckelavee, Kevin, Isla, Benji, Max, Peggy — but none of the Marauders have contacted me and I get that. We need a break. I figure if I'm wanted Benji will come get me. In the meantime, I've an essay to polish and my legs need a walk.

It takes me forever to crack the mystery of how the *Jeanie Johnston* got her name. It starts with me contacting the *Jeanie Johnston* in Dublin asking about the name. Emer replies saying, we don't know but we think the man who built the ship, John Munn in Quebec City — he came from Scotland — was a big fan of Robbie Burns who was always going on about Bonnie Jean.

I google Robbie Burns and Jeanie Johnston but it's all dead ends. So, I toss that out and start researching John Munn. He turns out to be a good guy employing Irish immigrants in his shipyard even when times were tough trying his best not to lay anybody off. He even built the *Jeanie Johnston* with his own money hoping it would sell so he could keep all the men working. He never married, no kids, and lived with his cousin, Elizabeth Allan, who looked after the household.

I pretend to be John Munn needing to name my ship and I picture him thinking about a little girl who always smiles at him as he walks to the shipyard so I start searching the directories for Quebec City and find a William Johnston living near the docks and then I find his family tree (not easy!) and doesn't he have seven kids — (YES!) — none of them named Jean. (Rats!)

I reread John Munn's biography looking for clues. At the bottom it says he left his estate to his cousin Elizabeth and his brother's son, David, who was living with him working at the shipyard as a carpenter. I research David Munn (costs me twenty Euros on a genealogy site!) and he turns out to be married to Marie Elizabeth Johnston and they have three children, two boys — Luke and Gabriel — and the youngest a girl named — wait for it! — Jean Johnston Munn.

Here's where you picture me flying around the room like my knickers have sprouted wings!

My essay's as good as it's going to get and I've walked to the tower and back. There were four Canadian tourists enjoying the view. They asked me questions so I broke into my tour guide act. Canadians are like Americans just not as pushy like they can see their place in the world. I asked them what they knew about the quarantine station at Grosse Isle, Quebec, explaining that so many Irish died there waiting to be cleared. They ended up apologizing, saying they weren't taught anything about the Irish Potato Famine, *but we celebrate St. Patrick's Day* says the cute boy with the scar above his eye. *Green beer,* says his g.f., getting me to take their photo.

I listen at the door of the Honeymoon Suite and don't hear any grunting so I assume Father McKenna and Ol' Man O'Reilly are still in Faeryland. The key's gone so they've learned that lesson. I kept wondering which of them threw Darcy over? When the Dullahan showed Karen and me what happened that night I was sure I saw two heaving and more watching from the shadows but Karen didn't see the ones looking on. So, was it Crash and Burn doing the heaving, or Adriana and her brother, or Father McKenna and Ol' Man O'Reilly, or some combination? My money's on Crash and Burn, with Father McKenna and Ol' Man O'Reilly watching, though I'm only saying this because I don't want it to be Adriana and her brother.

Bandit and I have dinner together. I'm still feeling guilty about not going back to help Max and Benji but no one's showed up saying they need me which means things are either under control or so bad no one has the time to get me. Billy texts and he's feeling guilty too but his mum is watching him like a hawk so he's not going anywhere. I run a bath letting the hot water soak into my bones. There's a lot to think about but my brain says we're out of steam — let's take the night off — and I'm too tired to argue.

I'm trying to stay awake to greet Gran so Bandit and I curl up on the chesterfield watching an old episode of *Game of Thrones.*

I must have fallen asleep because the next thing I know it's black out. I hear a vehicle pulling up outside so I get to my feet grinning like an eejit because I'm expecting Gran to come bursting through the door, but it's not Gran it's Father McKenna with Ol' Man O'Reilly right behind. *Shite!*

'So, Father, did you conclude your business with Queen Caelia?' asks me buying time.

'We're not sure yet Fiona,' Father McKenna answers. 'Adriana and her brother stayed behind to ingratiate themselves.'

'Has Queen Hebrides's army landed?'

'I believe so. We left before anything had transpired.'

Bandit walks by my feet and goes right to Ol' Man O'Reilly who picks her up. Bandit likes strangers because they're always good for strokes.

'So why are you here?'

'We need Gran's book.'

'It's not here.'

'I don't believe you.'

The Father and me stare at each other.

'We could pay you for it but I know you won't take money.'

'It's not mine to sell.'

Ol' Man O'Reilly walks to the kitchen counter. He's holding Bandit with one hand his other reaching out to the block of wood holds Gran's kitchen knives. He pulls one out and holds it up so I can see it. Then he moves it under Bandit's throat. Bandit's squirming now digging his claws into Ol' Man O'Reilly's sleeve but Ol' Man O'Reilly isn't letting go.

Most blokes would be bluffing but Ol' Man O'Reilly isn't. He's as tough as jail bars and as heartless as a Mafia hit man. I run upstairs and return with Gran's book. I hold it out to Father Wanker but he shakes his head.

'Sit down. Now open it to the faery spell page. Now say it.'

I sit down glancing at my left arm. My long bath has all but erased the words to undo the spell. Three times I read the words at the bottom of the page desperate to engrave them in my memory.

'Say it now!'

Just like the first time I'm back in Faeryland wearing my armor, sword in hand, crouched over running uphill through waist high grass. It's nighttime and the others around me are more shadow than real. I know something horrible just happened at home but I can't quite pull it in.

Something to do with Bandit...

Benji and Mally are in front of me so I catch up.

'What's going on?'

'You're back!'

I don't think I meant to be but here I am.

'What's going on?' I ask again.

'Where are the others?'

No idea. 'What's goin on?' I ask for the third time.

Benji doesn't answer because we've come to the edge of the bluff. He falls onto his stomach and the rest of us follow suit. Now I can see the ocean sparkling black in the moonlight and fires on the beach and dozens of sailors moving around holding torches. My eyes find Queen Hebrides standing at the water's edge watching as a hundred of her ships approach the beach.

'Where's Max?' I ask.

'I'm not sure,' Benji answers. 'She said she was going to swim to the raft holding the Nuckelavee.'

'And then what?'

'Cut the rope and pull the raft away so the Queen can't use her monster.'

It sounds like a good plan but I'll wager Max didn't figure on the other hundred ships arriving. 'Where are The Unseelie?'

'They're here.'

'If the Nuckelavee is out of it can we beat that many Seelies?'

'Could go either way but Max is hoping to use the Nuckelavee against Queen Hebrides.'

Now my eyebrows are heading for the stars above. Better Max than me that's for sure. Or is it?

'I can't die here,' says me squeezing Benji's arm. He doesn't get it. 'I should be the one dealing with the Nuckelavee. He can't kill me.'

'You're right! C'mon!'

Now Benji and I are hurtling back the way we've come and racing around the side till we're past the beach and running toward the water of a different bay. I can see shadows turning when they hear us coming. Unseelies. Not that many but all holding a spear in one hand and an amulet in the other. We pass through them and soon reach the water's edge where we find King Kade pacing back and forth and Max wearing a silver one-piece that makes her look like she's auditioning for the cover of the Sports Illustrated Swimsuit Calendar.

'Fiona!'

Max has me in a bear hug and she's kissing me like a sister I haven't seen for three years.

'The Nuckelavee can't kill me,' I splutter.

Now Max is staring at me, thinking. Her hair's wet so she's already been in the water. Probably saw the other ships arriving and came back.

'Come with me' she says heading for the water.

I start taking off my armor hoping I'm wearing okay underwear which it turns out I am. Crimson low-riders with bra to match.

Max is in the water up to her knees. She holds her hand out and I wade in.

The water's cool but doable, not frigid like the Atlantic pounding in on Gloire Bay. As I round the point of land into the adjoining bay I bump into Max treading water, scoping out the situation.

About a third of Queen Hebrides's fleet is pulled up on the beach the remainder anchored just offshore. On the beach a huge crowd is gathered around the Queen who's handing out things, probably amulets. It finally hits me why she waited for her army. The Nuckelavee will win the battle but she'll need her army to occupy Faeryland. Then she'll be Queen of Scotland and Ireland.

That's when the bagpipe music starts! Honestly, along with everything else, Queen H has brought four bagpipers and if they put on amulets I'm all for waving the white flag right now. You don't need a Nuckelavee when you've got four Scottish hoovers assaulting your eardrums!

Max reaches the raft before me. She's a strong swimmer and quiet reminding me of Darcy who could move through the water like a porpoise. Me, I have to go slower, otherwise I'm noisy not that that matters now with a quartet of bagpipers bombarding the bay. By the time I get there, Max has the anchor rope untied. We get on the same side of the raft and start kicking underwater pushing the raft away from the Queen's ships back toward The Unseelie.

We're halfway to the point of land separates the bays when the bagpipers stop abruptly and shouts erupt from the beach. A bloke taking a leak in the ocean has spotted us. Now the Queen's sailors are rushing around pushing one of the ships back into the water. I figure we've got two minutes max.

Max's hand comes up holding the bracelet with the brass key; the one Queen H gave her to open the other cage.

'Might work, right?'

'It better,' says me grabbing it. 'Hide under the raft.'

'I love you,' Max says grinning. Then she gives me another kiss and disappears. I pull myself up onto the raft and put the key in the padlock. Then I get as close as I can to one of the air holes and I say, 'Hi Mr. Nuckelavee. I love you! I really do. I *really, really* love you!'

I turn the key and the padlock springs open. This is it.

'I LOVE YOU!'

I open the door.

I'm stretched out riding in the bucket of Fungal's digger but unlike the last time I'm conscious or sort of. It's still black out and I can hear the Atlantic's waves crashing off to my left. What the hell just happened? I close my eyes. *Concentrate.*

I open the crate door and the Nuckelavee jumps me, wrapping his arms around me, and we fall into the water the Nuckelavee heading for the bottom like a concrete pier. I open my mouth to scream and that's when I drown. Shite! So much for *I love you!*

I've got to get back. I say the words.

Someone's kissing me and someone's pounding on my chest. The one's nice the other isn't. Suddenly I'm sitting up barfing seawater all over Kevin.

'What are you doin here?' asks me between throw-ups.

'Rescuing you,' he says grinning like an alley cat with a fat mouse.

'Where's Max?'

'Here.'

'What happened?'

'The *I love you* didn't work.'

This is just about the worst news you can ever have.

'Where is he?'

'Let's go see.'

I put my clothes/armor back on and we scramble up the rocks that separate us from the other bay. It's chaos on the beach because the Nuckelavee is running around chasing everybody. He's not hurting anybody, he's just chasing them, knocking them over when he catches them.

'He's playing,' Benji says and I can hear the wonder in his voice. A monster playing! Go figure. Maybe my *I love you* worked after all or maybe he's trying to get away from the bagpipers playing their hearts out. Now the Nuckelavee is chasing Queen Hebrides who's shrieking, waving her arms in the air like this is so undignified, so un-Queen-like! (Yes, I know she has wings. No, I don't know why she isn't using them.) The Nuckelavee catches her and holds her up the Queen kicking him in the stomach, which makes him laugh. Then he pulls her down and gives her one of his toilet plunger kisses. He releases her and the Queen tumbles into the sand. The Nuckelavee is gone again chasing one of the Queen's attendants — squealing! — down the beach.

'This is our chance,' Max says jumping to her feet. 'Once the Queen puts an amulet around his neck we're done.'

Benji sticks a firecracker between the rocks and lights it. Pffft! Pfft! Pfft! Seconds later fiery red balls appear high in the night sky. Queen Caelia's forces, led by Major Domo, come hurtling down the bluff as The Unseelie attack from either end of the beach. I stand up getting ready to clamber down the rocks with Benji and Kevin when Max puts her hands on my shoulders and says, 'I want you up there.' Her head swivels toward the bluff. 'I need someone watching.'

'That should be you.'

'No, I don't think so. You heard Peggy. One of us has the power.'

'That's not me.'

'I need you up there. *Please.*'

It's the *please* that does it. It's so un-Max-like it stops me in my tracks. Grandad Sky can do that. Stop me in my tracks. It's not easy when you're as bullheaded as I am. Finally, I nod and Max grins at me. She doesn't say, *good girl,* but I can practically feel her patting my head.

Now everybody but me is racing down the incline screaming their lungs out, waving their weapons in the air. Every eye is on the Nuckelavee who's standing still, bewildered, watching shrieking bodies coming at him from all directions. I clamber up the rocks heading for the bluff.

Everybody's putting on amulets and what was a good-sized battle multiplies tenfold. Now it's Culloden or Waterloo or Gettysburg.

Max has reached the beach when I hear the Queen screaming at the bagpipers to stop, then she puts her fingers to her mouth. Even with all the battle noise I can hear the Queen's wolf whistle. The Nuckelavee turns listening. The Queen whistles again and now the Nuckelavee is bounding toward her running on all fours like a gorilla. One of Major Domo's soldiers takes a swipe at the Nuckelavee but the monster just swats him away like he's nothing.

For a second I'm wondering what would have happened if we'd left the Nuckelavee playing? Would the Queen have been able to turn him into a weapon of mass destruction or is it us rushing him, scaring him that's doin that? We'll never know.

To my right, led by a limping King Kade, The Unseelie are fighting hard to get to Queen Hebrides before the Nuckelavee can reach her. Straight ahead the other half of King Kade's army is hurtling into battle running near the water where the sand is harder. In the middle Major Domo's forces are engaged with Queen Hebrides's sailors. I see Adriana and her brother fighting alongside the Major, swinging their swords like they know what they're doing.

Queen Hebrides is standing near her ships so she can get away, if necessary I'm figuring, but then I see her grab a sword from a young soldier and that forces me to rethink my perception of Her Royal Highness. She's not a girlie queen like Queen Caelia, hiding in her castle waiting for the news; Queen Hebrides's not afraid to fight her own battles.

The Nuckelavee is battling now, trying to reach the Queen but enough of Major Domo's soldiers have gotten between him and Her Royal Highness that he has no choice but to deal with these obstacles first. Then I see Max shouting at the female warriors around her. Next thing I know they're lined up Max's sword in the air and as she whips it down they shout out together, 'WE LOVE YOU!'

The Nuckelavee puts on the brakes staring at them.

'WE LOVE YOU!'

Then Queen Hebrides whistles again. The Nuckelavee is flummoxed his misshapen body leaning first one way then the other. Which way should he go?

'WE LOVE YOU!'

The Queen whistles!

'WE LOVE YOU!'

The Queen whistles!

King Kade is approaching the Nuckelavee. Just leave him be, I'm thinking. Leave him be! But of course, that's not what happens. King Kade puts on his amulet and now there are eleven Kades approaching the

Nuckelavee with swords drawn. I want to shout, 'C'mon Max, one more WE LOVE YOU will do it!' but it's not to be. King Kade attacks and his clones follow. Kade's first swing slashes the bewildered Nuckelavee across his belly and everything changes again. The Nuckelavee goes berserk. With one swipe he knocks King Kade unconscious sending him sprawling facedown into the sand. Kade's clones hesitate not sure what to do.

Then my heart jumps into my mouth as the Nuckelavee reaches down and removes the amulet from around King Kade's neck. Anyone thinking the Nuckelavee lacks intelligence will have to rethink that as firstly he zeroes in on the real Kade like a kid spying the toy he wants and secondly, he knows the amulet will make him unbeatable. I want to scream but what good will it do? No one will hear me.

Then there's a blinding flash and I'm knocked off my feet by an explosion of air. A hand reaches out of the blinding light and pulls me to my feet. I can't believe it. It's The Dullahan, his head under his arm, grinning at me like we're best buds who haven't seen each other for a dog's age.

'Hi Fiona, having fun are we?'

'No! We can't stop the Nuckelavee.'

'Which one?'

The Dullahan is right. Now there are eleven Nuckelavees wreaking havoc.

'The one wearin the amulet. But don't hurt him, he's a nice guy.'

The Dullahan raises his eyebrows at this like, *really?*

'He's just confused.'

'Actually Fiona,' the head says still grinning, 'we have more pressing matters at the moment.'

What could be more pressing than having eleven Nuckelavees threatening to tear your friends' heads off?

Before I can ask there's another blinding flash and my world goes black.

Have you ever woken up and not known where you are? Personally, it's been happening all too regularly lately and I'm sick of it.

This time it only takes me a nanosecond to realize someone is holding my wrists and someone else my ankles. The moon's looming over me; I can hear the ocean crashing around me; and I'm in motion swinging up toward the tower but knowing I'll soon be going the other way.

MOTHER OF GOD! I'm about to do a Darcy!

'STOP!'

If the hands let go now, I'm sailing over the edge but they don't, they hold on bringing me back and I come to rest my butt scraping the ground. The light from the Dullahan is headlight strong and I can see it's Father McKenna and Ol' Man O'Reilly clutching my extremities. They're staring at The Dullahan like this can't be happening.

'Put her down.'

They let go and my head and feet thud to the ground.

'Was it you two that threw that unfortunate boy over?'

'We thought he was dead,' Father McKenna says not quite believing he's conversing with a severed head.

'It was an accident,' offers Ol' Man O'Reilly trying to look contrite but not managing it.

'And throwing Fiona over? How do you justify that?'

'She'll be a faery forever.'

'She'll like that.'

'No, I won't.' I roll away from the edge of the cliff getting to my feet moving beside The Dullahan who hands me his head. The Dullahan takes two steps forward and lifts his arms. Now the light is shining directly onto the two men's faces blinding them. Ol' Man O'Reilly lifts his arm trying to shield his eyes while Father McKenna tries to move away from the cliff edge but his feet seem rooted to the spot.

The Dullahan takes another step forward and the head in my hands says, 'Sean Walter Liam McKenna, Patrick Malone Singer O'Reilly, your time has come.'

Now both men are trying to get away from the cliff edge but the harder they try the stronger the wind becomes until finally The Dullahan throws his arms forward like a conductor reaching the crescendo and an explosion of air sends Father McKenna and Ol' Man O'Reilly sailing over the edge.

I'm in shock, my mind a whirl of images, but frozen too, like there's too much information assaulting my brain all at once. My body's shaking knowing how close I came to going over the edge. And the irony of Father McKenna and Ol' Man O'Reilly going over the cliff instead isn't lost on me. It won't bring Darcy back but there's a rough justice here that seems right. But poor Darcy, the fall must have been beyond horrible knowing what was waiting at the bottom.

'Your friends are here,' The Dullahan says pulling me back to the present.

'Friends?'

The Dullahan doesn't answer because an ATV roars up to the tower skidding to a stop beside the digger. Out jump Fungal, Gail, Billy and Karen.

'What are you doin here?' It's me asking but no one's paying attention because they're too busy staring at The Dullahan's head grinning at them.

'Karen, how nice to see you again.'

'Dullahan,' Karen says cool as a cucumber, like conversing with a severed head is an everyday thing. 'This is Billy, Fergus and Gail.'

'Nice to meet you,' replies The Dullahan enjoying himself.

'Where are Father McKenna and Ol' Man O'Reilly?' Fungal keeps looking around expecting the two men to step out of the shadows. 'Me and Gail saw 'em go by the Inn driving my digger.'

Billy says, 'Maybe they're up in their love nest.'

'Love nest?'

'There's a room in the tower with a bed and bottles of wine.'

I watch Fungal and Gail wrestle with this information their attention still overwhelmed with The Dullahan and his severed head.

Karen says to me, 'Gran called looking for you, so I called Billy.'

'And I called Fergus,' Billy says tearing his eyes from The Dullahan's head long enough to find mine staring back.

'They need us back in Faeryland,' says me. 'There's a battle going on and we're losing badly. Dullahan?'

Just like that we're back at the beach. Karen and Gail looked stunned, staring at their armor and swords like *what is going on here?* I ignore them and try to figure out the battle raging around us. The Nuckelavee are everywhere. I try to count them. Seven. So Major Domo, Max and The Unseelie have managed to take down four but not the one that matters.

Everybody on the beach is fighting somebody and nobody's running away. All of the Nuckelavees are encircled by Unseelies, mostly clones, holding spears out, not trying to kill the monsters so much as keep them from killing them. I can see Max and Benji and Kevin battling their way toward Queen Hebrides. If they can capture her the battle should end will be their thinking.

The Dullahan moves up beside me.

'What do you think, Fiona?'

'We need to capture the Queen.'

'How very chess like. Here, hold me, will you?'

The Dullahan throws me his head then reaches around me putting his fingers in his mouth and whistles, not a wolf whistle like Queen H, but a whistle that sounds like every whistle that's ever been whistled has been brought together for one last gala performance. For a second everything happening on the beach stops and everyone is staring up at the bluff. And what do they see?

A huge, black horse is what they see with The Dullahan on top holding on with one hand as Bess rears up kicking the sky.

'I love that bit,' the head says and for reasons that will never be known I hold the head up and kiss him.

'Me too!'

Bess starts down the hill as The Dullahan draws his sword.

'Fiona!' I turn looking at Karen. Beside her stands Bess's colt watching his mum plunge through the sand.

When I turn back The Dullahan is swinging his sword in a circle and it's making a sound so primeval I can see the sand rising up.

'What's he doing?'

'What am I doing?'

'Yes, what are you doing?'

'I'm calling the Nightmares.'

'The Nightmares?'

The head doesn't answer because I can see the answer, dozens of hairy monkey-like creatures dropping out of thin air like spinning playing cards — two dimensional demons off a comic book page — landing on the Nuckelavee tearing the human from the horse. I can't watch but even my hands over my ears can't stop the sound of the Nuckelavee screaming.

Then it's quiet. I open my eyes. The Nuckelavee's clones are gone; only the real Nuckelavee is left surrounded by Nightmares itching to attack. Everyone else has stopped fighting mesmerized by the Nightmares and the approach of The Dullahan riding Bess unhurriedly across the beach.

'C'mon!' cries me starting down the hill.

It's like The Dullahan is sucking all the players in because I see Queen Hebrides heading for the Nuckelavee, coming by herself, waving her sailors back, dropping her sword. I see Max and Kevin helping King Kade to his feet then all three following in the Queen's footsteps.

It's deathly quiet as we reach the gathering around the Nuckelavee who's kneeling in the sand, his head bowed crying silent tears. The Nuckelavee's breathing hard but otherwise it's as still as a thousand beings can be. I step forward and hand his head to The Dullahan and he takes charge.

'I won't use your proper names for reasons you all know. Queen, if you do not surrender your Nuckelavee will be torn apart. Is that what you want?'

'No! He's done nothing to deserve death. I surrender.'

'Good. You must leave this place and not return.'

'But you can't go home,' King Kade says. 'The Highlands belong to us.'

I expect the Queen to be enraged by this but instead she leans her head back and laughs, a real laugh full of joy.

'You know Kade, I'm sick of that miserable castle. It's damp, cold, and foul with mold. It's all yours and good luck to you.'

Now Queen Hebrides is looking at her sailors and grinning. 'No, I think we'll be heading to sunnier climes. Like Sicily or Malta or maybe the Seychelles. What say you Seelies?'

A cheer goes up loud enough to make the sand jiggle.

'But! I want Princess Isla returned.'

Now it's Max that steps forward. 'Queen Caelia wishes to adopt Isla. She has no children of her own as you know. She wishes to make Isla her daughter and heir. You on the other hand have four other children. This way your daughter will become Queen of Ireland. Surely you will marry your children off to form alliances, so here's one readymade. What say you?'

Let history record that Queen Hebrides doesn't say anything. Instead, she walks toward the ring of Nightmares who part for her and enters the circle taking the Nuckelavee by the hand. She pulls him to his feet and whispers something in his ear. His tears stop replaced by a wicked grin that makes my broken heart whole again. In less time than the telling Queen Hebrides, her army, her sailors, and the Nuckelavee are specks on the horizon. The only Seelies left are the four bagpipers standing on the beach staring at each other like, *was it something we played?*

The Nightmares fly away in formation like a deck of cards comin back together. The Unseelie — including a dazed King Kade — limp off heading for their camp. Major Domo takes his leave dying to return to Sí Dún to bring Queen Caelia the news. Soon the beach is empty but for a bonfire surrounded by The Dullahan, me, Max, Alonzo, Benji, Mally, Kevin, Billy, Fungal, Gail and Karen.

'That went rather well,' The Dullahan says making the rest of us laugh.

'Did you see Adriana and her brother?' I ask the gathering. 'They fought like fiends.'

'They're staying,' Max says. 'They like it here.'

'As far away from their father as possible,' Mally adds and we all laugh again.

'What about you Max?' I ask. 'What will you do now?'

'I plan to do what Sir Max has always done. Travel the world with Alonzo, righting wrongs, defending those who can't defend themselves. I'm rather hoping Benji and Mally will join us. Knights Errant!'

Benji and Mally share a look then Mally and Benji shout together, 'One for all, all for one!'

Max has been waving her sword around but now she plunges it into the sand beside me. I take it as my opportunity to read the words inscribed on the blade.

I AM THE STORM!

I love that quote! I have it on a piece of card stuck on my door at Stonehaven: *The Devil whispered in my ear, 'You're not strong enough to withstand the storm.'*

Today I whispered in the Devil's ear, 'I am the storm!'

No one gets credit for saying the words so I always picture some scruffy graffiti poet spraying it on the wall of the Pentagon. Max sees me reading the words and grins.

'And what about you, Fiona? What will you be doing?'

Before I can answer something hits me. I turn to Fungal.

'Where's Gran's book?'

'It's in my digger, Fiona. I saw it lying on the seat.'

I can see Fungal is worried about Father McKenna and Ol' Man O'Reilly stealing it but I'm not. 'It'll be fine, Fergus. Don't worry about it.' I turn to Max thinking how best to answer her question.

'I think I'd like to be a doctor like my mum and dad, maybe travel the world as they did.' I'm staring at Billy now, him smiling at me like, *I don't know if I'm smart enough to be a doctor but I could try.* Then I turn to Kevin who's smiling at me too. 'But I'd like to visit if that's okay? I want to keep up with my mates here and I'd like to babysit Isla. She's special.'

Max gives me a grin. 'I'm sure Queen C will be happy with that. Without you and The Dullahan, the Nuckelavee would have defeated us.'

'I liked the monster,' says me, but before I can say more The Dullahan claps his hands three times. The next thing I know I'm hugging Gran, her *Book of Faery Spells* lying on the table beside us.

SOME TIME LATER

It's my sweet sixteenth birthday and me and Billy have ridden Sally to the beach at Beg Head to celebrate. I have lots to be thankful for that's for sure.

Let's start with Billy. He's growing up in front of my eyes and pulling me along with him. I mean, we're still beyond silly half the time, but it's good craic not stupid silly. We're doing great at school, egging each other on, the medical school in Dublin our goal. I asked Billy if he was doin it for me but he said he knew he wanted to do something good with his life he just didn't know what it would be. He said he'd be scared to take on the world on his own but with me alongside he figures there isn't anything we can't do.

Sweet, eh?

And we've been working on our default positions; y'know the place you start from. Here's what we have so far: be honest; be loyal; be kind.

'You're not feeding those to me.'

I'm sitting on the sand, minding my own business, and now Billy's standing behind me dripping on me on purpose and he's dropped his bucket full of razorfish in my lap so I can inspect them.

'Gran said she wanted some.'

'Ugh.'

Billy flops down beside me and says, 'There's a lot of heavy thinking going on here. I can see heat waves risin.'

'Nope. Just happy is all.'

'Are you missin Darcy?'

'I am. We always celebrated our birthdays together. Darcy's becoming a fading memory and I don't like that.'

Billy doesn't say anything and it's one of his greatest strengths. He knows when to be quiet.

Okay, while we're being quiet, I'm going to update you on everybody.

Adriana and Alessandro are still in Sí Dún and doing just fine. They're writing songs like crazy and traveling around singing them. I asked Sandro why he was hiding out in Gloire Bay and he said his father was insisting he come into the hotel business and Sandro wanted no part of that saying he wanted to be a singer/songwriter and/or a craftsman making metal toys using gears and levers. Whose idea was it to build a faeryland near the fairy fort? Adriana, he says. She's smart that way. Then I asked how he knew to make his faeryland wonky and he said it just seemed right. And what was he looking for that day Inspector Mike and I saw him in Adriana's boat? My *giacca a vento* (anorak), he says, meaning it flew over the cliff the night Darcy died. We didn't want the police finding it, Adriana says. Then Sandro says, we thought Darcy was dead, Fiona. We're so sorry for what happened.

The whole thing makes me beyond sad, but there's no changing it.

Adriana's and Alessandro's bodies were taken to the hospital in Sligo, then Dublin, both on life support nobody understanding what happened to them. Gail called Adriana's father in Italy and he hurried to Dublin. Then he showed up at the Inn demanding to know what the hell was going on? So, Gail told him.

'Impossibile!'

'No, it's not,' answered Gail. 'If I take you to your son and daughter will you sell me and Fergus the Inn?'

'No! I'll give it to you!'

Fungal asked Gran if he could borrow the spell book but she suggested he bring Mr. de Santis to Stonehaven so that's what Fungal did. Fungal, Gail and Mr. de Santis said the spell together but only Fungal and Gail made the jump leaving Adriana's dad sitting at Gran's kitchen table with two corpses. Now Mr. de Santis is a believer and he looks at me for help. I sit down and we say the spell together. This time Adriana's father lands feet first in Sí Dún dressed like a rich merchant from medieval times. Fungal and Gail take us to a warehouse full of wings — new, broken and experimental — where we find Adriana and Sandro in a back room practicing their music for a show they're putting on.

At first Adriana isn't happy to see her dad — he's one of the reasons they're staying in Faeryland — and then Alessandro lets his dad have it — you're a horrible father. All us kids, three wives — you're never around! — all you care about is making money. And what do you do with it? Nothing good. Buy another hotel, another stupid car.

It's embarrassing being there and I'm thinking of sneaking off when Mr. de Santis starts crying, real tears from a place so deep inside only your soul lives there. Then we're all crying and hugging, part of something so big you can't see it at all. Like standing so close to a leprechaun all you can see is green.

(And freckles! Kevin will like that!)

'It was like he rediscovered the child within,' Gail offered later. 'Like he realized he didn't have to always be a hardass. That it was okay to be silly, to have fun.'

The short of it is Mr. de Santis stayed with his kids long enough to attend their show — Gail says he loved it! — and when he came back he kept his promise, he gave the Inn to Gail and Fungal. They had to pay a Euro to make it legal and Gran had to promise to make the spell book available to Mr. de Santis whenever he wanted to visit his kids. Gran and Grandad really like Adriana's dad so that was easy. Then he took the twins' bodies off life support because he knew they weren't ever coming back.

What about the bog, right?

He sold it to the Irish Peatland Conservation Council for more than he had invested in the Inn so he was happy about that. He might no longer be a hardass but he was still a businessman.

Of course, word of our adventures in Faeryland got out on social media so the Inn is packed with fairy enthusiasts visiting the bog hoping for a glimpse of Queen Caelia or Princess Isla. They visit the excavation site — Ten Euros each proceeds helping to buy more bogs! — viewing Sandro's faeryland and because Queen C has a soft spot for Fungal and Gail, and all the attention she's getting, she makes sure there's something to see at the faery fort on nights like Beltane when legend — and the Fairy Guidebook — says the veil between our world and the otherworld is at its thinnest.

Karen's decided to stay in Gloire Bay — 'I like it here' — and she's still seeing Inspector Mike. Karen and Mike's son, Jamie, get on well so that helps. I keep urging Karen to record her songs but so far I'm just a *whisper in the wind*. We'll see.

Inspector Mike got the job of figuring out the mysterious disappearance of Father McKenna and Ol' Man O'Reilly. I tried to tell him the truth but as soon as I mentioned The Dullahan he wanted none of it; but he did listen when I said it was Father McKenna and Ol' Man O'Reilly using the love nest in the tower. Inspector Mike assumed they'd run off together but couldn't find any evidence to support that. Then two weeks later what was left of Ol' Man O'Reilly's body washed up in a fisherman's net. The official report declared all three deaths — Darcy, Father McKenna and Ol' Man O'Reilly — as misadventures. Cases closed. Close enough, I guess.

Crash and Burn O'Reilly used some of their inheritance to buy Fungal's digger. Their first job was digging up Mrs. Smythe's ancient sewerage. Rumor is Crash went forward when he should have been backing up and the backhoe fell onto the tank breaking the lid and sending shite for fifty meters. Crash & Burn Construction — Use At Your Own Risk! Too funny!

Speaking of sewerage my Greek chorus, *Wide Arse* McDonogh and *Big Mouth* McLeish, have had a falling out. Apparently Wide Arse had the shared clothesline filled end-to-end with newly washed clothing and says to Big Mouth, I'm goin out, if it starts raining could you bring me clothes in? Sure, no bother, replies Big Mouth. It starts pouring but Big Mouth doesn't notice cos she's got a plugged toilet to which Brian-the-Plumber is given his rapt attention except Big Mouth is talking his ear off and not paying attention to the downpour outside. The clothes get so heavy the clothesline snaps and Wide Arse comes home to find her washing lying in the mud. Now there's two clotheslines and a fence with Wide Arse and Big Mouth firing insults back and forth Gloire Bay's equivalent of Donald Trump and Kim Jong-un. Too funny again.

You remember Liang, the locksmith from China? He and I have become good mates. We email once a week telling each other the latest news. I like getting Liang's take on things coming from the other side of the world. We'll never be lovers but we're growing into something better: Good Friends.

I babysit Isla every Sunday morning. Holding her in my arms is like holding the sun, the stars and the planets. She's the *Secret of the Universe* everybody's looking for but too blind to see. (I have this dream where the leaders of the world are makin this huge decision on climate change or nuclear disarmament and each of them is holding a baby in his or her arms!)

Sometimes Billy and I go to visit Kevin and Peggy. I took Gran to visit Peggy. They're best buds now Gran trading her Guinness Chocolate Cake recipe for Peggy's Butterfly Melts. Peggy's going to visit King Kade in Scotland. The news is he's still the badest of the badasses but Peggy doesn't seem to mind. She says he's misunderstood — he's just playing his part! —which is what we females do to justify things.

Grandad Sky visited Faeryland once, just to see for himself, but said it was too far from Texas. Well, what he said was, we're not in Kansas anymore, but it was Texas he was meaning.

'I got you something,' Billy says jumping up heading for his backpack, which is behind us somewhere. Me, I'm leaning on my elbows, my head back letting the sun warm my face.

'Holy shite!'

Now I'm turning wondering what could have happened to Billy to elicit a *holy shite!* There's no snakes in Ireland so he hasn't come face-to-face with a three-meter anaconda. St. Patrick gets credit for the no snakes, if you can believe it. Maybe he can rid the world of asshats, now that would be something.

'Fiona!'

Okay, okay. I'm on my feet heading for Billy who's standing there like an eejit grinning and pointing at something hiding behind Sally.

Billy's right! HOLY SHITE! It's Bess's colt! With a red ribbon tied around his neck! A birthday present from The Dullahan! I doubt there's anybody else can be saying that!

My arms wrap around the horse's neck; my nose buries in his hair; my eyes turn into a watering can.

'Oh, you are so handsome.'

'He needs a name.'

Now I'm hugging Billy too, kissing him, makin his face wet.

'What do you think?'

'Midnight.'

'Midnight, it is!'

Half an hour later, when there isn't a centimeter of Midnight that hasn't been touched, Billy hands me a little, dark-blue velvet box, the kind jewelers use. I untie the ribbon. Inside is a beautiful silver necklace the spitting image of King Kade's amulet.

'Oh Billy, it's beyond beautiful!'

'Queen Caelia had it made for me to give you. It's enchanted. Tap it three times and you're in Faeryland.'

Half an hour later when there's not a centimeter of Billy that hasn't been touched (!!!!) Billy says, 'There's one more present. It's from Max.'

'Max?'

I haven't seen Max since the night she told me to stay on the bluff watching.

'I thought she and Benji and Mally and Alonzo were in Tuscany helping Queen Hebrides fight the Fata?'

'It was the night of the battle. Just before we headed home Max told me to say these four words to you on your birthday.'

'Four words? That rules out *I love you.*'

'This might be better.'

'What could be better than I love you?'

Billy makes me wait. And wait. Wanker! He wants me to beg. Now I'm going for him, faking high, heading low, wrapping my arms around his legs and pushing him over. 'Say the words Billy.'

'I'll be needin a kiss first.'

'Now say 'em.'

'Happy Birthday Simply Fiona.'

DARCY!

Grandad Sky's Texas Chili

1 lb. chicken or beef chunks
2 sweet peppers
2 garlic cloves
1 large onion
1/8 cup olive oil
2 tbsp chili powder
2 tsp cumin
¼ tsp cayenne pepper
1 can diced tomatoes
½ cup chicken or beef broth
1 can red kidney beans
1 jar of salsa (hot)
1 pkg frozen corn
Salt & pepper to taste

Must be wearing cowboy hat!

Cook the meat and onion in the olive oil then throw everything together in a large pot. Simmer forever. Add stuff, like more chili powder, to taste.